THE
ROPE

THE
ROPE

CATHEMAE CECCHIN

TATE PUBLISHING
AND **ENTERPRISES**, LLC

Published by Tate Publishing & Enterprises, LLC
127 E. Trade Center Terrace | Mustang, Oklahoma 73064 USA
1.888.361.9473 | www.tatepublishing.com

Tate Publishing is committed to excellence in the publishing industry. The company reflects the philosophy established by the founders, based on Psalm 68:11,
"The Lord gave the word and great was the company of those who published it."

Book design copyright © 2016 by Tate Publishing, LLC. All rights reserved.
Cover design by Joana Quilantang
Interior design by Gram Telen

WISHFUL THINKING: A THEOLOGICAL ABC by FREDERICK BUECHNER.
Copyright © 1973 by Frederick Buechner. Reprinted by Permission of HarperCollins Publishers.

Published in the United States of America

ISBN: 978-1-68270-174-4
1. Fiction / Christian / General
2. Fiction / Family Life
16.03.15

Acknowledgments

I could never have written this novel without the support of several individuals, and I want to thank each one of them.

Patty, when the idea for this story first came to me, I was filled with doubts that I could do it justice. You were the first one I shared the idea with, and your response was immediate: "You have to write it!" Thank you for that first push! And thank you for your support and encouragement every step of the way since.

Kathy, from the moment I told you about this new story I was working on, you have been a wonderful cheerleader. Through all the highs and (especially) the lows of trying to turn an idea into a full-fledged novel, you were always present and encouraging. Thank you, and thank you also for sharing your own expertise in writing, which has helped me to become a better writer.

Char, the first time I read one of your stories, I recognized a wonderful gift for storytelling, and I thank you for sharing that gift with me. In our countless conversations, you have inspired me, enlarged my thinking, and helped me to believe I could do more than I thought I could. I am a better writer—and person—for your presence in my life. Thank you.

Steve and Paula, without your prayerful support, this novel would never have happened. Steve, thank you for always being willing to provide a listening ear (even when you had a dozen other things you needed to be doing). Paula, thank you for your encouraging spirit, and thank you both for believing in me and in *The Rope*.

Everyone I've mentioned here has had a significant impact in my life and in my writing. However, there's one other person whose influence has been even greater and who means the world to me. Mom, thank you for your unwavering support and belief in me every day of my life (especially during those times when I didn't make it easy for you!). This book is for you. I hope you like it.

1

A brilliant flash of lightning exploded across the dark sky, and Mark Newman flinched. His hands tightened involuntarily on the steering wheel, and he muttered a curse as he squinted in an effort to see better through the rain pounding against the windows of his Lexus.

"Of all the stupid timing," he growled.

If only he had left his office an hour earlier, he could have avoided this mess. Except he had an important deposition tomorrow. Mark had tangled before with the law firm representing the other side and knew their attorneys would be prepared. He needed to be better prepared.

Lightning blazed again, and he winced as the brightness stung his night-adapted eyes. It was after midnight, and he hadn't seen any cars since he turned onto a secondary road to avoid the accident on the freeway and resulting backup. There was nothing outside the windows but darkness and the storm, the intensity of which occasionally shook even his well-built car.

This was ridiculous. Mark was tempted to turn around and go back to his office. He had a comfortable couch on which he could spend the night. It wouldn't be the first time he had done so. But he was slightly more than halfway home. Better to keep going.

Visibility was so poor Mark was going slower than the speed limit, another reason for irritation. Leaving the freeway had seemed like a good idea at the time, but as he traveled along the frontage road feeling the power of the storm smashing into his car, he couldn't help thinking he might have done better to stay on the more-heavily traveled freeway, delays notwithstanding. Especially at this time of night when he seemed to be the only person on the road.

Thunder rumbled directly overhead, immediately followed by another crack of lightning. As if it had been a signal, the driving rain intensified and everything outside the windows turned into a blur.

Mark swore and hit the high beams but instantly realized his mistake. The brilliant light reflected back in his eyes, blinding him.

He cried out in pain and surprise and threw a hand over his face. Simultaneously, his foot found the brake, and he stamped down hard. He felt the antilock braking system kick in and thought to help it by yanking at the steering wheel.

The Lexus swerved. He tried to correct it but failed.

He felt himself thrown forward, only to be yanked back by his seatbelt. The car lurched as it sideswiped something large and immovable and kept going.

It lurched again, the tires bumping hard over a suddenly rough surface.

Mark gripped the steering wheel more fiercely, his heart in his throat.

"No!"

His world tilted, twisted, turned upside down as the out-of-control car rolled over and over, going down, down.

Impact was like an explosion; his senses reeled.

Darkness descended, then nothingness.

Eons later, someone groaned.

Another groan sent a stab of pain through his head, and he tried to lift his hand. Strangely, his hand was reluctant to obey. It took all his energy to raise it, only to accidentally slap himself in the face.

The pain yanked Mark out of his stupor. He blinked and slowly turned his head. It was pitch-black outside the cracked window.

He blinked again. What happened? Where was he?

Mark looked around to discover that he was surrounded by airbags.

Memory returned with a rush. His car had gone off the road. He had had an accident, but thanks to the car's safety features, he was alive.

He had gone off the road. He had rolled down the embankment. Thankfully, the car had ended right side up.

Mark pushed aside the side airbag and peered out. Only darkness met his gaze. After some fumbling, he found the door handle and pulled. Nothing happened. A thrill of fear cut through his confusion, and he pulled harder. Still nothing. He reached down for his seatbelt and tried to unlatch. It wouldn't work.

He had to get out. Panic bubbled up, and he fought it back. He had to stay calm. He had to stay in control. Leaning back in his seat, Mark concentrated on taking slow, deep breaths. One step at a time. That's what he needed to do.

The cell phone!

Mark reached inside his jacket, but the pocket was empty. He ran a hand swiftly over himself before remembering he had been talking on it earlier and set it in the console beside his seat. Fumbling in the darkness, he discovered the console was empty.

"Idiot!" he snarled. Of course, everything that had been loose in the car had been thrown around when the car went over the embankment.

Mark swallowed fresh panic. He knew if he gave into the fear, he would be lost.

More slow, deep breaths. Gradually, he felt his pulse slowing. Good, now he just had to think this through.

Lightning exploded almost on top of him, and he cried out in surprise. In that split-instant, his surroundings were revealed with brilliant, terrifying clarity.

He had rolled all the way down the embankment. Worse, his vehicle had landed at an acute angle with the front third now submerged in the raging river. That fast, logic pointed him toward the inexorable resolution of his situation. Gravity would continue to pull his car downward, ever further into the fierce torrent of water. Soon, the current would get a good grip on the vehicle and drag it into the river and him to a watery death.

"No!" he gasped, scrabbling frantically at his seatbelt. "No! Help! Someone help!"

Even as he cried out, Mark knew no one could hear. He was out of sight, down below the road that had been empty of all other traffic. There were no businesses or other dwellings around here. He was isolated. Alone. And soon he would be dead.

He fought with the unyielding seatbelt, something created to save his life, but which now held him while his life slipped away. He yanked at it with all his strength, managed to get a piece in his mouth and tried to bite through it.

Fiercely as he struggled, the seatbelt only seemed to tighten further. Gasping, cursing, Mark fought with everything he had. By the time his strength gave out, nothing had changed. He fell back with a frustrated sob and one last futile tug. He had to take a break, a brief rest, then he would try again. Eventually, it would have to...

Mark caught his breath, gripped by new terror. His feet were wet. He jerked them back convulsively and felt water swirl around them. He pulled mindlessly against the seatbelt, banging intermittently against the unyielding door. The assault didn't last long before his adrenalin-fueled strength faded again, this time into an exhaustion he couldn't fight through.

Surrounded by blackness that was only occasionally and briefly split by flashes of lightning, Mark felt as if he was being swallowed whole by the earth. He was going to die.

"No," he whispered, "please…no."

Not like this. No fine final speeches at the end of a long, illustrious life. He was trapped like an ant in a drop of honey, unseen by the world. Above, hidden by the storm, stretched out an infinite universe, beneath which he was utterly insignificant, less than an ant.

But he was significant! He was Mark Newman, highly respected attorney, feared by his opponents and, and… Except now, at the end of a life far shorter than he had expected, what did his reputation in the legal community matter? What did his large bank accounts matter? His entire life had been focused on achieving what he now had. Along the way, he had acquired a wife and later children, only to allow them to fall by the wayside. Would they care that he was dead? Would anyone mourn him?

Mark turned his head restlessly. Where were these thoughts coming from? If he had had any strength left, he would have pushed them away. Instead, they filled his mind, demanding answers he did not have.

"I don't want to die," he said into the darkness, for the first time feeling the tears sliding down his face.

Light stabbed his eyes, and he closed them automatically. Even closed, he was aware of the persistent glare. What did it matter? He was going to die. Very soon. He, Mark Newman.

Something tickled the edge of his thoughts. He tried to ignore it, not wanting to be bothered by any more irritating notions during the last minutes of his life.

Last minutes? How could that be?

Mark realized he was still aware of the reflection of light against his closed eyes and felt oddly annoyed. Since he was about to die, it seemed unfair that he should be bothered by such minor aggravation.

The something niggling at the edge of his thoughts grew more insistent, and he was too tired to resist it any longer. Something about the light.

The light in his face was lasting a long time. That made no sense. Lightning didn't linger. No natural light lingered like this, apart from the sun. Since it was after midnight, it couldn't be the sun.

Understanding exploded through his brain. This was *artificial* light! His eyelids flew open, and he winced under the penetrating gleam of a narrow beam of light.

For a moment, disbelief held him still. It couldn't be. He was hallucinating.

The beam moved erratically as the person holding it made their slow way down the steep embankment. Lightning flashed, a brief, brilliant flash of light, and Mark caught a glimpse of a tall figure, drenched by the downpour but real and alive!

Excitement jerked him upright in the seat, and he banged on the window. "I'm here!" he yelled. "Help me! Please, help me!"

Mark knew the figure wouldn't be able to hear him. His voice was too muffled by the glass, and he was competing against the fury of the storm. Still he yelled.

Salvation was approaching, slowly, cautiously, struggling against the fierce elements of nature. He prayed his would-be rescuer would make it safely down and help him to escape from his prison, a prison that was rapidly becoming ever more terrifying as he felt the wet coldness creeping up to his knees. Soon, the car would be fully under water.

Years seemed to pass as the narrow light moved slowly down the embankment, yet with every passing minute, it drew closer. The rain streaming down his car windows made a clear view impossible, but Mark had the impression of a husky figure. He was torn between anticipation and fear. Rescue was almost upon him. He couldn't die now. Not now.

The dark, drenched form stumbled down the last few feet and stopped just beyond the car. The beam of light disappeared as Mark's rescuer laid the flashlight down before gripping the door handle.

Eagerly Mark yanked at the handle inside while he threw his weight against the door. He sensed more than saw the figure outside pulling hard; they struggled together to force the door open. Within a couple of minutes, Mark's strength gave out and more fear surged into his throat when he glimpsed his rescuer draw back.

"We can do this!" he shouted desperately. "Please!"

The figure seemed to be gesturing at him, and Mark stared in perplexity. He was waving at him. Waving? Then his rescuer picked up the flashlight and pretended to swing it at the back window.

"Oh!" Mark exclaimed in relief and nodded vigorously. He leaned forward as far as the seatbelt allowed and wrapped his arms around his head.

There was a *thump* behind him, and Mark suppressed the desire to look around. More thumps followed, harder, louder, before a flat crack startled him. Suddenly the sounds of the storm resounded inside the car.

"Come on!" he whispered frantically.

The sounds of more thumps and glass reluctantly breaking under the force of the assault made his heart pound as if in sync. The boom of thunder overhead deafened him, yet even in the midst of his shock, Mark rejoiced. Finally, he dared to lower his arms and peer over his shoulder. His rescuer was in the process of breaking the rest of the glass out, the sounds of which weren't loud enough to overcome the tumult of weather.

Abruptly frantic to escape, Mark reached back with one hand to try to help…

"Don't!"

For the first time, he heard the voice of his rescuer, deep and harsh with warning. Mark knew then what he hadn't been certain of before. He wasn't hallucinating. This was really happening. He wasn't going to die.

"I can't move!" he yelled. "The seatbelt won't release!"

"Wait a minute."

Despite the urgency of the situation and the need to shout to be heard over the storm, the stranger's voice was calm, and the sound of it sent reassurance rushing through Mark. He kept watch over his shoulder so he saw when the last of the glass fell away under the rescuer's assault. To Mark's surprise, the other man didn't even try to open the door. He simply leaned inside until their heads were almost touching.

"Lean over," the stranger instructed.

As Mark obeyed, he caught a glimpse of something glinting in the man's hand. A knife. He was holding a small knife. Mark felt the seatbelt being tugged as the stranger sawed away at it. Without warning, it went loose, and he fell forward a few inches before he caught himself.

"Here!" his rescuer handed the knife over.

Mark grabbed the belt that still held him tightly across his hips and cut furiously at it. The task was made more difficult because the water had risen to his waist and his hands were numb. The tough fabric yielded only grudgingly under the assault, but hope and fear gave him the strength to saw away until suddenly the belt was gone.

"I'm free!" he yelled jubilantly.

"Come on!"

Mark pulled himself out of his prison and struggled to force his body through the narrow space between the front seats. Strong hands gripped his shoulders and pulled fiercely, and he fell through into the backseat.

He felt the car lurch forward. So did the stranger.

"Outta there *now!*"

Mark grabbed his rescuer's hands which pulled him through the window. Scrabbling for purchase, he pushed hard against the seat. Suddenly he found himself on the ground, facedown in the mud while the storm thundered over him. Panting in relief, he felt the stranger's hands pulling at him again.

"Get up! We have to get out of here!"

Out of where? He had escaped from his prison. Blinking in an effort to clear his vision, Mark's breath caught when he realized their predicament. They were on a narrow strip of land a few feet above the surging river. If they stayed, the rising water would sweep them away. Fighting back his terror, he heard his rescuer talking.

"Take this!"

He was holding out a thick length of rope. Mark stared at it blankly.

"Hang on to the rope," the man ordered.

Hang on? Mark looked at his hands. They were so numb he could barely flex his fingers. Seconds ago, he was exhilarated at his escape. Now despair sapped him of strength.

"I…I don't think I can."

"You have to," his rescuer insisted. "You have to grab on to it and climb!"

Mark stared up the steep embankment. It looked like a hundred feet high, and he shook his head hopelessly. "I can't."

"You have to! Or you'll die."

Die? After everything he had gone through?

"Come on," the stranger urged. "I'll help you." He took Mark's hands and wrapped them around the rope. Despite being soaked by the rain, the rope felt strong.

Mark didn't know if he could do it, but he had come too far not to try. With his rescuer's help, he stumbled to his feet.

"Go!" the man urged with a slap on his shoulder.

The embankment was not as steep as he had thought. He took one halting step after another, clinging more tightly to the rope when his foot slipped in the deepening mud, climbing slowly. He was acutely aware of his rescuer just behind him, shouting encouragement while demanding he take another step, another, and another.

Annoyance began to grow at the other's unrelenting nagging. Didn't the man know what Mark had been through? Still he demanded more. Annoyance hardened, turned to anger. He had to get up to the road so he could turn around and tell the stranger what he thought of him.

Suddenly he fell forward, the impact knocking the breath out of him. Surprise and lack of air kept him still until the same strong hands that had broken through his prison and pulled him out of his car patted his arm.

"Good job," said his rescuer. Though he still had to shout to be heard over the storm, his voice was warm with approval. "You can relax now. You made it."

Mark lay where he had fallen, not caring about the tears of relief that rolled down his cheeks and were instantly swept away by the hard rain. As he rested, his breathing grew easier, and he realized he was cold, numbingly cold. It wasn't important. He was alive.

"Thank you," he choked out to the figure still kneeling beside him.

"You're welcome."

"You saved my life. How can I ever repay you?"

"I'm glad I happened by. You're alive. That's enough payment."

"No, it's not." Mark squinted through the downpour, trying to see his rescuer's face. "I would have died if you hadn't risked your life to save me."

There was a long silence punctuated by thunder. Though he wasn't paying attention to the weather, he realized that the thunder was not as loud; the storm was passing.

The stranger said, "If you really want to thank me, the next time you run across someone who needs a hand, give him yours."

Mark blinked. Had he heard correctly? "My...my hand?"

"Good," his rescuer said unexpectedly.

"What?"

"You hear that? Help's coming."

Mark was having a hard time focusing, but when he listened, he heard the faint sound of approaching sirens. Never had they sounded so beautiful.

The noise of powerful engines died. Doors slammed, and voices erupted around him. He lay unmoving, swamped by relief, not caring he was shivering violently. New hands touched him.

"Hey, buddy," a new voice said. "We're here to help. How're you doing?"

Mark's smile was weak, but it felt wonderful on his frozen face. "I'm fine, thanks to him."

"To who?"

He gestured feebly. "To him. He saved my life." As he spoke, he turned his head. In that instant, every thought fled. There was no one beside him.

"Buddy?"

Mark looked up into the worried faces of the uniformed figures. "He was...he was right here. You must have seen him when you drove up."

The uniforms exchanged looks before the first man said, "There was no one here when we arrived except you."

He knew that wasn't true. His rescuer had been right beside him. Later when he wasn't so exhausted, he would figure out what had happened. For now, he sank gratefully into unconsciousness.

2

It had been years since Mark's last trip to a hospital, and he had forgotten how much he hated them. All he wanted to do was leave.

"I don't think that's a good idea, Mr. Newman," the doctor—Mark hadn't bothered to catch his name—insisted. "You should stay overnight for observation."

"I'm all right," he insisted.

"At least wait until someone can come pick you up."

Mark swallowed an angry response. He had called home and got the answering machine. Geneva should be home from her meeting by now; she probably turned off the telephone in her bedroom. Or else, he thought bleakly, she ignored the persistent ringing. He left a brief message, but now he wondered why he bothered. He did not expect her to come. It would be much easier to call a taxi.

"Why don't you rest for another hour?" the doctor suggested. "If your condition hasn't changed, then I'll okay your leaving."

He didn't want to stay. It was his decision, not the physician's. Unfortunately, though Mark would never admit it, he was hurting all over and exhausted; he wanted nothing more than to sleep for a week.

"Fine," he snapped.

"Are you sure you don't want to change out of those clothes? We can at least—"

"No," Mark said shortly. Giving up his clothes would make it that much harder to leave this place.

"Well, all right. Just relax. I'll be back in a while." The doctor walked away, stopping when he reached the door to allow another man to come in. "Pastor Joe." He smiled. "What are you doing here this time of night?"

Mark scowled at the tall, slender man shaking hands with the physician.

"The usual. Is everything okay, Jim? I missed you at church this morning."

"Everything's fine. We had car trouble, if you can believe that."

Mark tried to tune out the conversation. Of all the people who might have walked in, this man was one of the last he wanted to see.

He stiffened when his brother-in-law approached. The physician was gone, so he didn't bother being polite. "What are you doing here?"

Joe Ridgeway smiled, his green eyes darker than normal. "Geneva called me when she heard your message, and I said I'd come over. How are you?"

One of the things he disliked most about the older man was his unshakable calm. It always made Mark suspect his brother-in-law was hiding something.

"I'm fine," he said, then regretted his ungracious tone. Ridgeway was here; Mark had a ride home. He sat up, only to fall back as dizziness swept over him.

Joe put a hand on his arm. "Not so fast, take it easy," he said.

Nausea rose in Mark's throat, and he swallowed. For a minute, he feared he was going to throw up.

"Take deep breaths," Joe said as if he sensed his distress. "Deep and slow."

Mark obeyed and was relieved to feel his discomfort subside. At the same time, he realized Ridgeway still had a hand on his shoulder. As much as he wanted to pull away, he didn't. The strong hand helped to ground him.

"I'm all right," he said again, keeping his eyes closed.

"I'm glad to hear it. Can you tell me what happened?"

For some reason, the concern in his brother-in-law's voice irritated him. "I lost control of my car and went off the road."

"Your clothes are wet."

"I went into the river."

A beat of silence followed before Ridgeway said, "Then these should help."

Mark opened his eyes. For the first time, he noticed the bag Joe was holding and relief replaced his irritation. He sat up more slowly this time. The dizziness faded, and he shifted his weight until his legs were hanging over the bed. When he felt secure, he reached for the bag.

Joe handed it over. "You went off the road. Anything else?"

Mark didn't want to think about it. The memories were too fresh. He wasn't ready to speak dispassionately about his experience.

One look at his brother-in-law's set expression told him he had to say something. Joe Ridgeway might be a soft-spoken, easygoing man, but Mark discovered years ago that the older man possessed a strong, stubborn streak. It was impossible to discourage him from his chosen path, though Mark had tried more than once.

Tonight he was too exhausted to resist that quiet determination. "I couldn't get out of my car," he admitted. "Some passing stranger pulled me out before the river carried it away."

Joe's eyes widened. "I had no idea. Your message only said—"

"I know what it said. Now if you'll excuse me, I'll change."

"Can I help?"

Mark glared. "No."

Ridgeway nodded, his face giving nothing away. As soon as he was gone, Mark opened the bag and pulled out the clothes. His eyebrows rose when he recognized them as his own. Joe must have gone by his house before coming to the hospital.

His brother-in-law returned just as Mark was shoving his feet into his shoes. "Are you ready to go?"

Mark frowned at his untied laces. He was still light-headed; bending down to tie them did not seem like a good idea.

Before he could decide what to do, Joe knelt and quickly tied them, then rose with a smile. "Now you're ready."

Suddenly Mark wasn't certain what to say. When he met his brother-in-law's warm green gaze, his anxiety faded and words he didn't use often escaped. "Thank you."

Joe's smile softened. "You're welcome. Let's get you home."

They had to negotiate a maze of corridors before reaching the elevator that took them down to the main level. As they walked toward the exit, a young man wearing surgical scrubs came around the corner. His eyes widened when he saw them.

"Pastor Joe! What are you doing here this time of night?"

"I could ask you the same thing, Scott," Ridgeway said, shaking the younger man's hand. "It seems as if I'm running into half of my congregation here."

Scott laughed. "I wouldn't have been here tonight except I switched shifts with a friend so he could go home." His smile faded. "His father was in an accident yesterday." He glanced at Mark, who looked away, too weary to be interested in the discussion.

"Serious?"

"I'm afraid so."

"I'm sorry," Joe said softly. "Have you contacted the Prayer Circle?"

"No." Scott sighed. "So much has happened so fast, I forgot."

"I'll call them as soon as I get home."

The younger man looked relieved then concerned. "It's awfully late."

"That doesn't matter."

"Thank you."

"I'm glad to do it," Joe said. "Let me know as soon as you hear anything more, okay?"

"I will."

They shook hands again before the young man walked away.

Ridgeway gave Mark an apologetic smile. "I'm sorry about that. I couldn't just walk away, and I didn't think this was the time for introductions."

Mark shrugged, and Joe's smile turned sympathetic. "Let's get out of here."

The drive was a silent one. The adrenalin surge Mark had felt during his escape and again when he realized he had survived the accident was long gone, and with it had gone the last of his energy. He didn't exactly fall asleep, but Ridgeway still had to give him a shake to get his attention.

"We're here. Do you need a hand getting out?"

"No."

He climbed out of the car, staggering momentarily when he straightened. The storm had passed while he was in the hospital, and stars were beginning to twinkle in the night sky. The temperature had dropped, and he shivered.

A yawn escaped, and he bent down to look inside the car. For the second time in less than an hour, Mark said, "Thank you." For some reason, it wasn't as hard to say as it usually was.

"You're welcome. Here you go." Joe handed him the bag that held his still-wet clothes. "I put your prescriptions inside too. Are you going to be all right?"

"Yes," he said and turned away.

Mark never clearly remembered walking through his house, climbing the stairs, passing Geneva's bedroom—the door was closed as usual—and finally turning into his own bedroom. *Just a few more steps*, he kept telling himself.

He lasted long enough to pull off his clothes and fall into bed before sleep claimed him.

3

Early morning light edged the drawn curtains when Mark finally gave up on sleep. Between the nightmares and the bruises and strained muscles clamoring for attention, he felt more exhausted now than when he went to bed.

A hot shower would help, if he could gather together enough energy to drag himself to his feet. The bathroom was attached to the bedroom, a short walk, but at the moment, it seemed much farther.

Faint sounds intruded—a door closing, feet on the stairs, and, briefly, voices. One of the boys, although he couldn't be sure which one because it was too faint. Or maybe he just wasn't used to hearing them this way. Mark was never home at this time of the day. His usual routine had him in the office shortly after the sun rose.

The office!

Mark groaned. With everything that had happened, he had forgotten about the Ashmore deposition. He started to sit up and fell back with another groan as abused muscles protested. Breathing shallowly, he didn't try to move again until the pain eased.

In the end, determination and temper got him to his feet and enabled him to stumble into the bathroom. Once inside the spacious shower, he turned the handles and moaned in pained pleasure as the hot water rained down on him. As much as it hurt, it felt even better, and he leaned against the tiled wall with his eyes closed, letting the healing heat restore him. Only the nagging thought of the office made him eventually, reluctantly, turn it off.

A few minutes later, Mark stood in front of the bathroom vanity, staring at his battered reflection in the mirror. He swore under his breath as he ran a hand over his face, wincing when he touched a tender spot. The thought of shaving was too painful to contemplate. There was no way he could hold a deposition today. Not only did he look as if he had gone ten rounds in a boxing ring, strained muscles and exhaustion made every move a painful effort.

Muttering more curses, Mark shuffled back to his bed and sat down, then picked up his cell phone and pressed the speed dial. Seconds later, he heard the recording begin. "You have reached the Law Offices of Newman, Buchanan, and Welch. Please note that our hours are—" Impatiently, he punched in the code to bypass the recording, and another recording began. "You have reached the desk of Carolyn Colby, assistant to Mr. Newman—"

Mark punched in another code and was finally able to speak. "Carolyn, this is Mark Newman. I was in an automobile accident last night and won't be able to make the deposition this morning. Please call the other side's attorney—Mattingly—and reschedule." He shifted position and winced at another stab of discomfort. "I'm not sure I'll be in today. I'll let you know later."

After setting the phone aside, he sat still, trying to ignore the multitude of aches that seemed to make up his entire body. Out of nowhere, he heard his brother-in-law's voice. "Take deep breaths...deep and slow."

Mark tried it again, and after a few minutes, he felt a little better. He had a vague memory of Joe mentioning prescriptions the hospital had provided. As much as he disliked taking medicine, he knew he wasn't going to be good for anything today in his current state. Where had he put it?

He found the plastic bag his brother-in-law had given to Mark on the floor just inside the bedroom door where he had dropped it. Inside, his clothes were still wet, and he pulled them out one piece at a time. There at the bottom of the bag were two small green plastic bottles. He studied the labels and snorted. One was for sleep; it was too bad he hadn't realized that last night. The other bottle—yes, it was what he wanted.

Mark dragged himself back to the bathroom and filled a glass with water. After downing a pill, he turned away from his reflection and moved cautiously to the corner of the bedroom to sit carefully in the overstuffed leather chair in front of the small fireplace. He sighed in relief and let himself sink into the embrace of his favorite chair.

"No!" He sat up with a jerk and looked around wildly.

The serene bedroom was all that met his gaze, and he leaned weakly back while trying to catch his breath. He realized he had fallen asleep.

"A bad dream," he muttered. "It was just a bad dream."

As his pounding heart began to slow, Mark took stock of his situation. He was still sitting in the chair, and—he stretched cautiously—the pill had kicked in; he was no longer in pain. With that realization came another—he was hungry. Mark glanced at the clock on the table, and his eyes widened. He had slept away the morning. No wonder he was hungry.

He rose and took a few steps before relaxing. Still no pain. Excellent. To the accompaniment of a growling stomach, Mark made his way downstairs. As he entered the kitchen, he heard a gasp and the *clang* of a dropped pot. He stopped, shocked, before another emotion took over.

"Who are you?" he demanded angrily.

A woman stood by the stove, still clutching the lid of the pot she had dropped while she stared at him with wide eyes and open mouth. She was of medium height and medium build with short, graying hair, dressed in jeans and a flannel shirt.

"I said, who are you? And what are you doing in my house?" Mark demanded. He reached for his cell phone before he remembered he had left it on his bedside table.

His words or action seemed to shake the woman out of her shock. Her eyes narrowed, and she snapped, "I work here."

"You what?"

"My name is Amy Kittredge. I've worked as Mrs. Newman's housekeeper for the last five years."

Five years? Mark shook his head. "That's impossible. I've never seen you before."

"And I've never seen you either," the woman—Amy Kittredge—said coldly. "How do I know you really live here?"

Mark's mouth opened and closed in fresh outrage. Of all the… "I think you're lying," he snarled.

"I can prove I work here," she said calmly. "All I have to do is call Mrs. Newman. She'll vouch for me."

"At what number?" Mark said suspiciously.

"She's at the museum's open house today." Amy Kittredge rattled off the number for the museum.

At least Mark assumed it was the museum. He wasn't about to admit he would have to look up the number to confirm the woman's claim. If nothing else, her confidence supported her words.

"I was just about to have lunch," she said unexpectedly. "Would you like some?"

"Lunch?"

"I've been here since 9:00 a.m." Amy Kittredge studied him with a surprisingly sharp eye. "Cleaning." She waved a hand to encompass the house. "Mrs. Newman left a note that you were home sick, so I haven't gone up to the second floor yet."

Geneva had left a note? Mark was unexpectedly moved. She must have checked on him before she left. He realized the housekeeper was still talking.

"The beef stew is almost ready and—" The timer on the stove dinged, and she smiled. "How's that for timing? The rolls are ready too."

Now that he wasn't distracted by a stranger in the kitchen, Mark smelled the delicious aromas wafting through the room, and his stomach growled again, more loudly this time. Amy Kittredge heard it too and laughed.

"I'll take that as a yes. Let me set another place," she said.

For the first time, he noticed the single place setting on the table in the breakfast nook. In all the years he had lived in this house, he had never eaten there, only at the dining-room table. He didn't know why the thought struck him so hard.

"Mr. Newman?"

A hand patting his arm pulled him out of his preoccupation, and he looked down to see concerned brown eyes. "Yes, uh"—Mark coughed in an effort to clear his throat—"I'm fine," and pulled away.

Amy Kittredge didn't take the hint. She stayed uncomfortably close and watched him carefully. "No, I don't think you are," she said. "Why don't you sit down."

It was a statement, not a question. Mark wasn't used to taking orders, and he was surprised to find himself obeying. Thanks to the pill he had taken earlier, he wasn't in pain, but he was increasingly aware of a stubborn exhaustion that made moving, much less thinking, difficult.

He was content to sit and let his mind drift, only vaguely aware of the housekeeper setting the table in front of him. After an indeterminate time, Mark felt someone standing over him and opened his eyes to see the housekeeper.

"Eat," she said.

Another order. But looking at the plate filled with beef stew and rolls still hot from the oven she had set before him, he was happy to obey.

"Here's the butter," she offered.

The butter melted into the rolls, and when Mark took his first bite of the stew, his taste buds hummed with approval. It was hard to suppress his exclamation of satisfaction and even harder to keep from gobbling. Such mouth-watering food insisted on being appreciated, and eating slowly allowed him to do that.

"Would you like something to drink?"

The voice startled him out of his pleasurable daze. Amy Kittredge had risen again and was looking at Mark expectantly; he had forgotten she was sitting across the table.

"Yes, coffee."

She pursed her lips. "I think milk would be better for you right now."

Mark's eyebrows rose. For a minute, he didn't know whether to be amused or annoyed by her high-handedness, but amusement won out, and he drank the glass of milk she handed him. When Amy Kittredge finished her meal, she began gathering together the dishes.

Glancing at the pot that was still half-filled with stew, he asked, "Why did you make so much?"

The housekeeper smiled. "I always do. The rest is for the boys' dinner, and Mrs. Newman if she wants."

The boys' dinner? Mark looked blankly at the woman as he realized he was hearing a part of his family's life that he hadn't been aware of for many years. A wave of dizziness rolled over him, and he caught hold of the edge of the table before he could be swept away with it. Gradually, the light-headedness faded, and he heard a worried voice.

"Mr. Newman, say something. Talk to me right now, or I'm calling an ambulance."

"I'm all right," he said and pushed away her hand on his shoulder. He stood up slowly, cautiously, and the housekeeper backed away a few steps.

"Are you sure?" she asked.

"Yes, I'm sure." He ignored her worried expression. "Excuse me."

4

Mark didn't go back upstairs. Instead, he went through the living room, dining room, and then out through the french doors into the backyard. When he reached the patio he sank down into the first chair he encountered.

He deliberately blanked his mind of all thoughts and allowed his senses to take over. It was quiet in the yard and pleasantly warm, surprisingly so, considering the weather of the last week. Birds were singing, and he felt a light breeze caress his face. It also brought to his nose the fragrance of flowers, and he looked around to find out where the scent was coming from.

Considering the ferocity of last night's storm, Mark saw surprising little damage. The pool covering was sprinkled with debris from the surrounding garden. Still-damp leaves were scattered over the flagstone patio and walkways, but otherwise, it looked as usual.

His wandering eyes fell on the rosebushes lining the far wall of the garden. There was the source of some of the sweet-smelling scents. The budding orange tree in the corner of the yard was also sending its fragrance through the air. And there, the beautiful bank of white flowers edging the walkway waved merrily in the light breeze, having also weathered the storm with astonishingly little damage. Narcissus, he thought it was called.

Mark took a deep breath, enjoying himself. On some level he didn't care to analyze, he knew it was the mingled scents of the narcissus and the roses and the orange blossoms that were providing an oddly soothing, fragrant backdrop to the garden.

Soothing? He stiffened. What was wrong with him? Where were all these stray thoughts coming from? It had to be because he was so tired, maybe partly the effect of the pain medication. He mentally shrugged aside the inconsequential, irritating thoughts and relaxed, but a few minutes later, he opened his eyes again in fresh irritation. Why couldn't he relax?

The answer was slow in coming. Relaxation was impossible because, as much as he didn't want to think about what had happened last night, the memories refused to leave him. He could only be grateful for small mercies. Thanks to the medication, he wasn't in pain. In the shower, Mark had seen the evidence of the accident in the bruises covering his body. It was more than enough evidence to remind him of how he would be feeling without the pills.

All right, so be it. It was time to gain some perspective. He'd been in an almost fatal accident, but he had survived. It was time to move on.

Much to his annoyance, logic didn't chase away the memories. He had nearly died last night. He would have died if not for a stranger's help. The stranger had risked his life to save Mark, only to disappear when official help arrived.

Wait a minute. He sat up mentally and physically. Who had notified the authorities about his plight?

He rubbed his forehead hard. Thanks to years of hard work, he was a wealthy man. He would happily have given the man who saved him money or some other expensive gift. That would have been an appropriate resolution. Instead, when Mark asked him how he could repay him, his rescuer had made only one request: "If you really want to thank me, the next time you run across someone who needs a hand, give him yours."

Mark swore. The stranger hadn't asked for money or other kind of material reward. That would have made sense. But this, no. Of all the stupid, confusing requests…

He shook his head in an attempt to dispel the useless thoughts and leaned back in the chair, rubbing his eyes. They ached as they always did when he didn't get enough sleep. Ordinarily, it didn't matter. Ordinarily, Mark Newman could work through exhaustion, illness, and whatever else life threw at him. But somehow in the last twelve hours, ordinariness seemed to have flown out the window. Now he was feeling...what was he feeling?

Unsettled.

Why?

Be logical, Newman, he told himself. Though terrifying when it happened, the accident was over, behind him. He had survived and now it was time to move on, to get back to the life waiting for him.

You almost died last night.

The words seemed to fill every atom of his being. Mark was on his feet before he realized it, trying to breathe despite his suddenly racing heart. He clenched his hands to try to stop their shaking. This was ridiculous. He was stronger than this.

He couldn't shake the memory of the stranger who had risked death to save him. Mark hadn't even had a chance to ask him his name before he was gone. The paramedics claimed they hadn't seen him. There were no homes along that area of the road. Where had the stranger disappeared to so fast? And why? Why not stick around?

He groaned and rubbed his aching head again. Enough of this. He needed to get out of here and away from his uncomfortable thoughts. For the first time in his adult life, he couldn't seem to control them, and he was a little frightened by the knowledge.

Mark jumped to his feet and hurried back inside. As he strode through the house he heard the distant roar of the vacuum cleaner coming from upstairs and was grateful not to run into the housekeeper again. He called a car rental place he had used before and fifteen minutes later he was picked up and driven to the lot. Ten minutes after that he headed out in a rented Lexus.

He had no destination in mind; he just needed to get away from the house. As he drove, Mark paid only partial attention to the passing scenery. Houses gave way to shopping malls, and for no reason he could put his finger on, the changing landscape made him feel better. It was a relief to feel his tension ease; he deliberately loosened his grip on the steering wheel and leaned back in his seat. This had been a good idea.

He saw a ramp for the freeway just up ahead, and though he hadn't originally planned on it, Mark went up it. Ordinarily he would have moved immediately to the fast lane, but oddly, he didn't feel the need. Now he realized he had a destination after all. Strange, he hadn't been aware of it earlier.

What are you doing?

The words seemed to come from the deepest recesses of his mind. Mark detected a note of criticism in them. Instead of getting defensive, he mentally thumbed his nose at them. He was going back to the place where he had almost died last night to get some questions answered. There was nothing wrong, nothing abnormal, in wanting answers.

He also wanted—needed—to find that stranger to thank him properly. The least Mark could do for his rescuer was to reward him.

Not that he expected to find his rescuer hanging around the site. All he was certain of at the moment was that he needed to go back. Once he had his answers, he could move on.

It was midday, so traffic was light, a rare event on these freeways. When he saw the exit sign he had been watching for, Mark moved over and, minutes later, was driving along the frontage road again.

Unlike the violent storm of last night, there were no ominous shadows to distract or confuse a driver today. Huge old oak trees lined the road and provided a shady canopy, along with flowering bushes that, though overgrown, offered pleasing splashes of color. Under a crystal blue sky and warm sun, the road was without threat, even inviting.

Mark slowed as he traveled, then lowered the window. The breeze of the car's passing carried with it the scent of fresh grass and the invigorating scent of rain-washed air. He took a deep breath and exhaled slowly, feeling the last of his tension fading away. It was amazing, the difference a few hours could make.

His foot hit the brake before his eyes recognized what they were seeing. The broken fence was stark, silent evidence of what had happened. His heart began to pound when he saw the deep gashes torn into the turf. They cut across the broad expanse of grass and up the shallow slope to disappear over the top of the embankment.

Mark pulled over and parked. When he removed his hands from the steering wheel, he tried not to notice they were shaking again. For an instant, he was overwhelmed with the desire to run away. He got as far as putting his hands back on the wheel before stopping. For another minute, he hesitated, indecisive, then he yanked the key out of the ignition and shoved the door open.

Once he was out of the car, Mark felt better. Now that he was moving, maybe he could shut up the small, irritating voice in the back of his mind, asking questions for which he had no answers.

"I'm here," he said out loud and marched up the slope. It was steeper than it looked, and he was breathing hard when he finally reached the crest. His gaze traveled down the other side of the embankment—and his heart stopped.

Tire tracks cut deeply into the earth, leading down to the water. What he saw now was not the gentle stream that normally traveled between the banks. It had become a raging river, rushing by with startling speed, the water crashing in on itself in wild, turbulent brown waves.

Where was his car?

Mark shivered, unable to stop the sudden chattering of his teeth. He winced at the pain in his hands and realized he was clenching his fists so tightly his fingernails were cutting into his palms. Once more, the truth of what happened slapped him in the face, more harshly this time with the evidence before his eyes. His legs gave way, and he sat down with a *thud*.

Mark had no idea how long he sat there before his heart stopped pounding. The ground was wet beneath him, but for once he didn't care what he might be doing to his Armani suit. How was he supposed to put this behind him?

A new thought broke through his swirling emotions. His firm had two private detectives on retainer. He would have one of them track down his rescuer, and once Mark had properly thanked the man, he was sure he would be able to return to his normal life.

Feeling better now that he had made a decision, he climbed to his feet and turned around to go back. He tried to avoid looking at the tire tracks but couldn't tear his eyes away. As hard as Mark tried, he couldn't shake off the implications of those tracks disappearing into the swiftly moving water.

When he reached the crest of the hill again, he paused to study the surrounding landscape. His memory hadn't played him false. Between the trees and overgrown bushes, it would have been a simple-enough process for his rescuer to hide.

It could have happened that way.

Mark followed the marks in the ground, walking carefully over the uneven ground and slowing as he neared a tree. There was something curled up by the base, something long and coiling. He caught his breath when he recognized what he was looking at. It wasn't a snake. It was rope—the rope that had saved his life.

Mark's heart beat faster. If his cuts and bruises weren't enough, here was solid, unequivocal proof that his memories of last night were genuine.

He crouched down beside the untidy pile of rope. One end was still tied around the base of the tree.

Mark stared at it for a long time before finally putting out a tentative hand. The rope was soaked through by the storm but otherwise seemed undamaged. He squeezed the fibers and felt them give slightly while moisture trickled out. Sitting back on his heels, he looked at his bandaged hands. They had been scoured and rubbed raw by this rope, and suddenly he was glad for the pain.

Mark Newman didn't believe in a lot of things. By training, by education, by experience, and by nature, he believed in what he saw, in what he could prove. This rope, the state of his hands, his cuts and bruises, were all proof of what happened last night. All the logic in the world couldn't change that truth.

He shivered again. Suddenly filled with resolve, he reached down to untie the knot. Swollen with moisture, the knot resisted, and with a muttered curse, Mark redoubled his efforts. Several unavailing minutes later, all he had to show for his efforts were fresh scrapes and throbbing fingers.

Cut it loose. That was the obvious, easy solution.

Something in Mark resisted. Instead, he had another idea. Rising, he went to the rental car and opened the trunk. Sure enough, wrapped in with the spare tire were some tools, including a crowbar. He hefted it and took it back to the tree. With slow, patient effort, Mark wedged one corner of the crowbar into the knot. He kept twisting and tugging and finally felt the knot began to give way. It still took a long time before the knot loosened enough to slide his fingers through it.

As if that had been what it was waiting for, the knot meekly gave way, and Mark finished untying the rope, then coiled it up. Wet, heavy, streaked with mud, it was not an attractive bundle; at least it wouldn't be if this was an ordinary day. Today was different. Slinging it half over one shoulder, he carried it triumphantly back to the car. After dropping the rope in the trunk, he stared at it. If he ever started doubting, all he would need to do was look at this tangible proof.

He was no nearer to finding his rescuer now than he had been when he woke up this morning. Still, Mark was glad he had returned.

5

When he walked into the house, the first thing Mark heard was laughter. It wasn't a sound he was used to hearing in his home. Frowning in confusion, he followed the noise to the kitchen and stopped in the doorway.

His sons, sixteen-year-old Brian and twelve-year-old Daniel, were sitting in the breakfast nook. By the taste-bud-tickling aroma, he knew they were eating the same stew he himself had eaten a few hours earlier.

Mark glanced at his watch. How could it almost be five o'clock? He knew he had driven aimlessly for quite a while after leaving the accident scene, but he hadn't realized so much time had passed.

Most astonishing was the sight of his sons joking with each other. Actually, it sounded as if Brian had been teasing Daniel, who appeared a little flushed under the kitchen lights. The younger boy was smiling and shaking his head, and Mark watched them in surprise. This wasn't usual.

Granted, he wasn't around them very much, but they were ordinarily much more serious and quiet…

His thoughts came to an abrupt halt when Brian saw him. In a split-second, the laughter faded from the boy's expression and was replaced by the solemn, serious face Mark was used to seeing. As if recognizing his brother's abrupt shift in mood, Daniel turned around. Like Brian, his smile vanished at the sight of his father.

"Dad." Brian spoke without expression, the word coming out oddly flat.

Before Mark could respond, another voice sounded behind him. "Mr. Newman?"

Mark turned to see the housekeeper, Amy Kittredge. Her eyes went from him to the boys and back. For a second, he thought he saw disapproval before she went on.

"I'm going to be leaving in a few minutes. Can I dish up some beef stew for you before I go?"

"No, thank you."

"I'll have some more," Brian said unexpectedly. He looked at his brother. "You want any more, Danny?"

Keeping his head down, Daniel shook his head, and Brian reached out to tousle his hair.

"Hey!" Daniel jerked away and glared at his big brother.

Brian grinned at him and said, "How about some more of Amy's delicious rolls?"

Mark's frown returned. Brian knew better than to call an adult by their first name. Before he could chastise him, the housekeeper laughed. "Stay put, both of you. Give me your plates, and I'll fill them up. Just don't expect such service next time," she said.

Brian chuckled, and Daniel's glare turned into a smile. "Umm," he said, with a quick look at his father, "thanks. I mean, thank you."

Mark struggled to hide his increasing discomfort. There was some kind of dynamic going on between the housekeeper and his sons, something from which he felt excluded. Why were the boys so focused on Amy Kittredge? Why were they ignoring him? Or was this normal behavior for a sixteen-year-old and a twelve-year-old?

"Excuse me," he said abruptly and walked out.

When he reached the living room, he stopped, suddenly unsure what to do next. What was wrong with him? The obvious answer was the same one he had been struggling with since he'd awakened this morning.

Mark swore under his breath. He hated this. He had thought the whole problem through and arrived at what he thought was a logical solution. Yet still he felt…ill at ease, oddly disconnected from life.

Swearing again, he stormed upstairs. When he reached his bedroom, he closed and locked the door. A look in the mirror was enough to convince him that, after wallowing in the mud at the accident scene, he needed another shower. Hopefully, the hot water would also help with the aches and pains that were resurfacing as the pain medication wore off.

The shower did help. By the time he toweled off, Mark felt well enough that he decided to wait on taking another pill. Wrapping his bathrobe around him, he went back out into the bedroom and sat down. His eyes fell on his cell phone that he had left on the bedside table. He picked it up and was unsurprised to find he had several messages.

Mark felt suddenly better. This was part of his normal, busy life, and he relished the reminder. Smiling to himself, he called up the messages.

The first one was from his assistant. "Hello, Mr. Newman, it's Carolyn Colby. I got your message and was able to reach Mr. Mattingly, and he agreed to continue the deposition. I checked with the court reporters and got several dates to run by you. I also rescheduled today's appointments. Please let me know if you want me to give the information over the telephone or…could you please let me know if you don't plan to come into the office tomorrow? If so, we'll need to reschedule several items. I hope you're feeling better and I'll talk to you later."

Mark nodded in satisfaction. As usual, his assistant was on the ball. She made his work much easier.

The second message was from one of his partners, Marty Welch. "Hi, Mark, what's this I hear about you being in an accident? What happened? Carolyn says it wasn't serious so that's good. This is the first day you've missed that I can remember. Let me know if I can help with anything, okay?"

Not only a partner but a friend. It was as if each voice Mark heard was calling him back to normalcy.

The next message was from the hospital pharmacy telling him he had another prescription waiting to be picked up. He didn't recall the doctor talking about more prescriptions, and now that he was feeling almost normal again, he was ready to forget about the accident.

The thought of the accident seemed to awaken all his aches and pains. Grimacing, Mark returned to the bathroom to take another pain pill, before listening to the rest of his messages. There was nothing of substance, but he felt more grounded in reality with each one.

By the time he was done, he was beginning to feel hungry. A glance at the clock told him the housekeeper must be gone by now. The boys should have finished their dinner, which would mean the kitchen was empty. Despite feeling better, he felt strangely reluctant to face anyone.

The house was quiet when Mark left his bedroom. Walking down the hall, he saw light under the boys' bedroom doors, and from Brian's, he heard faint music. At least that what Brian called it.

The sounds faded when he went downstairs. Someone, probably Amy Kittredge, had turned on the lights in the living room, and the lamps cast a cozy glow around the room. Mark passed through it, then through the dining room and into the kitchen. He breathed a sigh of relief at the neat, empty room. The housekeeper had cleaned up before leaving, and he was pleased by the tidiness almost as much by the fact that there was no one else there.

Amy Kittredge had said there was more beef stew. Feeling as if he was exploring uncharted territory, Mark rummaged around in the refrigerator. He found a small tub of barbecued chicken, another of coleslaw, the beef stew, and a smaller aluminum-foil-wrapped package that, when unwrapped, revealed three rolls. Another container held what appeared to be yellow mashed potatoes. Sweet potatoes? And in this one, his eyebrows rose as he recognized one of his childhood favorites—meat loaf. In the vegetable bins were lettuce, tomatoes, zucchini, carrots, and a bag of large mushrooms.

Mark was amazed at the contents of the refrigerator and then amused by his amazement. He couldn't remember the last time he had actually looked in a refrigerator, much less explored its contents. *You need to get out more, Newman,* he told himself, resisting a laugh. If anyone came in and found him laughing out loud while staring into a refrigerator, they would cart him off to a funny farm.

Suddenly feeling light-hearted, he pulled out the meat loaf and put it on the counter. In a bin on the floor of the pantry, Mark found unpeeled onions and potatoes, but that wasn't what he was looking for. The bread saver was on the third shelf, and he found two loaves of bread, one half-used.

Still smiling, Mark took out two slices of bread and laid them next to the container of meat loaf. After rummaging through a couple of drawers, he found a large knife and cut a thick piece of meat loaf and laid it between bread slices. He leaned against the counter, took a big bite, and chewed slowly, relishing the spices and other flavors that Amy Kittredge had expertly mixed together. It tasted slightly different from the meat loaf he remembered eating as a young boy but was still delicious.

Mark had almost finished his second meat loaf sandwich when the door bell chimed. He glanced at the clock. He wasn't expecting anyone. When he looked out the peephole in the front door, Mark's light spirits faded. On the other side of the door was the last person he wanted to see. He debated briefly ignoring the chimes, and then he heard Brian's voice floating down from the second floor. "Is anyone going to get the door?"

Mark's lips tightened. His son knew better than to yell in the house. "I have it," he returned, raising his voice just enough to be heard upstairs.

He heard the bedroom door close, just short of a slam, and his temper flared. Maybe being grounded for a weekend would remind Brian about house rules. After he got rid of the unwanted visitor, he would talk to the boy.

Opening the front door, he said, "Hello, Joe."

"Hi, Mark. I wanted to see how you were doing."

As tempting as it was not to let his brother-in-law inside, he couldn't think of a good excuse. And if Joe chose to mention the slight to his sister, Geneva would be furious. Mark wasn't in the mood for an argument with his wife.

Trying to hide his annoyance, he stepped aside. "Come in."

He didn't think it was his imagination that the corners of Joe's lips quirked slightly. If he didn't know better, he would have thought his brother-in-law knew what he was thinking.

Once inside, Ridgeway studied him with observant eyes. "How are you feeling?"

So much for small talk. That was his brother-in-law. Still irritated, Mark answered shortly. "I'd rather not stand in the foyer and talk."

"I'm sorry, standing probably isn't one of your favorite activities right now. Let's sit down." As if he was the host, Joe led the way into the living room.

Mark followed reluctantly, resisting the impulse to roll his eyes. In his own pleasant, low-key way, Joe Ridgeway could be one pushy character when he chose.

Ridgeway settled down on one end of the sofa. If he was expecting his brother-in-law to join him, he was disappointed. Mark deliberately sat in the deep, overstuffed chair opposite the sofa before realizing his mistake. In his current state, it was going to take considerable effort to lever himself out of the depths of the chair and probably result in more than a little discomfort. Well, he would worry about that later.

"I hope Beth isn't waiting dinner on you," he said, wanting to keep things casual.

Joe's eyes twinkled as if he recognized Mark's attempt to change the subject, but he responded easily. "No, I told her I would be dropping by here. She and the kids will go ahead and eat. I'll get something when I get home."

Mark was tempted to swear. Ridgeway's words eliminated any quick escape. The man wasn't about to leave until he got his questions answered. So be it.

"In answer to your first question, I'm fine."

Joe didn't look convinced. Even as Mark braced himself for a frontal attack, his brother-in-law said, "Geneva was quite upset last night when she called me about your message."

Mark blinked in surprise. Geneva had been upset? He hadn't talked to her since the accident. In fact, he had to think for a minute before he remembered the last time he saw his wife. Last Sunday afternoon, there had been a meeting here of the board of directors of one of the charities Geneva favored. Mark had come home from a meeting of his own just as they were breaking up, and his wife had introduced him around.

Over the years, he and Geneva had carved out their own separate lives, and Mark was used to not seeing his wife for several days at a time. Yet Joe claimed she had been upset when she called him last night. And, Mark suddenly remembered, she had left a message for Amy Kittredge warning the housekeeper that he was home, ill.

A strange little surge of warmth moved through him, and Mark didn't know what to make of it. He tried to shrug it aside and said matter-of-factly, "There was nothing to be upset about."

"Nothing to be upset about? You could have been killed!"

Mark flinched away from an echo of the fear that had dominated him during those terrifying moments. "Well, I wasn't. I'm fine."

"I don't think so." Ridgeway's eyes narrowed. "You're moving stiffly, your hands are bandaged, and I bet under your clothes you're covered in bruises."

Mark caught his temper a split second before it erupted. "That's none of your business. What are you really doing here?"

He had succeeded in surprising his brother-in-law. Joe stared at him for a long minute before his eyes softened. "As hard as it may be for you to believe, I really did come over here to see how you were doing. And to offer my help."

"Help with what?"

"With whatever you need."

The words were simple, the tone matter-of-fact, and Mark was momentarily at a loss for words. "I've already told you how I am," he said finally. Losing his temper would mean losing control, and he was determined not to allow that. "I don't know what else to tell you."

Ridgeway studied him with those too-observant green eyes. "I'd like to believe you but…" He let his voice trail off and raised his eyebrows.

Mark knew his words didn't match his appearance, but he didn't care. "Cuts and bruises always look worse the day after," he said dismissively.

"They do," Joe agreed. "It's not the cuts and bruises that worry me, Mark. You went through a terrifying ordeal." He sighed, a frustrated sound. "I'm thankful you survived, but I don't believe you can just set it aside and go on as if nothing happened."

Mark didn't know what to say. He wasn't about to admit the truth that he hadn't set anything aside, and his brother-in-law was ignoring his attempts to belittle the experience. Ridgeway's attitude must have something to do with being a minister. As that was the part of his brother-in-law to which Mark had always objected the most, the realization only increased his annoyance. If Joe was expecting some tearful confession, Mark was happy to disappoint him.

"It happened, it's over, life goes on," he said brusquely.

Joe sat back in his seat and considered his brother-in-law thoughtfully. Mark almost laughed. He had hit the nail on the head. Ridgeway had expected something, and Mark wasn't responding as he hoped.

"Praise God, it ended well," Joe said. "Thanks to the man who helped you."

Mark nodded. On that point, he agreed. "Yes."

"Have you found out who he was?"

"No. He hasn't come forward."

Mark thought again of his tentative plan to bring in one of the firm's private detectives to locate his rescuer. Was it even possible? He would let them decide since they were the experts. Abruptly, he realized his brother-in-law was speaking.

"Did he say anything at all last night that might help you identify him?"

It was Mark's turn to look thoughtfully at Ridgeway. It was almost as if the other man was reading his mind. "He didn't say much, nothing about who he was."

"But he did talk?"

What was his brother-in-law getting at? "Of course, he did," Mark said impatiently. "When he helped me get out of the car…" Despite himself, a shiver ran through him. He was grateful that Ridgeway didn't comment. "And when we climbed up the embankment…" Another shiver gripped him, and Mark barely swallowed a curse.

Joe's eyes were oddly intent. "So he really did save your life."

"Yes."

"Why did he leave?"

"How should I know?" Mark's temper rose again. "Once we were back up on the road…" He stopped, remembering that strange request.

"What?"

"I thanked him," Mark recalled. "I wanted to reward him in some way. But he said…" He stopped again, suddenly feeling awkward about repeating the words. Glancing at his brother-in-law, he met the calm green gaze and felt…what? Joe Ridgeway annoyed him on a regular basis because of his old-fashioned religious beliefs.

Mark wasn't used to feeling reassured by the man's presence, yet that was what he was feeling now. The anxiety that had been lurking on the edge of his thoughts all day had faded during their conversation and been replaced by a sense of…of comfort. How odd.

Joe was sitting quietly, watching him, but there was no demand in his expression. Maybe that was what broke through Mark's instinctive resistance, and he admitted to what he had thought he would always keep to himself.

"When I insisted that I wanted to reward him, he said if I really wanted to thank him"—he paused to ensure he remembered correctly—"he said, 'If you really want to thank me, the next time you run across someone who needs a hand, give him yours.'"

Joe's eyebrows rose. After a minute, a smile slowly curved his lips. "That's an intriguing comment."

Mark hadn't actually considered his rescuer's words in that light, but he had to agree and was freshly irritated. "I wanted to reward him. He risked his life to save mine. That deserves some kind of reward. But instead…" His voice trailed off because he wasn't sure how to finish the sentence.

"There's no 'instead,'" Joe said.

"What?"

"There's no 'instead.' What he asked for was in response to your offer of a reward. That's how you can reward him. By helping someone else."

"That doesn't make sense."

Joe chuckled. "Not to you, but it did to him. You said it yourself. He risked his life to save you. He's not your ordinary stranger, that's for sure. Maybe—" He stopped abruptly, and to Mark's surprise, his brother-in-law looked embarrassed.

"Maybe what?" he prompted.

Ridgeway gave him a self-deprecating smile. "I'm a product of my upbringing and my beliefs. I can't divorce my thoughts from them."

Mark stared at him between narrowed lids. "Is this going to be some religious mumbo jumbo? If so, never mind."

"I don't think it's mumbo jumbo," Joe said. "Your rescuer may be a man with a strong concern for others. But after listening to you, I can't help wondering if he was something more."

The antagonism Mark usually felt around his brother-in-law had been mostly absent tonight. Now he could feel it growing. "Whatever," he said dismissively. "As I said, it happened, it's over—"

"I remember what you said," Joe calmly interrupted. "I'm not sure it's accurate."

"I don't care what you think. I'm tired, and I'm going to bed. If you want to stay here by yourself, go ahead."

Ridgeway gave him a long, measuring look. "I'm sorry, I didn't mean to stay so long." He got to his feet. "I meant what I said earlier. If you need help with anything, please let me know, and I'll be happy to give you a hand."

Mark glared. He was sick and tired of hearing about helping hands. Maybe Joe sensed what he was thinking because his lips twitched, as if he was fighting back another smile.

"I'll let myself out. Good night."

Mark nodded curtly and listened to his brother-in-law's footsteps recede behind him. He heard the door open then close and relaxed in his seat. Finally. Now that he was alone, he sagged under the weight of an overpowering exhaustion. He had claimed to be tired simply to get rid of Ridgeway, but those words were more true than he had realized.

The thought of moving his battered body was not appealing, but remaining in the chair was not an option. Upstairs was his bedroom and, more importantly, the pills that would take away his pain. He just had to get out of this chair, ascend the stairs, and make his way down the hall.

Mark groaned, but there was no help for it.

Ten minutes later, he collapsed, panting, into bed. It felt as if every part of his body ached and he could only lie helpless, shivering, waiting for the pill to kick in. At least the discomfort kept him from thinking about that ridiculous conversation with his brother-in-law.

A stray thought broke through his misery. He had forgotten to chastise Brian for disregarding house rules. Another time, he decided, feeling the pill beginning to work. As the pain receded, exhaustion returned, and he gratefully embraced sleep.

6

The beautiful strains of Rachmaninoff's *Piano Concerto No. 2* drew him gently out of sleep. Mark opened his eyes a slit and was relieved to see it was still dark. His alarm had gone off at its usual time, so he would be able to begin his day with the rising sun.

Remembering what had happened the last time he tried to move swiftly, he cautiously stretched his arms and legs. The now familiar aches spread through his body, and he caught his breath in a hiss of pain and frustration. He had hoped to be done with the pain pills, but there was no way he was going to be able to show up at his office feeling the way he did.

After taking another pill, followed by a long hot shower, Mark emerged feeling fairly human. A short time later, he was driving to his office. The sun was just beginning to send rays of crimson, cobalt, and gold across the sky and he felt a rising sense of satisfaction. This was the way his life was supposed to be. The insanity of the last two days was finally fading, much to his relief.

As was usually the case, Mark was the first person to arrive. The Law Offices of Newman, Buchanan, and Welch occupied the entire ninth floor of the high-rise, and the mail room and storage rooms of the firm took up the eighth floor. Every so often when he was alone in the suite, Mark thought back to the beginning when he and Steve Buchanan, both recent law-school graduates, had left their safe if boring positions with one of the largest firms in Los Angeles to open their own. In less than twenty years, they had gone from that to this.

Smiling, Mark walked through the front doors, switched on the lights in the reception area, and turned right to go down the hall to his office. Just as he reached his door, he noticed light coming out from under the door of Buchanan's office at the far end of the hall. Steve wasn't an early bird. What on earth was he doing in the office at this time of the day?

Curious, he turned away from his office and walked to Buchanan's. He knocked lightly but didn't hear anything. He knocked again, and after a minute, he heard a faint voice from inside. Taking that as an invitation, Mark shoved the door open.

"Good morning," he said before frowning at the dimness of the room.

The drapes were still drawn across the windows, and only the desk lamp was on. It was enough light to see Steve Buchanan sitting behind his desk, staring down at a pristine desk blotter. There were no files on his desk, nothing to indicate why he came in so early.

"Morning."

Underlying Buchanan's voice was a shakiness he had never heard before, and Mark felt suddenly uneasy. "You're in early," he said.

Steve sat back in his chair, out of range of the light from the desk lamp. "I know."

Mark's concern grew. On impulse, he sat down in one of the two client chairs facing the desk. Then he noticed something he hadn't spotted earlier. A small picture frame was laying facedown by the telephone. He had seen the picture in the frame numerous times and knew it was of Melanie Buchanan and their three children.

Mark was a lawyer. He was used to putting together bits of information into an understandable picture, and he didn't like the preliminary picture these bits of information revealed. It was tempting to make some casual comment and walk away because he had never cared for emotional scenes. Yet he couldn't bring himself to leave. He and Steve Buchanan went back to law school, almost twenty-five years. Buchanan wasn't just an acquaintance; he was a friend. Mark didn't have all that many real friends that he felt he could walk away from this one.

"What's going on, Steve?"

"Melanie wants a divorce."

The words were soft, flat, containing a bone-deep weariness, and even in the midst of his shock, Mark was immediately sorry he had stayed. This was just the kind of emotional scene he tried to avoid; he had no idea how to respond. His first thought was to find someone else to listen to Buchanan. Maybe Marty Welch would be able to provide some kind of support. Then again, Welch's propensity for the opposite sex hardly qualified him as an expert in marital relations. Neither was Mark, but he was the only one here.

Mentally gritting his teeth, he said, "Do you want to talk about it?"

Only silence answered him, and he waited. Finally, Buchanan spoke, so softly Mark could barely hear him. "I came home last night to find she had packed all my clothes. She said she'd filed for divorce and wanted me out of the house immediately."

Mark had encountered Melanie Buchanan on countless occasions, but he had never had more than brief, superficial conversations with her. All he really knew about her was that she was an attractive redhead who was always stylishly dressed and seemed a perfect complement to her husband.

The Buchanans had been married for over fifteen years, almost as long as Mark had been married. He felt a sudden sense of disquiet that had nothing to do with Steve's situation.

"What about your children?"

"They weren't home. Melanie had sent them off to spend the night with friends." He stopped talking, and silence filled the emptiness.

Mark debated several responses before saying, "What did you do?"

For the first time, Steve raised his head and met his partner's gaze. "I spent the night at a hotel. Part of the night, anyway. I couldn't sleep, so I finally came here." He looked around as if he hadn't noticed his location before. "I know things haven't been that great between us. I mean, she's always complaining about how much I work. But she never said—I don't remember her ever threatening me with divorce if I didn't change."

The exhaustion was increasingly obvious the longer he spoke, and Mark had no idea how to respond. He had always been a big believer in the efficacy of work. Ordinarily, he would have encouraged his partner to try to bury himself in his cases and let things fall where they chose in regard to his marriage. He opened his mouth and closed it again, reluctantly acknowledging that his partner needed more than a pep talk. As much as Mark had embraced the returning normalcy of his life, he realized it wasn't going to be as simple as he thought. His terrifying ordeal of two nights ago had shattered his worldview; it was going to take time to regain it.

Mark suddenly felt betrayed. He didn't want that stupid accident continuing to affect him. But why else was he unable to voice his usual spiel of work being the solution to all problems?

"I…I'm sorry, Steve." Where had that come from?

His partner shrugged. His attempt at a smile was a poor effort. "Well, that's life." He took a deep breath. "I wanted to go over the responses to our discovery from Edgemont's attorney. Is this a good time for you?"

Thankful for the change of subject, Mark nodded quickly. "Sure. What've you got?"

Almost an hour later, he stood. "It looks good. Let me know if you want me to take another look after you finalize it."

"Thanks."

Walking back toward his office, Mark tried to shrug off an unusual depression. He noticed two of the firm's law clerks approaching and was reminded how long he had been in Steve's office. The workday had begun, and he needed to meet with his assistant to see what his day held.

"Good morning, Mr. Newman," the female clerk, Sara Reynolds, said brightly. "You're looking much better than the rumors suggested."

Rumors. Mark grimaced at the thought, and her smile faded.

"I'm sorry, sir. I didn't mean anything."

The other law clerk, Brad Fielding, simply nodded to his superior. This was his second year of clerking with the firm, and he had obviously learned that Mark Newman did not care for casual chit-chat. "Morning, sir," he said briefly, and Mark saw him nudge his fellow law clerk. She offered a weaker smile and hurried away.

Dismissing them from his thoughts, Mark pushed open the door to his office and went in, closing it firmly behind him. As one of the founding partners, his office was twice the size of the other attorneys' offices in the firm, and with it being a corner office, he enjoyed light from windows on both outer walls. Only Steve Buchanan, the other founding partner, enjoyed such space, though the office of the third partner, Marty Welch, came close.

He looked around the room, feeling as if he hadn't seen it for a long time. The largest piece of mahogany furniture was a massive bookcase that took up an entire wall. The long wall opposite the door was composed of several large windows and, since the firm was situated on the top floor, provided a beautiful view of the San Gabriel Mountains to the north and Old Town Pasadena below. A large ornamental palm tree was in the corner. Like all the greenery in the firm, it was maintained by an outside landscaping firm.

He turned slowly, drawing comfort from the familiar surroundings. On the right side of the room, a comfortable sofa in a soft blue-gray color was against the inner wall. Two small chairs upholstered in a rich blue watered silk and a small hand-carved coffee table rested in the center of the sitting space. Beyond that were two client chairs, also upholstered in blue watered silk, that faced his desk. On the desk was a computer monitor and keyboard, and beyond, nestled beneath the windows, was a large credenza on which files were stacked.

Mark rubbed the back of his neck, trying to massage away some of his tension. This had been his office since the firm moved into the building more than eight years ago when they had grown too large for their old space. It was filled with memories of past legal battles, tough negotiations, successful—more often than not—conclusions of difficult cases. It was his favorite place in the world. But not today.

"Ridiculous," he fumed and slung his briefcase with unusual violence on the desk before going around it and dropping heavily into his chair.

Was this, this aimless anxiety, the lingering results from his accident? Or was it a response to the upheaval in his partner's life? That Steve's marriage, something so long-standing, so much a part of the background of their joined lives, could suddenly explode without any warning was startling. And what about the implications? Would Buchanan still be able to pull his weight with the firm?

Or would he be unable to deal with the collapse of his marriage? The possible problems that could result from that scenario were even more unnerving.

Mark took a deep breath and exhaled slowly. He needed to talk to Marty Welch. Though the junior partner of the firm, Welch was still a partner and needed to know what was going on.

His intercom buzzed; he knew by the extension number who it was before anyone spoke.

"Yes, Carolyn?"

"Good morning, Mr. Newman," came his assistant's cool, crisp tones. "I have several items to discuss with you whenever you're ready."

Glad for the distraction, he said, "You can come in now."

"Yes, sir." A minute later, there was a gentle knock on the door before it opened. "Mr. Newman?"

"Come in, Carolyn."

She obeyed, shutting the door behind her. Watching as she approached, Mark thanked the fates for bringing the woman to the firm fourteen years ago just when he was looking for a new legal secretary. She was both experienced and highly intelligent, and it wasn't long before he knew Carolyn had it in her to be a first-rate assistant. At his recommendation and on the firm's dollar, she had taken a number of night classes that widened her abilities even more. Over the years, she had fulfilled all of Mark's expectations.

This morning, she wore an attractive dark-blue suit, and as usual, every strand of her short dark hair was perfectly in place. Not for the first time, Mark felt a touch of smug satisfaction at how well his gamble so many years before had paid off.

"Mr. Newman?"

He abruptly realized that she was already sitting down and looking at him with inquisitive eyebrows. Mark was annoyed all over again at the difficulty of controlling his thoughts.

"I'm sorry, Carolyn." He managed to smile. "I suppose I'm a little tired."

"That's perfectly understandable under the circumstances. I'm very relieved it wasn't worse."

"Yes." He cleared his throat. "What do you have for me this morning?"

Carolyn opened the file folder in her hands. "As I mentioned in the message I left for you, Mr. Mattingly agreed to continue the Ashmore deposition, but he wants it rescheduled as soon as possible."

Mark grunted. He couldn't blame Mattingly for his impatience. This particular deposition had already been continued three times. There was a pretrial hearing coming up soon, and they were running out of time.

"Get in touch with all the parties and find a date agreeable to everyone," he said.

"Yes, sir." Carolyn made a note. "Mr. Englander called late yesterday and also left a message early this morning. He's having second thoughts about settling."

Mark frowned. "If we go to trial, he's going to end up with a lot less. As soon as we're done here, give me his number, and I'll remind him of that little fact."

"Yes, sir," she repeated. For a second, a glint of amusement brightened her eyes, but she moved smoothly on to the next item of her list.

Forty minutes later, they were done. When Carolyn stood to leave, she said, "I'll get Mr. Englander's number and check for any new calls."

"Good, thank you."

Just as she reached the door, there was a sharp rap on the outside, and it was yanked open.

"Oops, sorry!" someone said. Carolyn took a step back, and Marty Welch bounced inside. "Good timing." He grinned.

She smiled faintly and left, once more closing the door behind her. Welch moved swiftly across the office and draped himself over one of the client chairs.

"Good morning, Marty," Mark said dryly.

"And good morning to you too. It's good to have you back."

"I was only out one day."

"I know, but that's practically a record for you." Welch leaned forward and planted his elbows on the desk. "You're looking good. How do you feel?"

"I feel fine. And I have a lot of work to do."

Welch chuckled. "Hint, hint, huh? I've got a couple things to run by you. First, we need to go over three new cases, or potential cases, that have come in. I don't think we should take one of them, but the other two have possibilities."

"Talk to Carolyn about how much time you think you'll need, and she'll check my calendar."

"You don't want to check it now?" Welch asked as he tapped the monitor.

Mark stifled his irritation. "I've got a lot on my plate right now, Marty. This isn't a good time to chat."

"Okay," the other man said easily. He stood up. "We can talk about the other matters when we get together. Just one last thing. Do you know what's going on with Steve?"

"With Steve?" Mark repeated, keeping his expression neutral.

"Uh-huh. I popped my head in his office to talk about the upcoming settlement conference for Stafford, and he looks like he just lost his best friend."

"Did you ask him about it?"

"He said he was just tired."

"I suppose that answers that, doesn't it?"

Welch frowned. "I suppose," he agreed, not looking convinced.

"Marty, I'm very busy right now."

"Oh, right." The younger attorney gave him a little salute. "I'll talk to you later."

When he was finally alone again, Mark felt relieved he had escaped so lightly. Rumors and gossip were endemic in any office, and this one was no exception. Hopefully, they could keep a lid on Buchanan's marital problems. As much as he knew he needed to talk to Welch about them, Steve had chosen not to say anything. For the moment, Mark was willing to respect his friend's wish for silence.

He gave his head a little shake. It was time to get to work. After one last thing.

Checking his electronic Rolodex gave Mark the number he wanted. A minute later, he heard a recording click in. "You have reached the office of Frank Adams, private investigator. Please leave a message after the tone, and Mr. Adams will return your call as soon as he is able."

"Adams, Mark Newman here. Please call me back on my cell phone." He left the number and hung up but continued to look at the telephone. Adams would probably figure this was a typical call from a law firm that had him on retainer. He would have no reason to think otherwise.

There was nothing more Mark could do about his mystery rescuer for now, and he was glad to turn his attention to the files Carolyn had left for him. He had only gotten through one of them before it was time for the first of three meetings scheduled for the day.

As the day wore on and Mark moved from one matter to the next, looking over what was happening with his own cases while reviewing the cases of several subordinates, the unsettling sense of dislocation gradually faded. It confirmed his earlier thought that getting back into his ordinary life would allow him to put his experience behind him.

The slightly smug relief lasted until late in the afternoon when he heard the soft buzz of his cell phone. Focused on a set of interrogatories that needed to be sent out before 5:00 p.m., he picked it up. "Newman."

"Mr. Newman, this is Frank Adams returning your call."

Abruptly yanked out of his preoccupation, Mark hesitated as he suddenly realized he hadn't thought through what he wanted to ask the investigator.

As the silence lengthened, Adams spoke again. "Mr. Newman? Are you there?"

"Yes," Mark said, annoyed by his uncharacteristic hesitancy. "I… have a job for you."

"Yes, sir?"

"I need you to find someone for me."

"A witness?"

"No." Mark paused again, but there was no getting around it. "It's a personal matter, not firm-related."

There was a brief silence before Adams said calmly, "All right. I need everything you have."

Mark was grateful the investigator hadn't asked any embarrassing questions, but he suddenly realized how little information he could provide. When he finished, there was a longer silence.

"That's not a lot to go on, Mr. Newman."

"I realize that. Can you find him?"

"At this point, I can't say. I'll take a look at the accident scene to see if I can find anything. And I'll talk to the paramedic crew, the police officer who responded, find out if they saw anything out of the ordinary. That may lead to something more. I'll let you know what I find."

"Do you need payment in advance?"

"You know my rate. You can drop a check in the mail for a couple of days' worth of my time. We'll see what I've got then, if anything."

"All right. As I said, this is a personal matter."

"I understand. It'll be just between us."

Mark hung up with mixed feelings. Adams was a good investigator; he knew that from previous dealings with the man. At the same time, reliving that terrifying night, even if he had limited himself to the bare facts, had brought back the turmoil of emotion he had been trying to distance himself from. The sense of calm the daily routine had given him was gone, and he didn't know how to get it back.

His intercom buzzed. "Yes?"

"Mark, do you know where Steve went?"

He frowned. "I haven't seen him since this morning, why?" His frown deepened when he heard Welch swear. "What's going on, Marty?"

"I was just passing the receptionist's desk when a call came in from the Superior Court building. Steve was attending an arbitration for the Sherriman case. They took a ten-minute break, but that ended a half-hour ago, and he hasn't come back and isn't answering his cell phone. He hadn't come back here, either."

It was Mark's turn to swear. "Who's the opposing attorney?"

"Lou Delgado. It was his office that called."

When Mark got his hands on his partner, he was going to kill him. Meanwhile, he needed to do some damage control. "Get me Delgado's number. I'll call him and tell him Buchanan's sick or something. I'll need the arbitrator's number, too. With any luck, they'll be willing to continue it."

"Sounds good," Welch said, relief in his voice.

"And, Marty, have Carolyn call her cousin at the police department."

"Cousin?"

"Her cousin is a police dispatcher. It's possible Steve was in an accident. If so, maybe she heard about it."

"Will do."

A little over two hours later, Mark finally put his phone down for what he hoped would be the last time today. It had taken longer than he had hoped to calm an annoyed Delgado and an even longer time to calm the retired Superior Court judge who was arbitrating the case. In the end, both men agreed to continue the arbitration, which was what ultimately counted and worth a sore ear.

There was no time to be satisfied. Mark immediately turned to his own delayed work, finalizing the interrogatories despite having to attend another meeting. Only afterward was he able to turn his attention to trying to track down his partner. That proved fruitless, and he was forced to leave a message on Buchanan's cell phone and, as a last resort, called both of Steve's home numbers. The answering machine for his home office picked up that one, and he left a terse message—"It's Mark. Call me ASAP."

It was only with the personal home number that Mark was able to talk to a human being.

"Buchanan residence."

He knew that voice, although he hadn't heard it often. "Melanie, it's Mark Newman at the office. I'm looking for Steve."

"He's not here," she said, suddenly cold. "And I told him not to come back so I wouldn't bother calling this number again the next time you're looking for him."

There were several things Mark wanted to say, but he held them back. Anger would only beget more anger and accomplish nothing.

"If you happen to hear from him, please ask him to call me."

"Sure."

Mark hung up slowly. At first he had been angry. Now he was worried. Steve Buchanan was an experienced and responsible attorney who would never suddenly disappear in the middle of a case. Again Mark wondered if his partner had been in an accident, but Carolyn's cousin hadn't heard anything at the police department.

However, Buchanan's life had been turned upside down less than twenty-four hours ago. How would Mark feel if he was in a similar situation? He swallowed. He knew exactly how he would feel because his life had also been turned upside down a few days ago. Was Buchanan feeling that same sense of disorientation, of being out of step with life?

Mark shivered involuntarily, and he mentally flung the thoughts from him. No! He was done with fretting over what had happened. His partner's situation had nothing to do with his. He strode angrily out of his office, only to slow when he reached the reception area. The lights had been turned down, and the receptionist was not at her desk. Glancing at his watch, Mark was surprised to see that it was after 7:00 p.m. He had a vague memory of Marty Welch suggesting dinner earlier in the day, which he had turned down. With no dinner plans and no meetings scheduled, Mark felt a little lost.

Having nothing better to do, he drove home. As he walked through the front door, he heard voices coming from the kitchen and felt a sense of déjà vu. But this time it wasn't his sons' voices, and when he reached the kitchen, he found his wife talking on her cell phone.

Her back was to him, and Mark stood still, watching her. He was startled by the feeling that he was looking at a stranger. She was of medium height, but because of her erect posture, she always appeared taller. Even after nearly twenty years of marriage and two children, she remained slim and looked younger than her years, an illusion helped by her short ash-blond hair, which hid any strands of gray.

Geneva wasn't conventionally beautiful; her nose was a bit large for her oval features and her chin jutted out slightly in what Mark used to laughingly refer to as a determined pose. Yet most people considered her to be extremely attractive. From the day he met her in college, Mark recognized in her a unique beauty, a beauty that hadn't diminished despite the years and a marriage that somewhere along the line had turned into simple convenience.

Mark was struck by a sudden stab of regret at how things had changed between them, an emotion quickly followed by annoyance. Yet again, it seemed as if each time he rejected one uncomfortable thought, another immediately took its place.

His inward gaze turned outward again, and he gazed at his wife, startled by a sense of loss. The hot words and arguments that had troubled their marriage early on had gradually faded over time. He and Geneva had come to an unspoken compromise years ago. He would live his life, and she would live hers, and they would treat each other like polite acquaintances when they encountered one another. The compromise had worked well for many years. Was he now questioning it? If so, why?

At that moment, Geneva turned and saw him. Her eyes widened briefly, and her voice turned crisp. "All right, Eleanor. Ten o'clock on the twenty-first." She lowered the cell phone and met his gaze squarely. Her blue eyes were cool, her features a calm mask. "You're home early."

"Yes," Mark returned inanely, suddenly bereft of speech.

Her eyes swept over him. "You don't look any worse for wear."

It took a second for him to realize that she was speaking of his accident. Though Mark would have preferred to ignore the subject, at least it provided a vehicle for conversation that was normally limited to hello and good-bye.

"I'm fine. And thank you," he added impulsively, "for calling your brother that night."

Geneva's eyes narrowed. "Is that sarcasm?"

Mark felt a twinge of pain, knowing too well where that defensiveness came from. "No, I mean it. Otherwise, I would have had to call a taxi."

She studied him for a minute, and her shoulders relaxed. Not until then did he realize how tense her posture had been.

"I wondered when I heard your message if you expected me to come and pick you up."

An unexpected wave of sadness swept through him. "I think I gave up the right to expect anything from you a long time ago."

Astonishment broke through Geneva's mask, and they stared at each other. Mark felt startlingly naked before her. After a minute, her expression smoothed, and she walked by him. He couldn't think of anything to say, but he half-turned to watch her go up the stairs. She never looked back, and he was grateful.

Mark yanked his tie loose and took a deep breath but couldn't seem to draw in enough air. On impulse, he shoved the door open and hurried outside. He needed to get away, to drive—somewhere.

As he stepped into the garage, the overhead light came on automatically. He had the driver's side door of the rental car open before he saw an unusual shadow in the corner. Surprise froze him in midstep, then he recognized it. The shadow morphed into the rope he had brought back from the accident scene that he had thrown in a pile in the corner of the garage.

Letting the car door swing shut again, he approached the rope slowly, feeling oddly hesitant, almost expecting something to leap out at him. When he reached the rope, he crouched down and put his hand on it. The fiber was rough and coarse to the touch, and cold and damp from the rainwater that still soaked it.

It was just an ordinary rope, yet without it, would he still be alive?

A new thought pierced him. How had the stranger happened to have rope with him? When they finally climbed up the embankment, Mark hadn't seen any vehicle. Had his rescuer just happened to be carrying rope as he walked along the road in the rainstorm? Without the rope, how could Mark have gotten up the embankment? For that matter, how would his rescuer? Between the storm, the steep incline, Mark's injuries and shock…

A shudder swept through him, and he dropped to his knees, wrapping his arms around his chest. Despite the best intentions in the world, his rescuer would probably not have succeeded in saving him without this rope.

When emotion finally loosed its grip on him, Mark was exhausted. No longer did he want to drive anywhere; he just wanted to go to bed. Slowly unwrapping his arms, he winced, then wondered if the new aches were genuine or just memories. No matter, another pill before he went to bed should take care of it.

He started to rise but paused to give the rope another look. It was a dirty, wet inanimate object. Since he wanted so badly to leave the events of a few nights ago in the past, he should throw out this vivid reminder of his close call. Even as the thought came to him, he discarded it. He could always throw it out later.

Stepping back outside, he noticed the corner window on the second story of the house was bright with light—Geneva's room. He stared at it, feeling exhaustion like an actual weight pressing down on him. Rubbing his eyes, he looked away from the window and went into the house.

7

The next morning, Mark was jerked awake not by music but by the sound of young voices arguing loudly outside his bedroom. He sat up, and all of his bruises and aches complained simultaneously. Growling under his breath, he awkwardly maneuvered himself out of bed and stood up. Discomfort added to his irritation, and he stomped across the room and yanked his door open.

A few yards down the hall, Brian and Daniel confronted each other, both flushed with temper.

"…And you can't come!" Brian finished before he realized he was no longer alone with his brother.

"What's going on here!" Mark demanded.

The boys faced him, suddenly silent. He glared from one to the other, but neither would meet his angry gaze.

"Fine," he snapped. "Get ready for school."

Brian raised his head. "We haven't had breakfast yet," he said. He spoke quietly, but there was an undertone Mark couldn't identify and didn't like.

"Then get moving."

He watched until the boys disappeared into their respective rooms, then returned to his own bedroom. Only then did Mark realize that the rays of the rising sun were peeking in around the drapes. With the awareness came fresh irritation, but this time it was directed at himself. Checking his alarm clock confirmed the dismal truth. Either he had turned off his alarm last night or else awakened just enough this morning to turn it off before falling back asleep.

Great.

An hour later, he pulled into his reserved parking spot. As he got out of the car, he stopped. Beside his spot was the reserved parking spot for Steve Buchanan, and his partner's sleek red Jaguar was there. Anger flared and took Mark swiftly through the lobby to the elevators. When he strode into the suite, he was distantly aware of people around but ignored them.

He spared a half-second to bang on Buchanan's office door before pushing it open. "Where the—"

He forgot what he was about to say at the sight of the other man.

Steve Buchanan normally took pride in his elegant attire. More than once, Mark had accused the man of taking longer to get ready in the morning than a Hollywood starlet, to which Buchanan always replied, "The end result is worth it."

The slumped figure standing in front of the glass wall bore little resemblance to the Steve Buchanan Mark had known for so many years. His rumpled suit was the same one he had worn yesterday. His longish hair obviously hadn't seen a brush in the last twenty-four hours, nor had he shaved recently. The pale, drawn features and red-rimmed eyes spoke eloquently of the man's distress.

Concern warred with anger and won. Blowing out a breath, Mark said, "Sit down before you fall down."

Buchanan obeyed, moving sluggishly, but instead of going to his own chair behind the desk, he dropped heavily into the one of the chairs normally reserved for clients. He kept his head down so Mark couldn't see his face.

After taking another minute to get his anger firmly under control, he spoke. "You look terrible. What's going on?"

He heard a long, shaky sigh but nothing more. Mark waited, refusing to break the lengthening silence. Finally, Steve said, "I couldn't find them."

"Find who?"

"My kids."

"What are you talking about?"

"I wanted to see them, to explain…" Buchanan waved a hand in the air. "That this had nothing to do with them, that I'd always be their dad…" A slight quaver distorted the last word, and he swallowed, an audible gulp.

Mark wished he was somewhere, anywhere else. This unguarded outpouring of emotion was something he had never been comfortable with, something he couldn't imagine doing. He shifted uncomfortably and wondered who in the suite he could grab that would be able to help his partner. Not Marty Welch, not that happy-go-lucky, superficial ladies' man. The junior attorneys? No. As a senior partner, Steve would never open up to them. A member of the staff? His mind ran swiftly over the firm's secretaries, paralegals, law students. They were all good people in their own areas, but he couldn't imagine confiding in any one of them about a personal matter.

He ran a hand over his face as he reluctantly concluded that as poor a confidant as he was, he was all that Buchanan had for now. Outside of the firm was another matter, and Mark didn't know what family or friends his partner might have. He would have to find out because Steve needed someone better than him to confide in.

Buchanan had remained silent while Mark considered the situation, and he decided to give him a little prod. "You said Melanie sent your kids to stay with friends."

Steve nodded. "I went back to the house to ask her where they were."

Mark felt a fresh spark of irritation. If his partner was telling the truth, and he had no reason to believe otherwise, then Melanie Buchanan had lied to him yesterday when she claimed she hadn't seen her husband.

"And?"

"She wouldn't tell me where they were."

Fresh anger surged, but Mark fought it down. This had gotten ugly very fast. Apart from everything else, Steve needed the services of a good family law attorney. Their firm didn't handle that area of law, but he knew a number of attorneys who did. It would take a little thought, but he was going to find the smartest, most experienced, toughest lawyer in the field for Buchanan. Whatever was between Steve and Melanie had nothing to do with their children. She had no right to keep her husband from his kids. Unless...

The idea that slipped into his thoughts made him recoil in disgust, but now that it had raised its head he had to ask. "She doesn't have a reason to keep them from you, does she?"

Despite his exhaustion and distress, Buchanan immediately picked up the implication, and he raised shocked eyes to his partner. "Of course not! I've never done anything to them except love them." He rubbed his eyes. "I admit I've never been father-of-the-year material. My work always became before them." Confusion darkened his eyes. "I don't know how it happened. I didn't plan for things to turn out this way. But no matter what, I've always loved my children."

The despair in his voice brought a new worrying idea to Mark. Just how distraught was his partner?

"Steve, let's take things one step at a time. We need to hook you up with a lawyer to represent your interests. Let him or her do the fighting for you. You need to focus on taking care of yourself."

"What?"

Mark sighed. "Did you hear what I just said?"

"I need to hire a lawyer…" He rubbed his temples as if he had a headache. "I am a lawyer."

"Your specialty is business and real estate law. You need a family law specialist. You know that."

Buchanan smiled faintly. "A lawyer who represents himself has a fool for a client."

Mark felt a touch of hope. Perhaps his partner hadn't sunk as low as he feared. "Something like that. Let me find a lawyer who can help you with Melanie. Meanwhile, when's the last time you ate?"

Steve rubbed his eyes. "I don't remember."

"When's the last time you slept?"

He shook his head. "Not sure."

"Who's your doctor?"

"I don't have one."

Mark sighed again. "Steve, I want you to listen to me."

Buchanan blinked and widened his eyes. "I am."

"I'm going to call my doctor's office and see if he can't squeeze you in today."

"I don't need—"

"Yes, you do. You're going to see him and let him check you out, and you're going to do what he tells you. Am I making myself clear?"

Buchanan was rubbing his head again. "You're about to burst my eardrums."

"Do you hear what I'm saying?"

"Yes, yes, I hear."

"Good. Stay here."

Mark shut the door behind him and took some deep breaths. He glanced at his watch, and when he saw the time, he was freshly annoyed. Because he had overslept, the official business day would begin in less than a half hour. Worse, he knew Buchanan's problem was likely going to throw off the rest of his day. Yesterday, when Steve failed to return to the arbitration, Mark had worked hard to calm down the opposing attorney, Lou Delgado, and the arbitrator, retired Judge Harold Waring. In order to avoid Buchanan being hit with sanctions, Mark agreed to reschedule the arbitration to today.

After talking to Steve, he knew his partner was in no shape to handle the matter. Marty Welch was in court today, and Mark wasn't about to pull in one of the junior attorneys at this late date. The arbitration was too important. That left him to reshuffle his day in order to take the case himself, which required that he review the files in-depth prior to the arbitration.

Thinking over what needed to be done was almost enough to give him a headache, and Mark retreated to his office. To his relief, when he buzzed Carolyn Colby, she was already in.

"Carolyn, the Sherriman arbitration has been rescheduled for this afternoon, and I'm taking it. Since I'm going to need the morning to familiarize myself with the case, you'll have to reschedule my appointments."

"I'll get on it right away, Mr. Newman. But first I'll make sure all of the files on that matter are delivered to you ASAP."

He thanked her and hung up, grateful for her lack of curiosity. Recalling another task he had set for himself, Mark pulled his phone closer to run through the addresses. Rob Aaron, his physician, was also an acquaintance. With only a little bullying, Mark was able to get an appointment for Steve Buchanan during what would otherwise have been Aaron's lunch hour.

"Thank you, Rob, I appreciate it."

"I'll remind you of your appreciation the next time I need a legal question answered," came the half-irritated, half-amused response.

"You have a deal."

Mark barely had time to hang up before there was a knock on his door and Carolyn Colby appeared, followed by a clerk who was juggling an armful of files.

"This is everything we have for the Sherriman case," she said, standing aside to allow the clerk to drop the files on the corner of Mark's desk, who swallowed a groan.

"Thank you."

"How about a cup of coffee?" Carolyn suggested.

Studying the pile of files, he said, "I think that's going to be a necessity, thank you."

Secretaries and/or assistants fetching coffee for the lawyers was a long-gone stereotype at Newman, Buchanan, and Welch. Clients were an exception, as were the three senior partners, who were still able to enjoy that perk. Mark didn't feel guilty about the indulgence. He had worked long and hard to reach this position and figured he deserved a few benefits.

Another thought made him say, "Carolyn, can I ask you for a favor?"

She stopped halfway out of the door. "Of course."

"Mr. Buchanan isn't feeling well. He has a doctor's appointment at twelve thirty. I know it's an imposition but—"

"I'll be glad to drive him, Mr. Newman," she interrupted with a smile.

Mark swallowed a sigh of relief. He could trust Carolyn to get the job done while knowing she wouldn't gossip about it. "Thank you."

It was a long, tension-filled and exhausting day. The arbitration ran long, but Mark expected that. By the end, he had a genuine headache, but he was pleased by his performance. The arbitrator, Judge Waring, advised him and the opposing counsel, Lou Delgado, that he would provide them with his written decision by the end of next week, which was the best result Mark could have hoped for.

After Waring vanished out the door, Delgado lingered. "You did a pretty good job for being a last-minute substitution," he admitted grudgingly.

Mark gave him a cold smile. "I know."

"So what happened to Buchanan?"

"I believe it's a stomach flu," Mark returned blandly.

"Better him than me." Delgado smirked.

It was after seven o'clock, and the staff had departed, so Mark escorted Delgado to the front of the suite and made sure the door was locked before he returned to his office. He noted in passing that light shone from under the closed doors of several offices and was pleased by this evidence of work continuing.

After trying fruitlessly to reach Rob Aaron at his office, Mark resorted to the physician's cell phone.

"Dr. Aaron."

"Mark Newman. I assume you saw my partner today?"

"Yes, I did. He's in reasonably good physical shape, though he needs some sleep and good food. But I am concerned about his emotional well-being." There was a brief silence before Aaron added cautiously, "He said you were aware of his current, ah, family situation?"

Despite the seriousness of the conversation, Mark almost smiled. Aaron might be a personal acquaintance, but he wasn't about to break doctor-client confidentiality.

"Yes, I am, if you're referring to his marital issues."

"Ah, good." The physician sounded relieved. "I recommended that he seek professional counseling and offered to give him the names of some therapists, but he wasn't interested."

Mark was tempted to swear. Steve was his own worst enemy right now. "Thank you for seeing him, Rob, especially on such short notice."

"He's a friend of yours, correct?"

"Yes."

"Then encourage him to get some professional help. If what I saw today is any indication, Mr. Buchanan is going to need it."

Once Mark hung up, he glared at the darkened windows. He wasn't Buchanan's brother; he shouldn't be the one having to shoulder the burden of the man's emotional problems. All right, he could do this one thing. He would push, insist, nag—whatever he had to do in order to ensure Steve got some professional help. Then he could wash his hands of the whole sorry affair.

Except that thought immediately led to a new issue. *Professional help.* What professional help? The firm had used medical specialists for a variety of cases in the past, but Mark immediately discarded the thought of contacting any of them. Steve wouldn't want to consult anyone on a personal basis who knew him through the firm. Neither would Mark if he had been in his partner's position. He realized belatedly that he should have gotten Aaron's list of referrals before hanging up, but after a moment's thought, he set aside that idea as well. Getting Buchanan to agree to professional help would require connecting him with someone not associated in any way with the firm. Granted, Rob Aaron wasn't officially connected to Newman, Buchanan, and Welch, but the physician knew Buchanan was.

Mark leaned back in his chair and rubbed his forehead. What he needed was an experienced, dependable stranger. He stared at the ceiling while another unwelcome thought made its presence known.

His brother-in-law, Joe Ridgeway, wasn't only the pastor of a church. Mark had learned through Geneva's occasional conversations about her brother that Ridgeway was also a trained marriage and family counselor. Apart from his work at his church, he volunteered one day a week at some local shelter, and Mark had a hazy memory that that volunteer position also involved some kind of counseling.

He shifted uncomfortably in his seat, not liking the idea of his brother-in-law counseling one of his partners. It was possible Ridgeway might find out things about Newman, Buchanan, and Welch that were none of his business.

You're being paranoid, Newman. Steve Buchanan's issues had nothing to do with the firm and everything to do with his marriage, which was a subject Joe Ridgeway was trained in.

He stood abruptly and began to pace. Was his brother-in-law any good as a counselor? Would Mark have to put himself in the position of asking for a favor of a man he had always disliked and avoided in order to get Buchanan the help he needed?

Maybe he could simply ask Ridgeway for a referral. As soon as the thought crossed his mind, Mark immediately felt better. Any referral by his brother-in-law would be unconnected to the firm, so Buchanan couldn't use that rationale to refuse. That would work on more than one level. He would get some names from Ridgeway and pass them along to his partner. If Steve refused to act on them, that would be his choice. Any obligation on Mark's part should be more than satisfied.

He stopped pacing to look at his watch. It was after seven thirty. Mark didn't have Joe's telephone number, but he knew Geneva must have it. She had no more interest in her brother's religious obsession than Mark did, but she had always kept in touch. The thought of calling her made him wince. After all these years of doing his best to avoid her brother, Mark would now be asking to contact him. He hated to think of her reaction.

Wait a minute. There was another, easier option. He could simply call information. And if Ridgeway's number happened to be unlisted, then he could try the man's church. What was its name? It was named after a street.

First something. *First Avenue*. That was it. First Avenue Community Church.

Mark called information and was relieved to find his brother-in-law listed, but he stared at the small phone lying in the middle of his desk for a long time before reluctantly picking it up.

He heard ringing on the other end, two, three, four times, then he heard a click followed by a familiar voice. "Hello, you've reached First Avenue Community Church. The church office is open from 8:30 a.m. to 5:00 p.m. Please leave a message, and we'll get back to you as soon as we can. If this is an emergency, you can reach Pastor Joe at…"

Mark grimaced as he listened to the recording. *Pastor Joe*. There was something so…off-putting about the nickname. He didn't like his brother-in-law, but he knew he had advanced academic and professional degrees, and a title that smacked of nineteenth-century religious hysteria lacked respect. Shrugging aside the thought, he dialed the new number. It barely had time to ring once before he heard his brother-in-law's voice.

"This is Pastor Joe. What can I do for you?"

Mark gritted his teeth before saying, "It's Mark. I need to talk to you about something."

"Sure." There was no surprise in the other man's voice, although Mark had never called him before. "Go ahead."

He started to speak but stopped. How to explain? How detailed did he need to get? What exactly should he say and what should he omit? Several seconds passed while Mark's thoughts squirreled around.

"Mark? Are you still there?"

"Yes."

"Look, I'm going to be home in about a half-hour. Why don't you come over and we can talk?"

Mark swallowed his instinctive refusal. As much as he didn't want to meet with his brother-in-law, he didn't see any other options. *Get it over with, Newman.*

"All right." He started to disconnect and stopped. "Thank you," he forced out.

"No problem. See you soon."

He hung up the receiver with more force than was needed and realized he was gritting his teeth again. Buchanan was going to owe him. A lot.

8

A half-hour later, he knocked on Ridgeway's front door. It was flung open almost immediately, and he found himself staring down at a little girl with brown pigtails, perhaps six years old.

"Hi!" she exclaimed, beaming.

The scampering of little feet grew louder, and two more small faces peered around the door. The faces were unnervingly alike, and he remembered that the two youngest Ridgeway's were twins.

"Sarah, Davy, Jonny, you know better than to open the door by yourselves!"

Beth Ridgeway appeared behind her children and shook her finger at them. They backed away, but not before offering their mother a trio of cheeky grins.

"Don't you give me that," she said sternly. "And the playroom is still a mess. I've already told you to put your toys away so we could eat dinner. If I have to tell you again, no dessert tonight!"

All three scattered, giggling loudly, and Beth gave Mark an apologetic smile. "I'm sorry about that. Please come in, Mark."

He obeyed, surprised by her casual greeting. The last time he had been at this house was for Thanksgiving dinner several years ago and then only because of Geneva's insistence. Joe must have called his wife to say that he was coming. Beth's next words confirmed Mark's suspicion.

"Joe just got home. He'll be down in a few minutes." She chuckled. "He got caught in the middle of a food fight at the preschool and needs to clean up."

Preschool? Food fight? Increasingly confused, Mark allowed her to lead him down the short, narrow hall to a small room.

"Can I get you something to drink?" she offered. "We've got milk, apple juice, orange juice"—her eyes narrowed in thought—"I think we may still have a little grape juice left too."

He shuddered inwardly. "No, thank you."

For the first time, her smile looked uncertain. "I can make some coffee if you prefer."

"Thank you, but I'm fine."

Mark was certain there was nothing in his tone of voice his sister-in-law would be able to read. Nonetheless, her smile faded, only to return too quickly to be genuine.

"Let me know if you change your mind. Joe should be right down."

He was relieved when she left, but it didn't ease his discomfort. What on earth was he doing here? Right, he was here because of Steve Buchanan's marital problems. Suddenly he was furious with his partner. Steve should be dealing with his own problems, not dragging Mark into them.

Trying to distract himself, he looked around the room. It wasn't very big and felt even smaller because of the floor-to-ceiling bookcases that covered two of the walls. He took a closer look and realized that although they looked sturdy enough, the bookshelves had not been built by a professional. The furniture itself had seen better days. The top of the small desk in the corner of the room was badly scratched, and the computer that sat atop it was several years old. There was a small loveseat in the corner, with a blanket thrown over it, and two overstuffed chairs facing each other. The skirt on one was coming off, and a bit of stuffing spilled out from the arm of the other chair.

He shook his head in disgust and wandered aimlessly around the small space. A closer look at some of the books made him frown. There were a lot of books on religion and theology; he had expected those, or would have, if he had thought about it. There were other books on counseling, on dysfunctional families, on problems faced by teenagers. Considering what Ridgeway did, those subjects also made sense.

What surprised him were books covering other topics—American and European history, the environment, biographies on individuals as diverse as Archimedes and Winston Churchill. There was also a section of world literature, as well as plays beginning with the ancient Greek Sophocles and moving forward in history to Shakespeare and Edward Albee.

Mark's frown deepened. This wasn't the library of some backward Bible thumper, some provincial hick, and the realization made him uncomfortable. He didn't want to think about it because it might force him to rethink his opinion of Joe Ridgeway. He pressed his fingers against his temples, feeling the beginnings of another headache. Abruptly, he dropped his hands when the door Beth had closed swung open.

"Hi, Mark." Ridgeway was smiling what looked like a genuine smile, and his hand was extended.

Reluctantly, Mark accepted it. "Thank you for seeing me on such short notice."

"Why don't you sit down? I recommend the chair on the left."

Mark obeyed; the sooner he had his say, the sooner he could leave.

Ridgeway sat down on the seat opposite. "I'm sorry, I should have offered you something to drink."

"Your wife already did. I'm fine."

"I'm glad to hear that." Ridgeway's voice was calm, without any innuendo, and his green eyes met his with equal calmness.

Mark felt increasingly uncomfortable. "You don't seem surprised that I called you." He swallowed a curse. He hadn't meant to say that. It felt as if he was giving an advantage to his brother-in-law.

"I was," Joe said, and it was Mark's turn to be surprised. "But in my line of work, surprises come with the territory. What can I do for you?"

Just like that. No preliminary small talk. This whole situation was so foreign; Mark was used to people coming to him for help. This time, he was the one in need of help and he hated the feeling.

"I'm here on behalf of one of my partners," he said abruptly, more harshly than he intended.

Joe nodded but otherwise didn't react, and Mark's irritation grew.

"His wife wants a divorce, and she's apparently hiding his children from him. He's…not handling it well."

His brother-in-law leaned forward, and Mark was pleased to see concern in the other man's expression.

"He's talked to you about the situation?"

"Yes. But I—" Mark stopped abruptly. Admitting his inability to fix the situation was something he rarely had to do. Even more rare was a growing feeling of inadequacy. He only hoped he didn't show anything of what he was feeling. "I'm going to find a good family law attorney for him," he added and wondered at the inane comment. It wasn't what he had intended to say.

"It sounds as if he needs one," Joe said quietly. "It also sounds as if he needs more immediate help. Is that why you're here?"

Mark was startled by the warmth in his brother-in-law's eyes and surprised to realize his discomfort was subsiding. "Yes," he admitted. "Can you refer me to someone who can help him?"

Ridgeway rubbed his chin, looking thoughtful. "Do you think he's willing to be helped?"

"Willing?"

"If he's not amenable to the idea, then the best counselor in the world isn't going to be able to help him."

Amenable to the idea? Mark's immediate impulse was to reply affirmatively, but he couldn't. Buchanan was in bad shape emotionally. Even Mark's regular physician had recommended, after a simple physical exam, that the man get professional help. But what about what Steve Buchanan wanted? Mark thought back over his conversations with his partner. Had Buchanan indicated at any point that he recognized he needed help? No. And according to Dr. Aaron, he had raised the possibility to Steve, who hadn't been interested in the idea. He was tempted to swear. As if Buchanan hadn't already complicated his life, now there was this to contend with.

"Maybe if I insisted," he said slowly. "If his behavior is negatively affecting the firm, I might have grounds to threaten him with—"

"No," Joe cut in. "No threats. That's no way to convince someone to get help."

Mark glared. "This can't go on. Not for him and not for the firm."

"No, it can't," Ridgeway agreed softly.

He was silent for a while, and because Mark didn't know what else to say, he kept his mouth shut. If his brother-in-law couldn't come up with a solution, Buchanan would just have to tough things out for himself. As far as Mark was concerned, life was hard, and the only honest way to get through it was to face it as it came and deal with it as best as one could. He had no time for people who preferred to use a crutch to deal with life. Whether alcohol, religion, drugs, a crutch was a crutch, and he had no respect for those who used them.

So what was he doing here? The answer was simple yet daunting. He was here because he hoped his brother-in-law would help him deal with the problem that Steve Buchanan had become.

Mark abruptly realized that his brother-in-law had spoken his name, and his tone of voice indicated he had said it more than once. Confused and annoyed, though he was no longer sure why, he looked at the other man. "Yes?" he spoke casually, pretending that he hadn't allowed his attention to wander.

Joe was watching him closely, and Mark drew on all his legal training and experience to keep his expression matter-of-fact.

"I said that I can't make a referral if you think he'd be unwilling to follow up with it. However, I would be willing to meet with him at least once, if you can persuade him to come. Maybe after he and I have talked, I'll have a better idea of what he needs, and so will he."

Buchanan talk to Ridgeway? Even though he had considered the possibility, it still rankled Mark. But if it was the only option before him... He couldn't help recalling his encounter with his partner this morning, an encounter marked by what appeared to be Buchanan's deepening depression. There didn't appear to be a way around it. Steve needed help, and right now Joe Ridgeway looked like the only game in town.

He met his brother-in-law's eyes and, despite himself, was reassured by the calm green gaze. "I'll see what I can do and let you know."

Ridgeway nodded. "You know how to reach me."

"Yes."

Mark's reason for coming here was now satisfied. There was no reason to linger. Yet now that he could leave, he felt oddly reluctant. The realization jolted him to his feet.

"I won't keep you any longer. I...um...thank you for being willing to help."

Joe stood up too. "Sure," he said. "And there's no need for you to hurry away unless you have plans."

"No, I don't—" Mark stopped too late. He shouldn't have admitted that. To his surprise, Ridgeway brightened.

"Then why don't you stay and have dinner with us?"

Dinner with someone he had done his best to avoid for years? Mark stared at his brother-in-law and resisted the desire to rub his head. It wouldn't help his worsening headache.

"Thank you for the offer but..." He hesitated, at a loss for a pleasant lie.

Joe smiled. "Another time, maybe."

Relief swelled in Mark, along with another unexpected emotion—gratitude. His brother-in-law's casual comment had removed any sense of awkwardness. Ridgeway was being far more gracious than Mark had ever been toward the man. Even more confused than earlier, he knew he had to get out of there.

"Thanks for your time."

"Anytime." Ridgeway extended his hand.

Mark shook hands and left precipitously. During the drive home, he tried hard not to think about the conversation. Remembering wouldn't help his headache. It wouldn't help anything.

Nothingness, that's what he wanted now. When he drove into his garage, he turned off the engine and leaned back against the seat, closing his eyes against the overhead light.

What *was* wrong with him? He felt out of step with his entire life, and he didn't know why or how to go back to the way things had been just a few days ago. No, it was four days ago tonight before the accident.

He took a deep breath and was annoyed at how shaky he suddenly felt. Why had he been feeling so out of control since the accident? It made no sense. It was unacceptable. Control was everything; control had enabled him to become who he was, to gain the life he wanted. How had he lost it? More importantly, how did he regain it?

Mark rubbed his eyes in frustration. He didn't know how many times he had told himself that he needed to put the accident out of his mind and get on with his life. The problem was, his life today seemed more complicated than it ever had.

Perhaps... A new thought made him swallow hard. Perhaps Steve Buchanan's problems were somehow intruding, making him more confused, more frustrated. After all, he wasn't used to getting involved in his associates' personal lives. Yet here he was, doing things he didn't want to do in order to help Buchanan—even spending time with his brother-in-law.

Mark shifted uncomfortably. Thinking back to that quiet time in Ridgeway's study filled him with a strange unease. Not because there had been something wrong, just the opposite. It had felt warm and...welcoming...and safe.

He straightened with a jerk. Where had that come from? Suddenly furious, he shoved his car door open and jumped out. As he slammed it shut and started to turn away, his eye fell on the corner of the garage, and he stopped in his tracks. Still coiled up where he had left it was the pile of rope.

He blew out a breath and took a step away, only to stop again. He wanted to walk out of the garage, but instead, he moved over to the rope and crouched down. Almost as if it had a life of its own, his hand reached out and settled on the topmost coil, still damp to the touch.

This had saved his life. Saved him.

Sudden light-headedness forced him to shift his stance before he overbalanced.

The rope hadn't saved him. He was still alive because of the actions of a stranger.

If you really want to thank me, the next time you run across someone who needs a hand, give him yours. His rescuer's words rang in his ears, and the breath caught in his throat. He wished the words would leave him alone; he didn't understand.

Mark rose a little unsteadily. His head was throbbing more fiercely, and he decided he had done enough thinking for the day. When he walked into the kitchen, he was relieved by the quiet. The last thing he was in the mood for was dealing with more people.

Mark went through the house and was almost at the stairs when he became aware of a faint mumble. He stopped and turned, listening. After a minute, he pinpointed where the sound was coming from—the hall leading to his study.

As he approached, the mumble grew louder and turned into a voice, though he still couldn't make out the words. Then he saw Brian talking on his cell phone.

"Yeah…I'll bring it with me—" Brian stopped abruptly at the sight of his father. After a frozen moment, he coughed and said, "Gotta go, talk to you later." He snapped the cell phone shut and stuck it in his pocket. "Hi, Dad."

"Hi."

The silence between them stretched, strained. Had this always been between them? Mark wondered suddenly.

No, not always.

The words came out of nowhere and brought with them a memory he hadn't thought about for years, a memory out of the past when Brian was a toddler and Mark had taken him to the zoo to give his wife a break. He had been hard put to answer the unending questions raised by the little boy, by his little boy. It had been a wonderful day; he remembered that clearly. The memory filled him with an inexpressible sadness.

As he stood there, not knowing what to say, Brian said, "I'd better get to my homework."

Before Mark could respond, the boy had slipped past him and hurried up the stairs. He looked after his son before closing his eyes. Maybe he needed something to eat; maybe that was the problem. His stomach stirred uneasily, and he immediately discarded the idea. Maybe he was just tired.

Glancing at his wristwatch, he was surprised to see it was only eight thirty. It seemed much later. Mark couldn't remember a time in his adult life when he had gone to bed so early, yet suddenly he was exhausted. He went up the stairs, and as he walked down the hall, his steps slowed. All of the doors were closed, but he could see light edging the bottom of the door to Geneva's bedroom. He stopped in front of it and heard, very faintly, music. So she was awake.

Of course, she was awake. Geneva had never been early to bed, at least not in the long-ago days when they had shared the same bedroom. When had that changed? He couldn't remember, and the realization sent another stab of pain through him.

Mark retreated to his room and made sure to lock the door behind him. He paused just long enough to take another pain pill before climbing into bed. Hopefully, the blasted pill would keep away the nightmares tonight.

9

The sun was just rising over the horizon when Mark pulled into his reserved parking spot the next morning. He saw Steve Buchanan's vehicle parked in its usual spot, and irritation sparked. It was one thing to have his partner come in to the office ready to work. It was another thing if Buchanan was still a muddled mess who would only disrupt the firm and the work that needed to be done.

Mark realized abruptly he had been so preoccupied with talking to his brother-in-law that he had failed to ensure that Steve had gone home last night. How much more disruption of his own life would he have to endure? He had already gone above and beyond the call of duty.

Swearing under his breath, he slammed his car door shut and stormed upstairs. The suite was dark; as usual, he was the first one in. When Mark reached Buchanan's office, he didn't bother knocking but simply flung the door open. The room was dark, and relief flooded through him until he switched on the lights. Curled up on the sofa was his partner, apparently fast asleep.

Fresh anger obliterated his relief, and he shoved roughly at an exposed shoulder. "Steve, wake up."

Buchanan mumbled something unintelligible. Mark was tempted to slap him but resisted the impulse. Instead, he pulled out the cup of coffee he had gotten on the way in and took off the top, then waved it under his partner's nose. For a minute, there was no reaction, then Steve's head turned and his eyelids fluttered.

"Wake up," Mark demanded.

This time the man obeyed. As he shifted position, he groaned and winced. Mark watched without sympathy, though he didn't withdraw the coffee. Buchanan reached blindly, and he allowed the man to take the cup.

Steve look a long drink of the hot liquid and sighed. "What did I do to feel so badly?"

"What did you do?"

His partner raised bloodshot eyes filled with confusion. "I don't know…I don't remember."

Mark took a deep breath and let it out slowly. With forced patience, he said, "What's the last thing you remember?"

Buchanan took another gulp of the coffee, apparently not noticing how hot it was, then rubbed his eyes with his free hand. "I'm not…sure. Everything is…" He squeezed his eyes shut. "It's all mixed up."

Anger warred with impatience, and Mark struggled to remain in control. "Have you eaten anything?"

"Eaten?" Steve dropped his head and rubbed it tenderly with his free hand. "I feel terrible." He spoke so softly Mark almost didn't hear him.

For a minute, Mark stared at the slumped figure and then went to the desk and dialed his assistant's extension. As soon as the recorded greeting ended, he started speaking. "Carolyn, I have a personal matter I need to deal with. I should be back before nine, but if not, please reschedule my appointment with McCarty. I also need Mr. Buchanan's schedule for the rest of the week on my desk when I return." He hung up and turned back to his partner. "This has gone on long enough, Steve. Come with me."

"Huh?"

Mark grasped the man's arm and hauled him to his feet. Buchanan staggered against him, and he had to brace himself to avoid being taken down.

"What are you doing?"

"What you've forced me to do," Mark snapped before marching the man through the suite. When they reached the elevators, his partner tried to pull away.

"Stop it. Let me go."

"Shut up and get in."

Mark's anger grew with every passing minute. Buchanan had not only thrown off his entire week, but the man's failure to deal with his personal problems had brought trouble to the firm. There was no way Mark was going to allow that to continue. But as tempting as it was to give his partner an ultimatum, he knew now was not the right time.

Once he had manhandled Buchanan into his car, Mark headed out. At the first stoplight he called a now familiar number. It rang several times but just as he expected a recording to click on, he heard a quiet "Pastor Joe here."

He grimaced at the nickname and said, "It's Mark. I'm bringing my partner over right now."

There was a long pause before Ridgeway answered. "All right, but I'm not at the church right now. I'll be there in an hour."

"An hour!" Mark glared at his cell phone. "Do you honestly expect me to sit in a car with him waiting on you for an hour?"

"I'm at the hospital dealing with an emergency," Joe spoke crisply, steel underlining each word. "I will be at the church as soon as I can, but don't expect me for an hour."

There was a *click*, then a dial tone. Mark stared at his cell phone in disbelief, his anger surging higher, threatening to swamp him. For a minute, he considered calling his brother-in-law back and chewing him out for hanging up on him, but the memory of Ridgeway's tone of voice made him hesitate. In all the years he had known the man, he had never heard him sound like that. In all of their encounters— not that there had been many—Ridgeway had always been pleasant and easygoing, impossible to annoy. That was not the man Mark had just spoken to.

Part of the reason for his success as an attorney was because of his skill in reading people. That skill was telling him now there were depths to his brother-in-law that he had never imagined. Joe Ridgeway was a much stronger character than he had thought.

Certain that Joe would only hang up on him again if he called back, Mark slowly returned the cell phone in his pocket. An hour. What on earth was he supposed to do with his partner for the next hour? After dragging him out of the suite, there was no way he was going to take him back. Glancing over, he saw that Buchanan had slumped down in his seat and his eyes were closed.

"Steve?"

Buchanan mumbled something and rubbed fretfully at his eyes. *Great.* Mark spotted a restaurant at the next corner, and the sight gave him an idea.

After he parked in the restaurant parking lot, he got out and went around the car to open the passenger door. "Time for breakfast, Steve."

Buchanan blinked up at him. "Breakfast?"

"Breakfast. You need to eat."

"Not hungry," Steve said and closed his eyes.

"Yes, you are. You just don't realize it."

When Buchanan refused to move, Mark grabbed his arm. "Out." He had leverage on his side, and Steve was so surprised he actually stood up on his own; although once he was standing, he protested.

"I don't want to eat."

"Too bad, you're eating."

Mark pulled him several paces before Steve jerked away. "All right," he snapped. "I can walk on my own."

Secretly pleased by this first sign of animation he had seen in his partner, Mark said only, "Then keep walking." He stayed a step behind in order to ensure Buchanan wouldn't run off.

When they entered the restaurant Mark smelled fresh coffee, bacon, and eggs. His stomach rumbled, reminding him that a piece of toast and coffee, most of which Steve had drunk, wasn't sufficient breakfast. He glanced at his partner and was glad to see the man looked awake, if not happy.

It was moderately crowded at this time of the morning, but they only waited a minute before the hostess approached them.

"Good morning," she greeted them with a too-perky smile. "Two for breakfast?"

"I…" Buchanan started, but Mark overrode him.

"Yes," he said firmly. "A booth, if you have one available."

"Certainly. This way."

She led them through the restaurant to a corner booth that a busboy was just finishing clearing. He hurried off, and the hostess gestured. "Please have a seat." She waited until they were sitting before handing them each a menu. "Would you care for some coffee?"

"Yes, thank you," Mark said, cutting off whatever his partner had been about to say. After she left them, he pointed at the menu that Steve had laid down on the table. "What do you want to eat?"

"Coffee's all I want."

"No." Mark narrowed his eyes. "Since you haven't been able to tell me when you last ate, I'm assuming it's been awhile."

Buchanan sighed. "To be honest, the last two or three days are kind of a blur."

The admission didn't surprise Mark. Stopping here had been a good idea after all because his partner was definitely more alert.

"Which makes it all the more important that you eat something now. If you don't choose, I will."

"Fine." Buchanan flapped a hand at him and closed his eyes.

Fine. Mark looked through the menu. If Steve actually hadn't eaten for a day or more, then his system probably wasn't ready for anything heavy. This eliminated a large part of the breakfast menu.

When a waitress appeared with coffee, Buchanan opened his eyes again. Mark handed her the menus and ordered for both of them. Sipping his coffee, he remained silent while waiting for their food; so did Steve. Mark suspected he had actually dozed off because he jumped when the waitress finally returned.

Buchanan actually ate half of his frittata with grilled vegetables and drank a little of the apple juice. Mark watched and resisted urging him to eat more. He ate heartily of his own breakfast and finished at approximately the same time Buchanan laid down his fork and pushed away his plate.

"All right," he said, "I've eaten. Can I go back to the office now?"

Eating hadn't done a lot for the man. Mark studied him, noting the deep-down exhaustion in Steve's eyes. Despite himself, he felt some of his irritation replaced by concern. He suspected his partner was not going to be pleased by the plans Mark had made for him, so he spoke with deliberate matter-of-factness.

"Not right now. You have an appointment"—he glanced at his watch—"in fifteen minutes." As he spoke, he picked up the bill, pulled out his wallet, and laid down enough money to cover it and a tip.

Steve frowned. "An appointment? What appointment?"

Mark decided not to tackle this straight on. "Have you seen your children?"

Buchanan's eyes fell. "No."

"Have you talked to Melanie?"

"No." This time, the response was so soft Mark barely heard it.

"Have you talked to anyone about what's happened?"

Steve took a deep, shaky breath. "Not really. Your doctor asked some questions when I was there but…I didn't want to talk about it."

"You have to talk about it."

"No, I don't." Steve raised his head and glared at his partner.

Mark glared back. "You're falling apart, can't you see that?"

"I'm not—"

"If you don't want to talk to anyone associated with the firm, then talk to someone else."

Confusion diluted some of Buchanan's anger. "I'm telling you, I don't need to—"

Mark leaned over the table and lowered his voice, but not his intensity. "You nearly committed malpractice the other day. Don't tell me you don't need to talk to anyone!"

"Malprac—" Steve's eyes widened in shock. "No, I wouldn't—"

"You walked out of an arbitration, leaving our client high and dry. If things had gone a little differently, we could be looking at a lawsuit."

"I would never—"

"You did. Are you telling me you don't even remember?"

Buchanan looked stricken. "I…I don't…I wouldn't—"

"Bottom line," Mark interrupted again, "either you get help or you're out of the firm."

Even as he spoke, he wondered if he would be able to follow through on the threat. Everything in his partner's life was falling down around him. The only thing it seemed he had left was their law firm. Could he take it away too?

Steve stared at him with wide eyes. "You don't mean that. You can't."

Mark took a deep breath, trying to calm himself. "You're falling apart. If you refuse to get help"—he paused deliberately, his eyes boring into his partner's—"I will not allow you to take the firm down with you."

Even in the state Buchanan was in, he couldn't miss Mark's determination. His face seemed to crumble, and he lowered his head again. Mark couldn't see his expression; he only hoped he had finally gotten through.

Another glance at his watch made him slide out of the booth. "Let's go," he said curtly.

Steve looked up again, and Mark was shocked to see tears in the man's eyes. In all the years they had known each other, he had never seen Buchanan cry, and for a minute, he didn't know how to respond.

Finally deciding to pretend he hadn't noticed anything, he simply gestured. "You have an appointment in less than ten minutes. You can come with me or not, but if you don't, then don't bother going back to the office."

He waited while Buchanan stared at nothing for a minute. Slowly, the man dragged himself upright and followed him back to the car. Neither man spoke during the five-minute drive. Not until Mark had parked again did Steve look around.

"Where are we?"

Mark got out and waited for Steve to do the same. When his partner was standing by the car, he said, "First Avenue Community Church."

Steve stared at him. "What?"

"Come on." He started toward the church office but immediately realized Buchanan wasn't following him. Mark whirled around, but his angry words died before they could escape. Steve was staring at the church, his expression one of utter confusion.

Mark felt a stab of unwilling sympathy. "Steve, come with me."

"Why are we here?"

"We're here because this is where your appointment is."

Buchanan dragged his eyes away from the building to stare at him. "I don't understand."

"Your appointment is with the pastor of this church, a man named Joe Ridgway."

"Pastor?" Anger sparked in Steve's eyes. "I'm not interested in talking to some Bible-thumping fanatic—"

"Shut up."

Mark was as surprised as Buchanan looked by his rough tone. Where had that emotion come from? His partner wasn't saying anything that Mark hadn't thought, yet the sentiment didn't feel right this morning.

"Ridgeway has all the degrees, training, and experience he needs. Now come on, I'm not going to say it again." At that moment, another vehicle drove into the parking lot, and Mark recognized the elderly Jeep. "He's here."

Buchanan sighed noisily and came around to stand beside his partner. The Jeep pulled into the next parking spot, and Ridgeway got out. Mark's first sight of his brother-in-law made him raise his eyebrows. Last night, Joe had looked fine. Now he looked ten years older, and for a split-second, Mark saw something in his eyes that made him catch his breath. Then it was gone, and Joe was smiling.

"Good morning, Mark."

"Joe." Mark gestured. "Steve Buchanan, Joe Ridgeway."

"I'm glad to meet you, Steve," Joe said, holding out his hand.

For a few seconds, Buchanan looked at the extended hand before accepting it. Mark wondered if Joe saw what he saw—the exhaustion, the depression, the general bewilderment over the unexpected turn his life had taken.

"Why don't we go in?" Joe suggested.

Steve actually took a step back, and Mark put a hand on the man's arm. "Good idea," he said.

Buchanan looked at him, and Mark jerked his head toward his brother-in-law. "Go on."

Steve looked back at Ridgeway, whose smile softened. "I don't bite, really," Joe said.

A loud putt-putt interrupted, and all three men turned to see an ancient Volkswagen approaching. By mutual consent, they moved aside, watching as it was parked, and a petite, young Hispanic woman got out.

She smiled brightly at them. "Good morning."

"Good morning, Inez." Ridgeway smiled back. "We'll see you inside."

Mark was surprised he hadn't introduced them but figured it had something to do with confidentiality. They followed her through the back door and down a narrow hall that opened up into a reception area. Glass windows fronted the room and allowed in the morning light. Inez immediately went over to the desk and laid down her purse.

Abruptly, Mark realized there had been no reason for him to come inside. The thought was a relief, and he immediately started to turn back.

"Wait a minute," Joe said with a light touch on his shoulder. "Steve, this way." He led him to a closed door on the opposite side of the room, pushed it open, and turned on the light.

Steve hesitated, throwing Mark an almost desperate look that blunted his annoyance.

"Go on," Mark said, more gently than he had intended. "It'll be okay."

Steve slowly entered the room and disappeared from sight. Joe said something to him as he passed before looking back at his brother-in-law.

"Should I call you when we're done?" Joe asked.

Fresh irritation surged through Mark. His first thought was to say no, but he realized he didn't have any alternate suggestions. "All right," he snapped, not caring that he sounded ungracious. He knew Ridgeway was doing him a favor, but it seemed the more he tried to untangle himself from his partner's problems, the more entangled he became.

"All right," Joe agreed.

Without another word, Mark turned and headed back down the corridor. Behind him, he heard the young woman's voice.

"How was it at the hospital?" she asked.

There was a few seconds of silence before Ridgeway answered. "We need to update the Prayer Circle."

The pain in his voice and the woman's soft gasp made Mark walk faster. He didn't want to know what happened. All he wanted to do was return to the safety of his office and get as much work done as possible before Ridgeway's unwelcome call.

He was sick and tired of other people's problems. He was especially sick and tired of having to deal with other people's problems that interfered with his own life. From here on out, those other people could deal with their own problems.

10

Walking into his suite calmed Mark's lingering temper. Staff and lawyers were bustling around, clients were being met, and the craziness of the past several days was fading before the welcome reality of normal life.

Respectful nods greeted his appearance, and a couple of "Good mornings" were offered. Mark knew there must be surprise at what appeared to be his uncharacteristic late arrival, but no one was rash enough to say anything.

Charlotte Ingram was sitting at the receptionist's desk, talking on the telephone. As he approached, he heard her say, "Then we'll see you at 10:00 a.m. on the twentieth, Mr. Ames… yes… all right, good-bye." She hung up and looked at him with a smile. "Good morning, Mr. Newman. You have some messages."

Mark took the small sheaf of phone messages from her. "Thank you. Is anything else going on that I should know about?"

Charlotte clicked on her computer, and he saw the main appointment calendar pop up. "The small conference room is being used by Mr. Francis for an arbitration. Otherwise, everything's as usual."

As usual. Welcome words. Pleased with this additional evidence of normalcy, Mark smiled. "Good."

Instead of turning down the hall toward his office, he impulsively went in the opposite direction, past additional offices and secretarial spaces, the small conference room— its door firmly closed, and past the library. At the end of the hall, he went around the corner into the kitchen.

Two secretaries were sitting at the table, chatting over their coffee cups. When he entered, their eyes widened almost simultaneously. Without looking at each other, they quickly rose. Their greetings came so close together they were garbled, and before he could respond, they were gone. Only then did he let out the smile he had been holding back. Apart from breaks and lunches, staff were not supposed to linger in the kitchen, but Mark was feeling so much better that he didn't care about the minor infraction.

As he lifted the coffee pot, he caught a whiff of the contents and frowned. Someone had brewed a pot of flavored coffee, one of his pet peeves. He wasn't about to drink something that smelled like it belonged in a flower garden. After pouring it out in the sink and rinsing out the pot, he rummaged through the cabinets until he found where the coffee was kept. A few minutes later, the aroma of freshly-brewed coffee filled the air and he inhaled appreciatively. This was what coffee was supposed to smell like. His mug was in his office, but that was no problem. Taking one of the community mugs out of a cabinet, Mark filled it and relaxed, leaning against the wall while sipping the hot liquid.

Absorbed in the enjoyment of the moment, it took a few minutes before he realized he was hearing a low-voiced conversation from the hallway outside the kitchen. Mark sighed in annoyance. Another interruption. He needed to return to his office; at least there he could ensure that he wouldn't be interrupted.

"I don't know what else to do." Despite being spoken in a near-whisper, the anguish in the young man's words startled Mark.

"How much time is left?" A woman's voice this time. Both voices sounded familiar, but he couldn't immediately put faces to them.

"She has to be out in thirty days. Thirty days!" The voice rose slightly. "Cassie's in no condition to move, even if she had a place to move to."

"Has she finished with the chemo treatments?"

"That depends on what the tests tomorrow show."

What had started out as mild annoyance was now a mixture of anger and discomfort. This was obviously a very personal conversation, and it shouldn't be held in a work environment. Mark coughed, deliberately loud, before walking out of the kitchen.

Standing just inside the entrance to the library were two people who stared at him with similar expressions of surprise. Now he recognized them. The young man was one of the firm's law students, Jay Russell. The woman he had been speaking to was a secretary, Amanda Sutherling. They drew apart as he approached, and he gave them a short nod before continuing down the hallway, through the reception area, and on to his office. Once inside he was relieved to be able to close his door, but the feeling couldn't erase his memory of Russell's pale, strained features.

What on earth was going on? It seemed like everyone around him suddenly had problems that were, in one way or another, interfering with his life.

Mark settled in his chair, leaning back and closing his eyes, trying to force away everything that could be upsetting or distracting. This was his sanctuary, and he resented the world's attempts to take that away from him. Finally, he felt calm enough to face the work on his desk. He leaned forward to pull off his jacket and heard a faint crunching sound. Frowning, he explored his pockets and discovered the messages the receptionist had given him. He had stuffed them in a pocket when he decided to go to the kitchen, and they were now crumpled although still legible.

Mark smoothed them out and went through them quickly. The third one stopped him short. It was from Frank

Adams, the private investigator he had hired to track down his rescuer. Something fluttered in his stomach, and he took a deep breath before punching the number Adams had left into his cell phone.

"You have reached the office of Frank Adams, private investigator. Please leave a message after the tone and—"

The recording stopped abruptly, and a few seconds later a husky, slightly rough voice spoke. "This is Adams."

"This is Mark Newman returning your call."

"Oh, yes, Mr. Newman. I was just walking into my office. Just a minute while I get around the desk." There was a brief silence before the man spoke again. "Okay. I talked to a lot of people, their names will be in my report, but long story short, no one knows anything about the guy who helped you out."

Disappointment settled heavily in Mark's stomach. "You talked to the paramedics?"

"Yes, sir." He heard paper rustle. "Felipe Delgado and Tim Hartwell are the paramedics who responded to your accident. When they arrived, the only one they saw was you. No one else and no other vehicles except for the police unit that also responded to the call. I talked to the police officer, name of Langley, and he said basically the same thing."

Police? Mark didn't remember seeing any police. Then again, his memories of those moments were hazy and darkened by terror, nothing he wanted to recall.

Only now that Adams was reporting his failure did Mark realize how much he had wanted to find his mysterious rescuer.

"What about at the hospital?"

"I spoke to the people in the ER who were on duty that night, but they didn't see any strangers hanging around. Then again, they couldn't have seen anything unless the guy decided to follow you to the hospital, and like I said, there were no other cars around where you were found."

Mark sagged back in his chair. "What"—he coughed and cleared his throat—"what steps would you suggest next?"

There was a long silence, then, "I'm sorry, Mr. Newman, but I don't see anywhere to go from here."

Nowhere to go. The words sounded bitter, then he realized that he was projecting his own feelings. Adams's voice was matter-of-fact, professional, and that recognition made the last of Mark's hope fade.

"I even tracked down the 911 call that sent help to you," the investigator added. "They keep recordings of all the calls. There was a lot of static, and you could hear the storm in the background, but it sounded like a man's voice. Other than telling the operator what happened and providing a location, he didn't offer any other information. Another dead end."

The voice of his rescuer? That was the obvious answer, except when would the man have had time to call? Certainly not during the rescue and probably not after, since Mark was sure he would have heard that. After seeing Mark's desperate predicament, would the stranger have taken the time to make the call *before* his rescue efforts? That seemed doubtful. Yet if he hadn't called, who had?

Unanswered questions. Which left him where?

Nowhere.

Trying to hide his disappointment, Mark said, "Thank you for your time. Do I owe you anything more?"

"No, sir, the check you sent will cover everything. I'll mail my report to you. Sorry I couldn't give you better news."

"That's all right." He hung up slowly, marveling at his calm delivery. It wasn't all right.

Less than a week ago, he had almost died. The thought still had the power to send chills through him. Nor were the events of the past several days helping him to return to his usual routine. Between Steve Buchanan, Mark's own unusual encounters with the members of his family, including dealings with a brother-in-law he had never voluntarily sought out before, all these experiences were keeping him feeling out of sorts and off balance.

Mark swore and rubbed his face hard. *Let it go, Newman. Just let it go and move on.*

He took a deep breath and sat up in his chair. Maybe the best way to move on was just to do it. He smiled ruefully. He sounded like a commercial.

All right. Moving on. He turned on his computer and checked his calendar. His first scheduled appointment had been moved to later in the day and he silently blessed his assistant. Carolyn hadn't taken any chances on when he might be returning. Two more back-to-back meetings would take him into the early afternoon, and a settlement conference would finish the day.

Mark turned to the files in his Inbox and nodded in satisfaction. Once again, Carolyn was on top of things. He had everything he needed. Opening the first file, he immediately immersed himself in the details of the case. It didn't matter that he already knew them; the upcoming meeting was important, and he wanted every detail fresh in his mind.

His cell phone rang, and he picked it up. "Newman," he said absently.

"Hi, it's Joe."

In an instant, Mark's calm vanished. He knew why his brother-in-law must be calling, but sheer perversity made him say, "Yes?"

"Steve gave me permission to tell you that he's agreed to check himself into a hospital."

Mark sat up with a start. He hadn't expected this twist. "Hospital?"

"Other than the breakfast you forced on him this morning, he hasn't eaten or slept in several days. We need to address that before we can address other issues."

"Such as his marriage?" Mark said resignedly.

"I just wanted you to know. I'll take him over so you don't need to concern yourself."

Mark's annoyance grew. Ridgeway hadn't answered his question, and what did he mean that Mark wouldn't have to concern himself? Buchanan had dragged him into his personal affairs.

He wanted his regular life back, he reminded himself. Washing his hands of Steve and letting him take up his brother-in-law's time was one step in that direction. "Fine," he snapped.

"We'll talk later," Joe said.

Mark glared at the receiver before hanging up. Talk about what? He'd done his good deed and then some. There was no need to waste any more of his time on Steve's sorry situation and certainly no need to talk to his brother-in-law again. Trying to set aside his irritation, he looked down at the file again. He had no time for distractions; he needed to finish reviewing the file before the meeting.

Sometime later, his intercom buzzed. Mark bit back a snappish comment when he answered. "Yes?"

"Mr. Newman?" It was his assistant. "I'm going over to Ming's. Can I bring you back something for lunch?"

Lunch? Mark looked at his watch in surprise, realizing how empty his stomach felt. "Yes, please, Carolyn. Do you need any money?"

"No, sir, I've got enough."

"All right. Make sure you get a receipt so I can reimburse you."

"Yes, sir."

Mark almost disconnected before he thought of something. "Thank you, Carolyn."

"You're welcome."

He stared at the telephone for a minute, thankful for her composure. Everything else in his life might be in turmoil, but he was fortunate his assistant was not part of that turmoil. No matter what, Carolyn Colby remained calm, unflustered, and always in control.

Over a half hour later, Mark had almost completed reviewing the file when he heard a gentle knock on his door.

"Come in."

Carolyn appeared, carrying a large white bag. She smiled as she set it on his desk. "I hope this will hit the spot."

"I'm sure it will. Did you get a receipt?"

She handed it to him and glanced at her watch. "You have forty minutes before the meeting."

Mark nodded. "More than enough time. Thank you again."

"You're welcome."

After she was gone, he investigated the bag—lo mein, egg rolls, sweet-and-sour soup, beef teriyaki. He smiled in pleasure. She had remembered his favorites.

After he had eaten, Mark went back over the notes he had made during his review of the file. He was ready for his meetings, both this one and the one to come. There wouldn't be much time between the second meeting and the settlement conference, but the latter had been his case from the beginning, and he was intimately acquainted with every detail. The other side wouldn't know what hit them.

Warmed by anticipation, Mark put on his suit jacket, adjusted his cuffs, and headed for the conference room.

It was six thirty by the time he was done for the day. Despite the hour, he was pleased with how his afternoon had gone, and he returned to his office with a spring in his step to find several new telephone messages waiting for him. Carolyn's doing, no doubt. Two tempted him to crumple them up and throw them away. One was from his brother-in-law, and the other was from Marty Welch, asking if the monthly partners' meeting scheduled for tomorrow was still on.

Mark's jaw clenched. Welch's question was a subtle request for information. Marty had to know Buchanan hadn't been in the office the past week, at least not for any time worth mentioning. He doubtless also knew by now that Steve's meetings, conferences, and court appearances had been rescheduled for the week.

What was he going to tell Welch? The man was one of the firm's partners; he deserved not to be kept in the dark. As annoyed as Mark was with Buchanan, he wasn't about to publicize Steve's problems. The firm's rumor mill was undoubtedly active with speculation. He would have to think of something to tell Welch without actually telling him anything. As for the rest of the firm, they could speculate to their heart's content.

He made a mental note to ask Carolyn about Buchanan's upcoming caseload. She would need to talk to Steve's secretary. Although everything was covered this week, who knew what next week would bring?

Well, he would deal with Welch tomorrow. As for the other messages, most of them would have to wait until the morning, but there were a couple he could take care of now. When he finished with them, he looked reluctantly at the message from his brother-in-law. This morning, he had thought he was done with Steve Buchanan's problems. Except that now he was thinking about it, he remembered that Joe had mentioned he would be calling him later. Hopefully, it was just some minor matter that could be resolved with a brief phone call.

He grudgingly dialed the phone number Joe had left. The recording clicked on, and Mark was both annoyed and pleased to hear it. Leaving a message was preferable to talking.

Once again, the message was interrupted by a genuine voice. "This is Pastor Joe."

"It's Mark. You called?"

"Yes, thanks for getting back to me. Can we talk?"

"That's what we're doing," Mark snapped.

"I mean face-to-face."

He swore silently. "I still have quite a bit of work to do."

That wasn't a lie. Mark wanted to finalize some notes to the files he had worked on today, plus he had quite a bit of dictation he needed to do. Of course, he could do that tomorrow, but he wasn't about to admit it to his brother-in-law. He would be perfectly happy to do it tonight if it would get him out of meeting with Ridgeway.

There was a long silence at the other end, and Mark let it stretch out.

Finally, Joe spoke. "What about tomorrow?"

Mark bit back the words he wanted to say and settled for, "Tomorrow won't work."

"The next day won't work for me," Ridgeway said. "What about this weekend?"

Mark suppressed another curse. "Aren't you busy with your church on weekends?"

Joe laughed, a relaxed, easy sound that increased Mark's annoyance. "Not every minute. How does Saturday look for you?"

The man wasn't going to give up. As much as Mark wanted to say he would never be available, that wasn't an option.

"Saturday's busy too. I could meet you around two o'clock, but it couldn't be for long." He hoped that giving his brother-in-law a definite time would conflict with something on Ridgeway's agenda.

"All right," Joe said promptly. "I'll see you at two. I can come over to your house."

"No," Mark said immediately. He didn't want his brother-in-law intruding in his personal space. "I'll be coming from the opposite direction," he lied.

"Opposite?" Joe sounded thoughtful. "We could meet at the church, but we're having a rummage sale in the parking lot so it'll be a zoo. What about meeting at my home?"

Rummage sale? Mark shuddered at the thought. He didn't like meeting Ridgeway on his own turf, but it would be preferable to the church. "All right."

"Good, I'll see you then."

Mark answered by pressing the END button. Dropping the cell phone on his desk, he glared at it. He realized too late that he had forgotten to ask Ridgeway what the topic of the meeting would be. For a minute, he considered calling back but rejected the idea. It must be something to do with Buchanan.

Had Steve already checked himself into a hospital? Mark guessed yes, which raised an obvious question. What hospital? A tiny voice in the back of Mark's mind told him he should find out, but he ignored it.

Since he was here and the day's events were still fresh in his mind, he decided to update the files now and do some dictation. There would plenty more to do tomorrow, and this way he would be able to get a little ahead. Opening the files once again, Mark was pleased to realize that he was spending an evening as he was used to doing, as he had done regularly for years, up until the accident that had turned his life upside down.

He suppressed the thought and focused on work.

11

When Mark woke up Saturday morning, his first thought was of his upcoming meeting with Joe Ridgeway. It had seemed like a good idea at the time to put off that meeting at least a couple of days. Now that the day had arrived, he regretted agreeing to meet with his brother-in-law.

At first he had been disappointed by Frank Adams's inability to find out anything about his rescuer. Now that more time had passed, he looked on it as a turning point. There was nothing more to be discovered from that night. It was past time to leave it behind and move forward. Mark was loathe to tackle anything that might interfere with his decision, and that included spending time with his brother-in-law. In the last week, he had spent more time with Ridgeway than he had in years. Now that he thought about it, he wondered if that had anything to do with all the ungovernable emotions he had been struggling with.

Though he didn't know what Ridgeway wanted to talk about, Mark assumed it had something to do with Steve

Buchanan. A twinge of discomfort needled him at the thought of his partner. Was Buchanan still hospitalized? He had no idea, for he had avoided finding out what hospital the man was in. If he knew that, he might have felt compelled to visit.

Mark felt uncomfortable whenever he thought of his partner, so he tried not to think about him. All of Steve's current cases had been reassigned, and everything was running smoothly at the firm. The last thing Mark wanted was to interfere with that. He fervently hoped his brother-in-law wouldn't do exactly that.

As usual, Mark spent Saturday morning in his office. Weekends were a good time to work because things were quiet, fewer people were around, which meant fewer distractions. Immersed in his work, Mark let time slip by unheeded. If not for the fact that he had reluctantly set the alarm on his watch, he probably would have worked right through the time he was supposed to meet with his brother-in-law. It was a tempting idea, but one he discarded.

Promptly at 2:00 p.m., he parked at the curb in front of Joe's house and glared at the modest bungalow. *Come on, Newman. Get it over with.* Taking a deep breath, he let it out slowly as he exited his car. When he reached the door, he raised a hand to knock, then paused at the sound of childish shrieks from inside. Just what he didn't need.

He knocked harder than necessary, tapping his foot while he waited. The seconds passed, and just as he was about to knock even more forcefully, the door was opened by Joe himself. He had a small boy draped over one shoulder and held another small boy like a sack of potatoes under his arm. Both children were giggling wildly, and Ridgeway himself was tousled and grinning like an idiot.

"Hi, Mark, welcome to the zoo." As he stepped aside the little boys began making animal noises, growling and barking, interspersed with more giggles.

"If this is a bad time," Mark started, seeing a possible escape.

"No, not at all." Joe laughed. "Beth!" he called over his shoulder.

Mark entered at the same time his sister-in-law appeared. Ridgeway lowered the children to the floor, and Beth caught two small grubby hands in her own.

"All right, you monsters." She chuckled. "Come with me."

"We's not monsters!" proclaimed one of the twins.

"Yeah!" insisted the other. "We's g'rillas!" Whereupon both boys tucked their free hands under their arms and made loud grunting noises.

"Fine, gorillas," Beth said good-naturedly as she led them away. "Let's see if we can find you some milk and bananas."

"Nanas!" both boys yelled enthusiastically.

Mark couldn't help a wince, and Joe smiled sympathetically. "Sorry about that." He gestured. "The decibels should decrease by the time we get to my study."

"After you," Mark said, unaccountably annoyed. It wasn't just because he didn't want to be here. It was because of something else, another feeling he couldn't put a name to, which only made him more irritated. He didn't try to hide his feelings, but Joe only nodded, still smiling, and led the way.

When they entered the room and the door was shut behind them, Mark got straight to the point. "Why were you so insistent we meet face-to-face? What was so important you couldn't tell me over the phone? Is it Buchanan?"

Ridgeway's smile faded. "Why don't you have a seat?"

"I don't plan to stay long enough to need to sit down."

"Fine." The older man sat on the edge of his desk and studied his brother-in-law with thoughtful green eyes. "This isn't about Steve Buchanan. I take it you weren't aware that he had been released from the hospital yesterday?"

Though both his expression and tone were neutral, Mark sensed disapproval. He didn't care. "I've been busy," he snapped. "In part because I've had to take on a lot of his work."

"I thought you were friends."

Suddenly furious, Mark started toward the door. Joe stepped quickly in his way, and he stopped with a jerk.

"I didn't come here to have you play holier than thou with me. If you have a point, get to it. Otherwise I'm leaving."

"All right," Joe said quietly. "Is Geneva all right?"

Mark stared at him. Geneva? Of all the topics his brother-in-law might have chosen, this was the last one he would have expected. He felt as if someone had punched him in the stomach, leaving him breathless.

Joe's expression changed to concern, and he caught his arm. "Sit down," he said, giving the arm a gentle pull.

Mark sat, not because Ridgeway said so, but because his legs felt weak. Joe sat opposite.

"I'm sorry to hit you like this. I didn't realize."

"Didn't realize what?" Mark took a deep breath, feeling his strength returning.

Joe looked down at his hands before meeting his brother-in-law's hard gaze. "I didn't mean to surprise you. The reason I asked is because the day I helped Steve Buchanan check into the hospital, I saw Geneva there. She was just getting out of the elevator and was so preoccupied she didn't even see me, although I was only twenty feet away."

"What did she say?"

"Nothing. I let her go by without calling to her."

Mark wanted to look away from the worry in the green eyes but couldn't. "Why?"

Joe sighed and rubbed a hand over his face. "That's a good question."

"Which you aren't answering."

"I'm not sure…" Ridgeway sighed again. "Geneva is my little sister, and I love her very much, but she's always been a very private person. And she's only become more private as the years have passed."

Though Mark didn't respond, he silently agreed. It was only back when they were seriously dating in college and later, early in their marriage, that Geneva had been open and approachable. When had that changed? When had she withdrawn behind invisible, unbreachable walls? He couldn't remember.

"I didn't want to approach her at the hospital," Joe continued. "It felt too much like an ambush, and I knew I'd never get anything out of her. But when I called her later, I got absolutely nothing. She finally said she had been visiting a friend at the hospital but"—his smile was painful—"I'm not sure she was telling the truth."

Mark didn't know what to think. When was the last time he had talked to her? It had been a few nights ago, when he surprised her in the kitchen. They had said nothing of substance before she walked out. And before then? He didn't remember. He felt a surge of sorrow but wasn't sure why. By mutual if unspoken consent, their marriage had become a matter of convenience years ago. Why was he feeling guilty now?

It was Ridgeway's fault. It was because of his brother-in-law's worry that Mark was feeling this way.

"Mark?"

He drew his thoughts back to the present and scowled at the minister. "If Geneva chooses not to talk about it, that's her business."

Joe's eyes widened. "She's my sister and your wife! Do you know what's wrong, or aren't you interested?" The disapproval was stronger, and now there was an edge of anger to it.

Mark stood again, and Ridgeway immediately followed suit.

"What is between me and my wife is my business," Mark said, trying but not able to suppress his own anger.

Joe took a deep breath, then another. He dropped his gaze for a minute, and when he raised his head again, his green eyes were calm. "That's true," he said quietly. "However, she's also my sister and I'm worried about her." He paused, then sighed. "I'm not asking you to reveal anything she might have told you in confidence, but I'd like to know if she's all right."

The logical, analytical part of Mark's mind couldn't argue with a brother wanting to know if his sister was okay. Except that Joe's question cut directly through the veil of apathy Mark had embraced years ago, which kept him from taking a close look at his marriage. He couldn't recall the last time he had sat down with Geneva and had a serious conversation. For that matter, he couldn't recall the last time he and Geneva actually had a genuine conversation.

Mark mentally flinched away from the thought. This wasn't the time for soul-searching. Nor was he about to admit the state of his marriage to his wife's brother. "I can't tell you anything," he said shortly.

"Because you can't or don't know?"

Mark bit back an angry retort. Joe was studying him now, and he suddenly felt naked under that searching gaze. If he didn't know better, he would think the man could read his mind. It was stupid and paranoid, but perhaps not without an element of truth. By training, by experience, maybe by his very nature, Joe Ridgeway must have learned a great deal about other people during his years as a minister.

As an attorney, Mark tried to do something along the same line with clients, opposing counsel and judges. But not like this, not with the intensity that he could now read in his brother-in-law's expression.

There was a gentle knock on the door, and Ridgeway turned to open it.

Beth was standing in the hall, looking apologetic. "I'm sorry to interrupt, honey, but the person you've been waiting to hear from is on the phone."

"All right, please tell him I'll be right with him." After she withdrew, Joe looked again at his brother-in-law. "I need to take this call, and it's going to take awhile. I'm sorry."

Mark tried to hide his relief. "That's fine," he lied. "I need to get to another appointment." He didn't look away from his brother-in-law's intent eyes.

After a minute, Ridgeway nodded again. "Thanks for coming over."

"Sure." Mark strode past him and down the hall.

"Mark?"

He stopped reluctantly and looked back.

Joe was standing in the doorway. "In case you're interested, Steve is staying at the St. Regis Hotel."

Mark swallowed another spurt of anger and walked away. He got in his car and started driving but a few minutes later pulled over and stopped. Anger struggled with worry, almost paralyzing in intensity.

Was something wrong with Geneva? He shuddered, barely able to withstand the flood of…of what? What was he feeling?

He thought back to his brief exchange with Geneva the other night. When he thanked her for calling her brother to come and pick him up at the hospital, her response carried an edge of bitterness, *Is that sarcasm?* Mark had been surprised by her words, and even his assurance didn't seem to help for her next words filled him with inexpressible sadness, *I wondered when I heard your message if you expected me to come and pick you up.* Surprised by emotion, he had responded with unguarded honesty, *I think I gave up the right to expect anything from you a long time ago.*

Remembering now, he wasn't sure who had been more shocked by his words, Geneva or Mark himself. When had things changed between them? When had that early, all-enveloping passion turned cold? He tried to swallow but a lump of pain in his throat made it impossible. This was a waste of time. Agonizing over what had happened in the past wouldn't change anything. There was no going back.

Childish laughter echoed in his memory, and irritation replaced the other emotion. Ridgeway was welcome to his young children. Mark was grateful that his boys were beyond that age.

Out of nowhere, a memory seared through him.

Geneva lay exhausted in the bed, drenched in perspiration, yet the joy in her eyes made her more beautiful than ever. In her arms she held their firstborn child, only a few minutes old. Mark leaned over them, one arm around her slim shoulders and the other hand gently caressing the tiny features of their son. His blue eyes—almost the exact shade of his mother's—were unfocused, and they squeezed shut when he gave a tiny yawn. "Welcome to the world, Brian," Mark whispered as he ran a tender hand over the damp curls.

Mark swallowed. On top of everything else, his emotional turmoil seemed to be triggering ancient memories that he hadn't recalled in years. He had struggled so hard to get back to his normal life. Suddenly he was stricken by a new thought. What if he couldn't return to that old normalcy? What if these unwanted thoughts and memories continued despite all his efforts to contain them? What then?

Mark mentally flung the thought away. He would gain control of them; he would return them to the depths of his mind or wherever they had come from. It might take longer than he had originally thought but he would succeed.

In case you're interested, Steve is staying at the St. Regis Hotel.

He swore. Ridgeway's last comment still rang in his ears. He didn't want to be bothered with his partner's problems. He had done his share, more than his share. There must be others Buchanan could lean on.

Was Ridgeway still counseling Steve? The man knew what hospital Steve had checked into, and he knew when Buchanan left. He also knew where Steve was staying. Obviously, Joe had kept in touch. If Steve had no one else, he could use Ridgeway's shoulder.

Mark tried again to shove away his unwelcome thoughts. He should go back to his office and all the work waiting for him. It was the way he had spent his weekends for many years, and yet it suddenly felt unappetizing. With the realization came a fresh spurt of anger. It was Ridgeway's fault. Something about his brother-in-law was interfering with his struggle to return to his old life. Or was it Buchanan's situation that had to do with Mark's emotional upheaval? Maybe it was both.

As much as he wanted to, Mark couldn't lay the blame entirely on the two men. This had all started the night he had almost died. Could it only have been a week ago? It seemed much longer. If the accident hadn't occurred, would he have been so troubled by Steve Buchanan's marital problems or Ridgeway's interference? Mark didn't know.

All he was certain of was that his life had been turned upside down a week ago, and everything that had happened since only added to his turmoil. His vaunted self-control was in shreds and everything he tried to do to shore it up was failing.

Mark Newman needed to reclaim his self-control. As far back as he could remember, it had been at the core of his character, driving him to succeed in everything he attempted. The affluence that had come about through his successful career was merely a by-product.

If a man cannot control himself, he cannot control his life.

Mark choked, shocked. The words came from his oldest memories, and the voice, though he had not heard it in decades, was instantly familiar. William Newman had not only lived his beliefs, but in the process, he had grown extremely wealthy and successful. As both chairman of the board and president of the city's largest bank, he had always been a figure to look up to and emulate.

Or so his son had thought. Mark grew up with his father's admonitions ringing in his ears. From his son's earliest years, William was always pushing him to do better, and Mark knew his father's influence was the reason he had grown up to be so successful.

Or was he? He was wealthy and successful in his chosen profession but at what cost to his personal life?

Mark realized he was shivering, even as he wondered where this newest, unpleasant thought had come from.

Then he realized he was still parked on the side of the street. Swallowing, he started the car and pulled back into traffic. He was going to go back to the office and work. And work. And keep working until he forced all the turmoil down so deep it would never see the light of day again.

His cell phone rang, and Mark yanked it out of his inner pocket. "Newman."

"Mark Newman?"

He frowned, not recognizing the voice. "Yes, who is this?"

"Mr. Newman, this is the admitting office at Mercy General Hospital. Your son, Brian Newman, was admitted a short time ago."

He nearly plowed into the car in front of him before he hit the brakes. Heedless of traffic, he yanked the steering wheel over and parked awkwardly. "Admitted? Why? What happened?"

"I'm sorry, I don't have that information. If you—"

"How is he?" Mark demanded, his heart hammering.

"Apparently his condition is not serious, but—"

"I'll be there in a few minutes." He turned off the phone, shoved it back into his pocket, and jammed his foot down on the accelerator.

Tires squealing, the car lurched back into the street.

12

Mark never remembered his drive to the hospital. His first clear recollection was when he hurried into the emergency entrance and made a beeline for the information desk.

"My son was just brought in. Where can I find him?"

The woman was apparently used to distraught people suddenly appearing before her because she turned calmly to her computer and clicked the keyboard. "His name?"

"Brian Newman."

She typed in the information. "He's still in emergency. That's just down around the corner." She pointed and offered him a reassuring smile.

Mark barely noticed, for he turned immediately and hurried down the hall as fast as he could walk. When he entered the large room, it was almost empty. There were a few nurses and a doctor or two, but he didn't see any sign of his son. One nurse was just walking out and almost ran into him.

"Can I help you?" the nurse said.

"Yes, my son is here."

Her eyebrows rose. "Mr. Newman?"

"Yes!" Finally, someone knew something.

The nursed gestured toward the back of the room. Curtains blocked his view, but trusting she knew what she was talking about, Mark went over and pushed the nearest curtain aside. The sight of his son sitting on the gurney stopped him in midstride. For a minute, he stood frozen while his eyes swept over the boy.

Brian was dressed, but his shirt hung open, revealing the white bandages wrapped around his torso. His left hand and wrist were also bandaged, and dark bruises were forming on the left side of his cheek and jaw.

For the first time since he had received the call from the hospital, Mark took a deep breath, his knees almost buckling under the weight of sudden relief. Before he had a chance to speak, two things happened simultaneously. Brian raised his head and saw him, and a strange voice said, "Mr. Newman?"

Startled, Mark turned away from his son's wide-eyed stare to find himself facing a police officer. Despite his surprise, he answered calmly, "Yes, I'm Mark Newman." His eyes flicked to the name tag on the uniform which read BELTRAN. "What happened?"

The officer glanced at Brian before looking back. "You're Brian Newman's father?"

Mark wasn't used to having his questions ignored. "I am. Once more, what happened?"

Beltran seemed unaffected by his curtness. "Your son was a passenger in a car that ran a stop sign. When we tried to pull it over it attempted to evade us—"

"What!"

"And after a brief pursuit, the driver of the vehicle lost control, and it overturned," the officer continued matter-of-factly. "The other passenger is in surgery, while the driver is in custody." His eyes returned to Brian who seemed to shrink under the scrutiny.

Mark followed his gaze while he tried to make sense of the information. "I don't understand."

Beltran met his eyes, and Mark thought he saw sympathy. "On top of the charges that will be filed against the driver, we found two open bottles of alcohol in the car. We're waiting for the results of blood tests to determine if additional charges need to be filed."

The words echoed oddly through Mark's mind. He couldn't be hearing right. There was no way his son could be involved in this...this... He realized he was shaking his head. "There must be some mistake."

"I'm afraid not," Beltran said. "Your son has already been read his rights and refused to tell us anything. But things might go easier on him if he was willing to cooperate."

"Easier." Mark bit his lip; he didn't mean to speak out loud.

The officer nodded. "The most serious charges will probably be against the driver. Your son was only a passenger, and he's also a minor with no prior charges."

Mark heard Beltran's words but something was interfering with his ability to process them. He tried to respond as instinct and training dictated. "I'm sure cooperation won't be an issue. However, I would like to discuss the matter with an attorney first. For now," he continued, "I'd like to take my son home."

Beltran's hesitation was obvious.

"Have you charged my son with anything?"

"Not yet."

Mark didn't allow his thankfulness to show. "Then there should be no problem with my taking him home."

Beltran eyed the forlorn young figure sitting on the gurney. "I'll need your contact information, sir. And the young man will need to remain available."

Mark wasn't about to look a gift horse in the mouth. "Certainly."

After providing the officer with his information and talking to the physician who had treated his son, Mark ordered Brian into the car, and it wasn't until he was driving out of the parking lot that he spoke. His fear was gone, replaced by anger.

"What did you think you were doing?"

Slumped in the passenger seat, Brian shrugged.

"Don't give me that!" Mark snapped. "How old are the other boys?"

"What difference does it make?"

The sullen note in the boy's voice only strengthened his father's anger. "I want to know if you were all underage. You're sixteen years old! Whatever possessed you to think that drinking was okay? Especially while in a car!"

Another shrug from Brian made his blood pressure soar.

"One more of those and I'll let the police take you to juvenile hall. I want some answers."

For the first time, his son gave him a quick, fleeting glance before turning his attention to his lap. "It's no big deal."

"Yes, it is!"

"We weren't drunk."

"That has nothing to do with anything! You were drinking. In a vehicle. You're underage. Do you have any idea of how much trouble you are in? Not to mention how much trouble you're in with me!"

Brian seemed to shrink in his seat but didn't respond, which only added fuel to Mark's fury.

"And running away when the police tried to pull you over—"

"I didn't do that," Brian protested. "Terry...he was driving. He panicked."

"You shouldn't have been in that car in the first place! And drinking—" Wrath closed Mark's throat, and he had to take several breaths before he could continue. "Of all the stupid stunts you could have pulled, this tops the list. You could be arrested and convicted. Do you understand that?"

The sudden pallor on his son's face told Mark that this was a new thought.

"Obviously, you haven't given a thought to any kind of consequences for your actions. Well, let me tell you something, mister. There are always consequences to our actions, especially stupid, unthinking actions."

Mark could feel the last of his control beginning to slip and snapped his mouth shut. He had never raised a hand to either of his sons, but at this moment he was closer to doing so than ever before in his life. The temptation to grab Brian and shake him until his teeth rattled was almost overwhelming.

What in the world had his sixteen-year-old son been thinking? Obviously, he hadn't thought at all. He had broken the law by drinking, broken it again by getting into a car with other underage boys who were drinking and *then* running when a police car tried to pull them over for ignoring a stop sign. The sheer stupidity of his actions was staggering, and every time Mark thought about it, his anger grew. He didn't dare say any more, and the rest of the drive was made in silence.

When they finally reached home and walked inside, Mark held out his hand. "Give me your cell phone."

Brian opened his mouth, caught his father's eye, and closed it again. Without a word, he handed his phone over.

"Go to your room," Mark ordered coldly. "I'll be up shortly to remove your computer and entertainment center."

His son stared at him with huge eyes, and Mark braced himself for an argument. Instead, the boy turned away and went up the stairs. Looking after him, Mark noted the drooping head and slumped shoulders and almost swore. The boy was acting like a victim when he had no one but himself to blame.

Mark retreated to his study and sat down, only to immediately jump to his feet and begin pacing while he tried to get a grip on his anger. *Focus, Newman.* There were things he needed to do. He needed to find an attorney to represent Brian, but before that, he needed to take everything Brian enjoyed out of his bedroom. Before anything else, however, he needed to get himself under control.

Control. The past week had seen his habitual control shredded until he didn't know how to put it back together. He felt adrift, and despite all his efforts, nothing he had done helped. Now this—this stupidity by his son. He gritted his teeth, fighting back fresh temptation to put angry hands on the boy.

He shook his head at himself, knowing he didn't dare go near Brian until he calmed down. Suddenly claustrophobic, he left his study and resumed his pacing through the foyer, the living room, dining room, kitchen, and back. He walked and walked while he struggled to change the direction of his thoughts, struggled to put aside the last few hours—no, the day. Apart from his time at the office this morning, the entire day was nothing he wanted to remember.

The memory of his confrontation with his brother-in-law slowed his pacing. As if Brian's situation wasn't enough of a problem to deal with, what was he going to do about his wife? What was he going to do about his brother-in-law's news about Geneva?

Mark closed his eyes in consternation. He was going to have to tell her what had happened with Brian, and he had no idea how she would react. Nor did he know how he was going to ask her why Joe had seen her leaving the hospital. And when should he ask? Before or after he broke the news about Brian?

Halfway through the living room. Mark stopped, suddenly realizing he was tired. Dropping into the nearest chair, he scrubbed at his face. What was happening? Every time he thought things couldn't get worse, they did. It felt as if one unforeseen problem was spiraling into another, dragging him ever further away from his effort of getting his life back.

As he sat there, he gradually became aware of how quiet the house was. No human voices broke the silence, and even the ordinary sounds of furnace and air conditioning were absent. It was so quiet, so unlike the turmoil in his heart. Mark rubbed his face absently and was startled to feel moisture on his cheeks. Hastily, he wiped it away and rose again. This was not acceptable.

Not taking the time to think about it, Mark went upstairs and entered Brian's room without knocking. The boy was lying facedown on his bed and didn't react to the sudden intrusion. Without speaking, Mark unplugged the laptop and carried it out to the hall. Then he returned to take out the television and stereo system.

It took two trips to carry everything into his bedroom. He put the electronics in one of the walk-in closets and then settled in his favorite chair. A glance at the window showed the sun was going down, and he closed his eyes in exhaustion.

The traitorous thoughts from earlier in the day slipped back into his consciousness. *What if he wasn't able to return to his normal life?*

A chill ran through Mark. If he wasn't able to regain his normal life, then what?

Ridiculous. How could he even think such foolishness? While a lot might have happened during the past week, he wasn't about to surrender control. It had taken years of hard, focused work to make his life what it was, and he would do whatever he had to in order to keep it.

A distant hum caught Mark's attention. He went to the window that looked down at the garage and part of the backyard and was in time to see the garage door closing.

Geneva was home. For a minute, he hesitated, then his lips tightened, and he got to his feet.

When Geneva walked into the kitchen a few minutes, she stopped in surprise at the sight of her husband standing in the doorway. "I wasn't expecting you to be here," she said as she pulled off her light jacket.

Mark watched her while he struggled to find the right words. Maybe something of his discomfort came through because her eyes narrowed when she met his gaze. There was no easy way to say it. Even as her lips parted, he spoke. "Something happened that we need to talk about."

Geneva looked him over more closely. "Were you in another accident? You don't look as if you were injured."

"No." Mark swallowed. "I'm fine. Why don't you sit down?" He gestured toward the breakfast nook.

She frowned. "If you have something to say, you can do it in a more civilized atmosphere than the kitchen."

"All right, let's go into the living room."

Geneva nodded shortly and walked out of the kitchen. Mark followed, studying the trim, elegant figure ahead of him. He suddenly felt as if they were separated by a thousand miles. He had known, when he bothered to think about it, that they had drifted apart over the years, but never before had he felt such intense loss over that separation.

She sat down in a chair, and he sat opposite her on the sofa while he thought about what to say.

"I'm waiting," she said.

Her voice was cool, without emotion, and Mark suppressed a wince. Her quiet reserve was something he had enjoyed breaking through when they were dating so many years ago. When had it returned, and how long had it taken for that reserve to become so hardened? He dared not linger over the thought because he feared where it would lead. Better just to speak the truth.

"Brian was in an accident today."

The color drained from Geneva's features, and she started to rise. "Where is he? In the hospital? Which one?"

"He's all right," Mark said hastily, waving her back down.

Geneva didn't move for a minute, then she slowly returned to her seat. "Where is he?"

"Upstairs in his room." He rubbed his jaw. "I don't know how else to say it except tell you what I know."

He relayed the same story that the police officer had told him. When Beltran explained what had happened at the hospital, Mark's overriding feeling had been anger with his son. Now as he repeated those words to his wife, the anger had vanished and been replaced by a fresh sense of loss and desolation, though he didn't know why.

Geneva listened silently. When he finished, she stood up again. "I suggest you find an attorney for our son, the sooner the better."

He watched her walk away, knowing she was going upstairs to see for herself that Brian was all right. His vision blurred, and he blinked rapidly. Gradually, he became aware of an ache deep inside, and with the knowledge came the certainty that he didn't want to deal with it. Instead, he took Geneva's advice and went into his study.

What had happened in their family wasn't something he was comfortable sharing with any current acquaintances, so he decided to look at past contacts. After more than an hour of going through old Rolodexes and computer files, Mark found a few possible names to follow up on. What he hadn't expected was for his search to add to his upset.

Looking for an attorney to protect Brian's interests had taken him on a journey into his past where Mark had been brought face-to-face with the beginning of his long-forgotten struggle to prove himself. To prove he was someone *worthwhile*.

Even during his search, Mark had known he didn't need to go back so far in time, but the knowledge couldn't stop him. Finally, he found himself kneeling in front of a box he had taken out of the attic that held all the detritus from his law school years.

He flipped through one of his yearbooks, trying to ignore the tightness of his throat. There were so many familiar faces, fellow classmates he hadn't seen or thought of in years. He frowned when he found a small envelope stuck in the back of the yearbook; he didn't remember it. But when he opened it, Mark was suddenly overwhelmed by long-forgotten memories.

The envelope held a photograph of Mark in his graduation gown, standing beside his father. William Newman was not smiling. Then again, Mark couldn't remember ever seeing his father smile. There was no hugging, no lightness in either man's face. Nor was there any lightheartedness in his memory of that day. He stared at the picture, struck by how much he looked like his father. He hadn't realized.

What's the matter with you? No son of mine would ever settle for second best.

Mark shook his head to try to dispel the familiar voice. He had spent years working to please William Newman, but no matter how hard he tried, he was never able to reach that mythical state of perfection his father had demanded from his only child. Mark had never been "good enough" to meet the man's exacting standards. He had worked hard throughout his childhood, throughout school, college, law school and beyond. But no matter how much effort he expended, his father saw him as a disappointment.

Mark threw the photograph back in the yearbook before slamming it shut and tossing it back into the box. What had possessed him to dig so deeply into a past he had no wish to remember? His stomach churned and nausea filled his throat. Jumping to his feet, he kicked the box into the closet and slammed the door shut.

A deep breath helped, so he took another, and another. His pounding pulse began to slow, and he looked at the names he had jotted down. One immediately stood out.

Stuart "Stretch" Ramsey had been one of the dark horses in law school. Without money or family, he had used a variety of grants and loans and a brilliant academic record to achieve his goal of becoming a lawyer. Though he hadn't seen the man since graduation, Mark had heard through the grapevine that Ramsey worked in the county legal-aid office for several years before setting up his own practice. While he didn't specialize in criminal law, it was a significant part of his practice. Remembering what he knew of the man in law school, as well as the stories that had filtered down of his successful practice, was the deciding factor for Mark.

What were the odds that Ramsey would be in his office Saturday evening? He got the number from information, dialed, and waited impatiently through the usual recorded message.

"Stretch, it's Mark Newman. I'd like to talk to you as soon as possible."

Mark left his cell number and, after a moment's thought, his office number in case Ramsey didn't call him over the weekend. Finished, he sat back in his chair and wondered what to do next. His eyes drifted away from the list, and he found himself looking around his study as if he had never seen it before.

It was good-sized room, like all of the rooms in the house. Floor-to-ceiling bookcases filled three of the walls. The fourth wall contained french doors that led out to the backyard. From his desk, Mark could see into the garden, and although he couldn't hear it with the doors closed, he knew the fountain would be going, splashing water in a musical medley that he hardly ever took the time to listen to.

Since night had fallen, there was nothing to see outside, and he turned his gaze back to the room. In front of one wall of books, he had placed a deep, roomy chair, beside which was a floor lamp that gave out a warm light that never bothered the eye and allowed for easy reading. The small table on the other side of the chair was just large enough for him to set a glass of whatever he was drinking while he read. Mark stared at the chair and wondered when he had last taken the time to relax in it. When had he last sat there and read just for pleasure?

The telephone rang, and he jumped.

"Hey, Newman, it's been a long time." The husky voice edged with laughter came straight out of the past and knocked the breath out of Mark for a few seconds.

"Yes, it has. Are you still handling criminal law?"

There was a beat of silence before Ramsey said, "That's right. What can I do for you?"

The laughter was gone from his voice, much to Mark's relief. Drawing on his years of training, he gave the other attorney a succinct, unemotional summary of Brian's situation. When he finished, Ramsey asked several questions, most of which Mark couldn't answer.

"I'll need to talk to Brian," the attorney said. "Is he available now?"

"No."

Mark wondered where that had come from. The sooner Ramsey talked to Brian the better. Although he knew that, something in him didn't want to do it now. Brian needed a break, not to mention Mark wanted to tell Geneva what was happening.

More silence greeted his answer until Ramsey said, "I try to avoid going into my office on Sundays, but I can meet the two of you there tomorrow. Would 9:00 a.m. work?"

"Yes, fine."

"I'll see you then."

"Thanks, Stretch." Mark struggled with unaccustomed gratitude.

"You're welcome." Ramsey's voice had softened, and Mark wasn't sure how to take it.

He went upstairs, and this time, he knocked on Brian's door before opening it. The sight that met his eyes tightened his throat.

The boy was facedown on the bed, apparently asleep. Geneva stood over him, her arms folded and her face unguarded as Mark hadn't seen in years. Obviously, she hadn't heard his knock for she didn't react to his entry. She was too focused on their son, and her expression...

Geneva lifted her head and looked at her husband, the emotion fading from her expression before Mark could identify it. He started to speak, but she shook her head brusquely and walked out of the room, gesturing at him as she passed. Mark followed her into the hall and shut the door behind them.

"Well?" she demanded coldly.

For a minute, he looked at her as he struggled with another unexpected surge of emotion—regret.

"Mark!"

Though Geneva kept her voice down, the sharpness was all too familiar. Firmly setting aside useless emotion, he answered her unasked question. "Brian and I have an appointment with an attorney I know tomorrow morning."

She blinked once before walking away.

Mark watched until she reached her bedroom door, then he went to his own room. He collapsed into the nearest chair and cradled his head in his hands. What was wrong with him? Why hadn't he asked Geneva about her recent visit to a hospital? The worst she could do was refuse to answer. Or was that the worst? What if she told him a truth he wasn't prepared to accept?

Once again the feeling of being out of control swept over him, except this time it was even stronger, invading his personal life with his son and his wife. Despite its fragile state, his marriage had been a constant in his life for nearly twenty years. He desperately wanted it to continue. The question was, why? Why remain in an unhappy, unsatisfactory relationship? One reason—the worst reason—struck at the very core of his being. Marrying the intelligent, beautiful young woman shortly after he graduated from law school was one more proof that he wasn't the failure his father had accused him of being.

Mark groaned. He hadn't thought of his father in years, but suddenly memories of the man were haunting his every thought. In his mind's eye he saw again the forlorn figure standing in the hospital room earlier in the day. Fresh anger stirred, but with it came a new feeling—fear. What had led to Brian drinking, to being in a car with friends who were also drinking? Was it simple teenage foolishness, or was it something more? And if it was something more, how much responsibility did Mark bear? He closed his eyes as a new emotion swept over him. It took him a few minutes to identify it because it wasn't one he was familiar with—despair.

Something touched his cheek. He started to brush it away only to freeze at the realization that it was wet. Barely able to breathe, Mark rubbed harder at his face, trying to ignore his growing panic at the realization that he was crying. The life he had fought so long and hard for was falling apart, and he felt helpless to stop it.

13

Mark desperately wanted a good night's sleep. Once again, he didn't get it. When his alarm went off the next morning, he was startled from an uncomfortable doze filled with vague dreams that had no beginning or end but which left him feeling unsettled.

He dragged himself into the shower and deliberately turned on the cold water. After several chilling, teeth-chattering minutes, he turned it off and grabbed for his bath towel. At least he was awake now.

When he finished dressing, Mark put on his watch and checked the time. They had almost two hours before their appointment with Ramsey. He went down to Brian's room and knocked on the door. There was no answer, and he pushed it open. There was no sign of his son, other than the large lump underneath the covers.

With growing irritation, Mark went to the bed and yanked back the covers. Brian groaned and rolled over to bury his face in his pillow. It suddenly struck Mark that his son might be suffering from a hangover. If so, part of him was glad. The more unpleasant this experience, the less likely it was that Brian would repeat it.

"Get up," he said crisply. There was no response, and his irritation sharpened. "We have an appointment in less than two hours. You're going to be ready to leave the house in an hour, is that clear?"

Brian turned his head. "Appointment?" he mumbled.

"Yes. Now get up unless you want me to help you get up."

Mark was certain his threat would be sufficient to get the kid moving. Sure enough, after a few more seconds, Brian raised himself and slowly swung his legs around until they were hanging off the side of his bed. He looked up at his father with bloodshot eyes, and Mark had a startling thought—had the boy been crying? No, ridiculous. He hadn't seen his son cry in years.

How do you know, Newman? When's the last time you spent time with Brian? Mark mentally shook the thought away. "I expect you to be downstairs in forty-five minutes."

As he turned away, Brian said, "What appointment?"

Mark paused at the door to look back and swallowed a gasp. For an instant, he saw before him an eight-year-old boy sitting on the edge of the bed, his hair tousled and dressed in rumpled pajamas, apprehensive and uncomprehending his father's anger with him. "I'll explain downstairs," he snapped and walked out.

An hour and a half later, Mark turned down the street on which Ramsey's office was located. Beside him, Brian sat silently. He hadn't said a word since his father explained where they were going this morning. Apart from half a glass of apple juice, the boy hadn't eaten breakfast. Suspecting the hangover was at fault, Mark hadn't demanded he eat, although he did insist that he take a couple of aspirin.

Stretch Ramsey's office was in one of the older sections of the city, where buildings nearly a century old bore the signs of careful restoration. There was lots of greenery, trees, shrubs, colorful gardens. Office buildings shared space with small stores. All in all, it was quite a contrast to the sleek, modern building that housed the offices of Newman, Buchanan, and Welch.

This early on a Sunday morning, there was no problem finding parking. Mark parked on the street, directly in front of 1321 Francisco Road. As he got out of the car, he realized Brian hadn't moved. "Let's go," he ordered.

Without a word, the teenager unfastened his seat belt and climbed out. The front door was unlocked, and when they went inside, the first thing Mark saw was a staircase directly in front of him. He paused by the directory and saw Ramsey's name; his office was on the second floor. He jerked his head at his son and went up the stairs.

Ramsey's office was the second door on the right, and he tried the door handle. It turned easily, and he pushed it open. A small reception area greeted him, although there was no one behind the desk. Three doors led off from the room. Two were partly open, and he could see inside. One led into a diminutive but functional kitchen. The second door revealed another office, also currently unoccupied. The door immediately behind the reception room was closed, but even as Mark took a step forward, it opened.

At six foot seven, the reason behind Stretch's old nickname was immediately obvious. In law school, people had assumed that he must play basketball, which always amused the easygoing student. "Klutz should be my middle name," he would always say whenever anyone brought up the subject. Although never an athlete, Ramsey was extremely intelligent and determined, which had enabled him to make it through college and law school despite the numerous odds against him. Those qualities probably had a lot to do with why he was so successful in his practice—or so claimed the legal grapevine. They were also the reason Mark had decided to contact him.

"It's great to see you, Mark," Ramsey said as he strode forward, hand extended.

"Stretch, this is my son, Brian," Mark said, shaking hands. "Brian, this is Mr. Ramsey."

The attorney turned to the youngster, a smile warming his angular features. "Hi, Brian."

Mark was sure it was only his stern look that made Brian accept Ramsey's hand, though he kept his gaze fixed firmly on the floor. Swallowing fresh annoyance, Mark said, "I appreciate you taking the time to meet with us this morning."

"No problem." Stretch gestured. "Come on in."

Upon entering the office, Mark's first thought was how small it was. A second look made him realize it was all the clutter that made it look small. The desk itself wasn't that large and, though in good condition, bore the marks of age. The top was almost hidden by piles of papers and files, the obligatory telephone and desk lamp that looked like the same one Stretch had kept in his dorm room in law school, a desk calendar, and several small picture frames. Two walls were taken up with bookshelves. A credenza on the opposite side of the room was also stacked high with files, and beside it two storage boxes were mute evidence of yet more files.

Mark was surprised to see on the shelves over the credenza several sports trophies. He knew instinctively they couldn't belong to Ramsey and wondered briefly what they were doing here. He would never be able to work in such a chaotic environment.

Ramsey gestured at the two chairs as he made his way behind his desk. Brian reluctantly sat down in one and his father sat down next to him.

"Brian, did your father explain why he wanted you to speak to me?"

The teen darted a swift, sidewise look at Mark and then focused on his hands in his lap. "He said I needed a lawyer," he muttered.

Mark almost told the boy to speak up but pressed his lips tightly together instead.

The other attorney appeared unfazed by the sullen response. "Do you know why he wants you to have a lawyer?"

Brian shrugged one shoulder, and Mark's temper slipped. "Brian—"

"It's all right," Ramsey cut in. His eyes met Mark's and flicked back to the figure slumped in the chair. "Brian, would you prefer that just you and I talk right now?"

Mark swallowed the words that wanted to escape. Brian was a minor; Ramsey couldn't talk to him without the presence of one of his parents. Unless, of course, Mark himself gave permission for Ramsey to talk to his son alone. He didn't want to do that; he wanted to know exactly what was going on with the teenager. He watched the bowed head and heard another murmur. This time he didn't catch the words, but apparently Ramsey did, for he looked at him with raised eyebrows.

"Mark?" Ramsey said quietly.

Mark knew it was up to him. As much as he didn't want to leave, he didn't see any alternative. With an abrupt nod, he rose and walked out, shutting the door behind him. Back in the reception area, he stood uncertainly. Now what? Maybe he should have brought a briefcase of work, but he hadn't thought this through. Without warning, the now familiar sense of disconnection swept over him. He wanted to shrug it off, laugh it away, ignore it. But it stood foursquare in front of his thoughts, immovable, demanding.

Demanding? Where had that come from? Demanding. Something was being demanded of him.

What was *this*? What was happening? Mark ran a nervous hand over his face and realized he was sweating. It had to be because Brian was in trouble.

Or was it?

Mark swallowed, belatedly aware that his heart was pounding. *Get a grip, Newman.* It was just a lack of sleep. Or maybe, in part, he was still reacting to all that had happened the past week—no, it was all that had happened in the past two weeks. Less than two weeks.

He shuddered. There it was again. Ever since his near-fatal accident, he had been feeling off balance, out of sync with life. Except there was more involved now than just the accident. Considering how Buchanan's chaotic marital problems had impacted his life, considering Joe Ridgeway's unwarranted nosiness and interference, considering Brian's out-of-character, criminal behavior, considering Geneva…

Without warning, panic knifed through him. Shaking, he fought back. He would not submit to rampant emotion! Almost in desperation, he focused his thoughts on his own office. There was no chaos there. Every inch of it was his. It had been logically thought out in every detail—from the position of the furniture, the bookshelves, even the palm tree in the corner. All carefully thought through and designed to assist in his thinking and his work.

The panic began to fade, and Mark was able to take a deep breath, then another, relieved to feel his heart rate returning to normal. That was the ticket—to concentrate on what was real and tangible. The strange, unnerving thoughts and emotions could not withstand logical reality.

The Ashmore deposition was rapidly approaching; that was something to think about. Mark took a seat and considered the facts of the case. One by one, he considered each point that had been raised through discovery, weighing each one against the opposition's arguments. He was so engrossed in his thoughts that he started when the door to Ramsey's office opened.

The attorney looked out. "Could you come in now, Mark?"

He obeyed. Despite the situation, he had to resist a smile, for he felt, once more, that he had regained control. Brian's situation would be dealt with, and afterward, Mark would go to his office, where he could focus on the work waiting for him.

Brian was still sitting in the same chair. Mark stopped in midstride and stared at his son. The boy was holding some tissues in one clenched hand. It looked like he had been crying.

Unease shot through Mark's hard-won calm. "Brian—"

"Sit down, Mark," Ramsey said. "Please."

Mark did so, even more reluctantly than when he left the room earlier. He was very aware of his son sitting beside him but kept his attention on the other attorney.

Ramsey returned to his own chair behind the desk. "Brian explained what happened, and he gave me permission to tell you. Long story short, the driver of the car had a six-pack of beer when he picked up Brian and the other boys. They all drank, were spotted by a police car, and you know the rest."

Mark struggled with a surge of anger and equally strong relief. Brian had behaved irresponsibly, stupidly, but it could have been much worse.

"Where do we go now?" Mark asked.

"I recommend that Brian give the police a full statement. I will be with him, of course. This is a first-time offense, so I think we can keep the sentence to a minimum."

Mark almost sighed in relief. Whatever ruling the judge might make, he would be adding his own punishment. Brian was never going to forget this. Whatever mistakes he might make in the future, this shouldn't be one of them.

"However," Ramsey went on, "another issue has come up that I believe is even more important and needs to be addressed immediately."

What? Mark blinked at the other man's expression, recognizing not only concern but sadness. "What are you talking about?"

Ramsey looked at the silent figure beside Mark. "Wouldn't you like to tell your father, Brian?" he said gently.

The bowed head shook once. Ramsey's gaze met Mark's confused one. "I'm afraid there's no easy way to say it. Brian's been drinking since he was twelve years old."

"What!" Mark was out of his chair before he realized it. "That's impossible!"

"Why?"

Mark was startled by the unexpected voice. It hadn't come from Ramsey but from his son. He turned to see Brian looking at him. If he had been crying earlier, he wasn't now. His eyes were hard.

"Why what?" Mark demanded.

"Why is it impossible?" Brian said hotly.

"Why…because it's…ridiculous!"

"How would you know?" The anger was stronger, and Mark was momentarily taken aback.

"I…you're my son!"

"Since when?" Brian jumped to his feet, and his chair fell backward. "When's the last time you treated me like your son?"

Mark's jaw dropped. "I…Brian…"

"No answer?" the boy said with more bitterness than his father had ever heard. "Why am I not surprised?" Now tears shimmered in his eyes. "I've been raiding your liquor cabinet since I was twelve, and you never noticed!"

Mark shook his head uncomprehendingly. He couldn't be hearing correctly; Brian couldn't be saying what it sounded like he was saying. "No…" It wasn't thought out, just the first word that broke through his jumbled disbelief.

"None of your big-shot friends ever noticed either!" Tears rolled down Brian's thin cheeks, but the boy seemed unaware of them. "All these years I've been stealing your expensive booze, watering down what was left so you wouldn't see it disappearing. I didn't even need to bother with that, did I? You never noticed anything!"

Beneath Brian's anger was another stronger emotion. Only when it pierced Mark's shock did he recognize it— pain. Without thinking, he reached out to his son. "Brian—"

"Don't!" Brian backed away. "Don't pretend now just because someone else knows."

"Easy now." Ramsey stood up, and Mark looked blankly at him, at a loss for words. The attorney's eyes went from father to son. "This is a tough time for both of you. I think we need to take things one step at a time."

"It doesn't matter." Brian threw himself back in his chair. "Nothing matters."

Ramsey looked at Mark as if expecting him to say or do something, but Mark felt bereft of thought. After a brief hesitation, the other attorney came around his desk and knelt beside the chair. He put a gentle hand on the boy's shoulder. Though Brian didn't raise his head, he didn't pull back from the touch, and Mark felt a sharp pang slice through his shock.

"Brian," Ramsey said quietly, "I don't know what it's like to be in your shoes, but I'm guessing right now you're feeling overwhelmed. This probably isn't the best time"— he threw a quick look at Mark before continuing—"for this conversation. Can I make a suggestion?"

As Mark watched the pair, he felt as if he should say something, but nothing came to mind. Brian's stunning revelation had knocked all the air out of him, along with all coherent thought. This couldn't be happening. It couldn't be real. Not his family. Not his son.

His son.

Brian's shoulders moved slightly under Ramsey's hand, but whatever he said was too quiet for Mark to hear.

"I'm going to call the police department and arrange for you to give your statement tomorrow," Ramsey said. "For today, I suggest you go home and try to relax. We're going to work out the legal issues, I promise. The other issues will take time to work through." He squeezed the boy's shoulder. "They can be worked through, Brian. Please try to hold on to that, okay?"

Brian responded by wiping his face with the sleeve of his shirt before standing up and tossing the tissues he had been holding in the trash can. Ramsey stood up with him.

"Mark, after I talk to the officer in charge I'll call you with the details."

Mark tried to swallow around the lump in his throat. "Thank you," he managed.

He walked out to his car, his son a silent shadow beside him. They didn't talk during the drive home, and as soon as Mark pulled into the garage, Brian shoved the door open and slipped out. He watched the boy disappear through the side door and winced when it slammed shut. As if the sound had been a signal, the numbness that had gripped him splintered and broke into pieces. Anguish greater than he had ever known before crashed through him and if he had been standing, he would have collapsed.

"Brian," he whispered, dropping his head to rest it on the steering wheel.

No amount of rationalizing could change the truths he was suddenly staring in the face. His sixteen-year-old son, his firstborn, was in serious trouble, not only legally but emotionally. How had Mark missed all the evidence? He prided himself on his deductive abilities, his logical thinking processes. His son had been drinking since he was twelve years old! How had he missed this?

Mark had spent his life working to reach this point. He was a successful and highly respected member in the legal field and in his community. He had more money than he would ever need. But suddenly all of that seemed to be a sham. What had happened to his marriage? How had his wife become a stranger? What about his children? They were strangers too, both of them. He didn't know what they liked or disliked, how they were doing in school, who their friends were. He knew nothing about any of the members of his family.

Mark Newman had succeeded brilliantly in his career and utterly failed as a husband and father. Just like his father.

Mark wrapped his arms around himself as if it could help against the grief that ripped through his heart. Tears burned his eyes. This couldn't be happening.

A buzzing sound broke through his turmoil, and he instinctively reached inside his jacket before he realized it. He didn't want to talk to anyone, but habit won out. After clearing his throat harshly, he thought it was safe to answer. "Newman," he snapped.

"Mark, it's Stretch. Is Brian still with you?"

"No."

"You're alone?"

"Yes."

"Good. I understand that this must be a very upsetting time for your family, but there's something I didn't want you to lose sight of."

Irritation at this interruption filled him and Mark was grateful for the distraction. "If you have something to say, just say it."

"Fair enough," Ramsey said calmly. "Brian needs counseling, and it needs to begin as soon as possible."

"I'm aware of what my son needs," Mark snapped, though cringing inwardly. That was a lie. He had been unaware of what his son needed for years.

"I hope so. He said some things when you weren't in the office that concerned me."

"Such as?"

"I don't want to break his confidences, but you need to get him help as soon as possible."

Fear swept through Mark. Was Ramsey hinting— no. Impossible. *You thought it was impossible that Brian could have been drinking for several years*, his unwelcome conscience reminded.

"Mark? Are you still there?"

Ramsey's voice drew Mark from the unwelcome thought. "Yes."

"I won't keep you any longer. I'll call again after I've spoken with the arresting officer to give you an update."

"All right," Mark said automatically and pressed the END button.

There were still too many emotions swirling through him to make sense while Ramsey's words continued to echo in his thoughts. *Brian needs counseling...as soon as possible....He said some things...that concern me.*

Brian. His son.

His son was in trouble, had been in trouble for years, and Mark hadn't noticed. He had been too busy making a success of his life to notice what was happening with his firstborn.

Guilt was a new emotion for Mark Newman, and it tasted bitter.

Brian needs counseling…as soon as possible.

This isn't the time to wallow in emotions, Newman.

Brian needed help. Mark had no idea how to help. How could he? He didn't even know his own son. Still, Brian needed help.

There was only one person who came to Mark's mind who could help. Days ago, he had been reluctant to call on that person for help. Now in the midst of pain and fear and guilt, Mark didn't hesitate to pull out his cell phone again. When the now-familiar recording came on, he said, "Joe, it's Mark. I need to talk to you, right away. Please." He ended the call and leaned back in his seat, closing his eyes, trying to hold back the tears that pressed against his lids.

Mark had fought his entire life to prove William Newman had been wrong about him. How on earth had he ended up to be a carbon copy of his father?

The muffled ring tone of his cell phone startled him. He wiped his face with one hand and juggled the phone with the other. As he lifted it to his ear, he saw the time on his watch and was shocked. He had been sitting here for more than a half hour?

"Newman," he said.

"Mark, it's Joe. I got your message. What's going on?"

Mark opened his mouth to answer, but several seconds passed before he could speak. "I need to see you."

"All right," Joe returned matter-of-factly. "I'm about to head back to the church. Can you meet me there?"

"Yes."

"See you there."

14

Mark drove to the church on autopilot. The tumult of emotions that had swept through him had left him feeling absolutely exhausted and drained—and something else. He didn't know what it was, but he was all too aware of how it made him feel, *adrift*, like a boat that had lost its mooring.

Lost.

A red light stopped him, and he wearily rubbed his forehead. He could feel a headache coming on but was too tired even to reach for the aspirin bottle in the glove compartment. No, there was no aspirin there; this car was a rental. His car had been washed down a raging river, and Mark had only escaped the same fate because of the intervention of a stranger.

The turmoil of the past twenty-four hours had suppressed the memory of almost dying, but now it was back, sharper than before. Why had a stranger risked everything to save him? And then just disappeared? *If you really want to thank me, the next time you run across someone who needs a hand, give him yours.*

"Mark?"

Jerked from his thoughts, he realized he was in the church parking lot, and Joe was standing by the driver's side door. Mark swallowed and unlatched his door. His brother-in-law drew back as he got out.

"You look terrible," Joe said, his eyes dark with concern.

Mark shrugged.

Joe gestured. "Come on in." He led Mark through the back door, down the hall toward his office. "You have good timing."

"What?"

Joe smiled. "It's Sunday. We had two church services this morning, not to mention Sunday school. There was no potluck today. Otherwise, there would still be a lot of people here."

Mark shuddered.

Joe noticed, and his lips tightened, but he didn't react. "Come in." He stood aside to allow his brother-in-law to enter the office first. "Have a seat."

Mark collapsed on the old couch against one wall.

Joe pulled over an arm chair and sat down in front of him. "What's up?"

Now that he was here, Mark had no idea where to begin and simply blurted it out. "Brian's in trouble."

Joe's eyes widened. "Where is he?"

"At home." Mark rubbed his burning eyes. "He was arrested with some other boys. They were drinking in the car."

Joe sighed out a long breath. After a minute of silence, he said softly, "Is he all right? And the other boys?"

Mark swallowed. "When the police tried to pull the car over, there was an accident. One of the boys is still unconscious in the hospital. Brian wasn't driving, so that's something, I suppose. At least according to the attorney I hired."

"Is he—the attorney—going to help Brian?"

"Yes."

Thinking of Ramsey reminded Mark why he was really here. Pain gripped him so tightly that he couldn't breathe. He was distantly aware of his brother-in-law's voice then felt a hand grip his arm.

"What's going on?" Joe demanded. "Talk to me."

Mark scrubbed more fiercely at his eyes. "How could I have been so blind?"

"I don't understand."

There was nothing to do but admit the bitter truth. "Brian has been drinking since he was twelve years old, and I never noticed anything was wrong!" He saw the shock in Joe's eyes, which was immediately followed by pain.

"I'm very sorry to hear that," Joe said so softly Mark almost didn't hear him.

"Sorry! This is all my fault! I called myself a father and I didn't see—"

"Don't," Joe said sharply. "Guilt accomplishes nothing except to paralyze us. We need to focus on Brian here. It's important to remember that he chose to tell you."

"No, he didn't." Mark had to force out the words. "He told Ramsey, the attorney. And then he gave permission to Ramsey to tell me."

Brian's young face was suddenly before him, filled with anger and pain. Closing his eyes would never erase that memory. His words echoed strangely in the room. Suddenly Mark wanted nothing so much as to run away from them and this unfathomable reality. This couldn't be happening, not to him, not to his family.

"Mark."

Mark blinked at the sight of his brother-in-law kneeling on the floor in front of him, gripping his arms. Even in the midst of his turmoil, he was struck by Joe's pallor.

"Your family is mine too. You know I'm here for you all, don't you?" He waited until Mark nodded before continuing. "As hard as it is to face, there's no other choice, not for Brian and not for you or Geneva. Even Danny is going to be affected." Joe spoke softly but urgency underlined his words. "I'll help in any way that I can, but I need to know you're not going to turn your back on this."

"How can I?" Mark demanded, suddenly furious.

Joe didn't react to his anger except to loosen his grip. "You can't," he agreed. "Have you and Geneva talked about this?"

Mark thought back to that brief, tense confrontation with his wife last night in Brian's room. He could hardly call that a conversation. "No."

"You need to do that right away so that you're on the same page."

"At this point," Mark said bitterly, "I don't even think we're in the same state." He was deadly serious, and Joe must have caught that, for he didn't smile.

After a minute of silence, Ridgeway said, "How can I help? What can I do?"

"I…" Mark swallowed.

After years of ignoring his brother-in-law, he was asking for his help. Again. He would have expected Joe to be reluctant to aid a man who had never wanted anything to do with him. If nothing else, Ridgeway had the right to feel smug that Mark had finally admitted he needed his brother-in-law's help. Surprisingly, there was nothing but concern in Joe's expression.

Clearing his throat, Mark tried again. "The attorney I hired will take care of Brian's legal needs but he, Brian, needs more…" His voice failed again. Thankfully, his brother-in-law somehow knew where he was going.

"Yes," Joe agreed quietly. "Give me a day to figure out who among the therapists I know would be best for Brian."

"Not you?" Mark was sure he knew the answer, but some part of him resisted the idea of strangers becoming privy to the inner workings of the Newman family.

"No." Joe shook his head. "I would be more than happy to talk to Brian, but he needs someone who can be objective. He's my nephew. I could never be objective enough to help him as he needs."

Mark's thoughts seem to tilt chaotically. His sixteen-year-old son needed a therapist. Suddenly he couldn't catch his breath and dropped his head into his hands. "Everything…everything's falling apart," he choked. "I don't know how to stop it, how to make it go back to the way…it used to be."

Silence met his confession. He didn't dare look up; he couldn't bear to see the look of judgment and condemnation in his father's eyes. Wait. What? His father's eyes? Confusion broke through his torment, but Mark was distracted by a strong hand on his shoulder.

"Maybe it is," Joe said quietly. "Maybe everything in your life is falling apart."

That wasn't what Mark wanted to hear. Instinctively, he tried to pull away, but the older man hung on.

"It's a very frightening time," Joe went on in that same soft tone, "when the life we've worked so hard to build falls apart around us. There's no way to go back, Mark. No way to make things the way they used to be. But that's not necessarily a bad thing."

Mark spoke between his fingers, unwilling to allow the other man to see his tears. "What do you mean, it's not bad?"

"It's very painful, I know. But it's possible to create something new out of the ashes of our old lives. It's not easy, but if we're willing to accept what's happened and work with it, we can be astonished by the results."

Anger began to rise in Mark. He gave his face a hard swipe and looked up. "You don't know what you're talking about."

"Yes, I do." Joe met his gaze squarely, and for the first time, Mark saw anger in his brother-in-law's eyes. "When Rachel died, everything I thought I knew, everything I thought I believed, blew up in my face."

Shame warmed Mark's cheeks. How could he have forgotten about Joe's first wife? She died in a car accident many years ago, not long after Mark married Geneva. One of his earliest memories as a married man was reluctantly agreeing to his wife's insistence that they attend Rachel's funeral. He hadn't wanted to go. Something big had been going on at the office. But what? He couldn't remember. Mark had gone, against his will. Thinking back, he remembered hardly anything about his sister-in-law's funeral because his thoughts were occupied with the office.

From out of the deepest recesses of his mind, a new thought pierced him. *You are one sorry piece of work,*

Newman. Perhaps because he was already overwhelmed, all Mark could do was agree with that judgment.

Unaware of his brother-in-law's thoughts, Joe continued. "The time after her death was the darkest, most difficult I'd ever known. I questioned everything, my life, my faith, God. I came very close to leaving the ministry. To this day, I'm still not sure what stopped me." He smiled faintly. "I take that back. I know what, who, stopped me—God. He and I battled toe-to-toe for years before I was finally able to begin to put the pieces of my life—and my faith—back together. I couldn't have done it without him, as much as I resisted him during that dark time."

Joe's eyes turned to Mark. "God brought me out of that darkness and restored me to life and eventually restored in me the ability to risk loving again. As wonderful a person as Beth is, if I had met her sooner, I wouldn't have been ready to fall in love with her. God knew that and made sure the timing was right."

Mark had never known, never cared, what his brother-in-law went through after the unexpected death of his young wife. Remorse stirred in his heart and strengthened his shame. As much as he disliked talk about God and religion, he couldn't deny that Joe had gone through his own time of "everything falling apart." The knowledge forced him to pay attention to words he normally would have disregarded.

"The darkness can be overwhelming," Joe went on. "Especially if someone is battling it on his own. It might very well have destroyed me if not for God. It took his stubborn love and his perfect light to help me break through it and regain my life—"

"I don't believe in the things you believe," Mark interrupted.

"I know," Joe said matter-of-factly. "You have the right to believe as you choose, but that doesn't negate my experience and belief."

Mark blinked. His brother-in-law didn't seem angry now, but his quiet response sounded like a rebuke.

"You're going to have to figure out how to work through what's happening to you and your family," Joe said. "You can't ignore it, Mark, because it's not going to go away. I know it's hard right now, but it won't always be hard. Not if you're willing to keep your heart and mind open. You need to recognize what works and doesn't work in your life and come to some kind of decision as to what you're going to do about it all." He paused, obviously thinking, before saying, "Give me a little time, and I'll provide you with a couple referrals to therapists I think can help Brian. However..." He hesitated, his eyes thoughtful as he gazed at his brother-in-law.

Mark was disturbed by his expression. "What?"

"I'd also like to recommend a therapist for the family—"

"No." Mark was on his feet.

Joe stood too. "Hear me out, please."

"I don't need—"

"Will you stop with the denial?" Joe demanded. "You've admitted your son is in trouble and it's obvious that your marriage is also in trouble."

"You don't—"

"And you've also admitted that you're overwhelmed with all that's happening in your life," Joe steamrollered on. "There's nothing wrong with acknowledging that you need help in dealing with it all. That's not an indication of mental illness, just the opposite."

Mark stared at the man. Where was all this coming from? He had come here to get Joe's recommendation for someone to counsel Brian. The rest of this... "I'm not you," he said finally. "I don't look at things the way you do."

"I know," Joe repeated, "and I'm not asking you to. But speaking as someone who has counseled many individuals and families for nearly twenty years, I can see that you and your family are not in a good place. It's not just Brian who needs help."

Mark shook his head as he struggled for words. "Everything was fine until that...that accident." He rubbed his forehead, immediately regretting his words.

"Your accident?"

Mark swore silently. The more he tried to pull his turbulent thoughts into some kind of order, the more chaotic they seemed to be.

When he didn't answer, Joe said slowly, as if choosing his words carefully, "I can't imagine how terrifying it must have been for you."

Terrifying—that was a good word, and despite all Mark's efforts, its ramifications were still reverberating through his life. As much as he wanted to deny it, he couldn't, and Joe's words were enough to pierce the emotional walls he had erected in an effort to keep his memories of the accident at bay. They flooded over him, almost as violent as the watery torrent that had nearly swallowed him up that night not quite two week ago.

Suddenly he was back in his car, helpless, trapped by his seat belt while the water rushed in, rising inexorably, freezing cold and chilling him through. His heart pounded frantically while all rational thought gave way to terror, to desperation, to hopelessness.

"Listen to me, Mark. You're safe, it's over. You're safe now."

Joe's voice broke through, and Mark returned to himself, shaking violently. When he raised his eyes, he found his brother-in-law in front of him again, once more gripping his arms. Instinctively, he pulled back, and Joe released him.

"I'm all right," he said hoarsely.

"No, you're not," Joe said. Steel underlined his quiet words. "Forgetting everything else that's happened, you need to talk to someone about that accident and what you went through."

"No, I don't—"

"You do. An experience such as the one you went through is enough to turn your life upside down. Add to that everything else that has happened to you and to those around you the last couple of weeks, and it's no wonder you're floundering."

Mark mentally recoiled from the quiet judgment. Did Joe realize how close to home his words were hitting? He couldn't because he couldn't read his brother-in-law's mind. Yet his words resonated deep within Mark, and he had no idea what to do with them. See a therapist? The idea was absurd. Or was it? He swallowed again, angry to realize he was still trembling.

"Mark," Joe interrupted his thoughts, "have you talked to Geneva about why she was at the hospital the day I saw her?"

Was his brother-in-law a mind reader? Mark suddenly felt trapped. He had to get out of here. This was not the place where he was going to be able to make sense of things. "I…I've taken enough of your time." He wanted to sound firm and in control, but to his dismay, the words came out in a stammer.

Joe rose with him. "No, you haven't. You don't have to go."

Now that the idea of escape had come to him, it was all Mark wanted. "Yes, I do." He walked briskly out of the office. To his annoyance, his brother-in-law walked with him.

"I'll call you about a therapist for Brian," Joe said calmly, as if he didn't know Mark was running away.

No, he wasn't running away. He was...

Running away, said a small, jeering voice in the back of his mind. Sternly suppressing the voice enabled Mark to answer calmly, "Thank you. I appreciate that."

They reached the back door, and he put his hand on the door knob.

Joe put his hand over Mark's, stopping him. "Please think about what we've talked about," he said. "And remember I'm just a phone call away. If I can do anything—"

"Thank you." Mark cut him off and strode outside.

15

Not until he was in his car and driving away from the church did he begin to relax. His focus on getting away from his brother-in-law had somehow helped him to regain some kind of control over his unruly thoughts. With that bit of distance, Mark managed to shove them, topsy-turvy, behind mental walls, where he hoped they would remain. The chaos of the past days had weakened those walls but he was determined to rebuild them even stronger. He didn't need or want this confusion, this chaos. Such unbridled turmoil was opposed to the calm, rational approach to life and work that Mark cherished.

Joe's voice echoed in his mind, *An experience such as the one you went through is enough to turn your life upside down and make you reevaluate everything.*

Mark flung the thought violently from him. "No," he whispered. "It's not."

But isn't that exactly what you've been doing the last two weeks?

For a second, he thought the words were coming from that jeering little voice in the back of his mind, except this time it wasn't jeering at him. For the first time, Mark sensed concern.

Concern? What was he thinking? What was the matter with him? Now he was imagining voices?

A loud honk behind him startled Mark from his dark thoughts. The light had changed, and he hadn't noticed. Accelerating, he tried to think what to do next. Work drew him, not a particular case, but the thought of the quiet, normal environment that was his office. Mark desperately wanted something quiet and normal, anything to keep back the chaos that his mental processes had become.

The drive to the office was familiar, which helped his precarious calm. Parking in his reserved spot, taking the elevator up to the ninth floor, and striding down the hall to his suite, all helped to begin to restore his habitual composure. He was even more relieved to realize he was no longer shaking and his breathing had returned to normal. Better. Much better.

Since it was Sunday afternoon, Mark doubted many people would be in the suite. He hoped that would be the case. The way he felt right now, the fewer the people the better. Unlocking the front door, he was pleased to find the reception area empty, the overhead lights turned off. When the door closed behind him, he stood still for a minute, listening. Faint voices drifted from the rear of the suite, too faint to make out. It was likely they hadn't heard him enter. Good. Someone had made coffee recently, and he inhaled in pleasure. After he settled into his office, he would have to go down to the kitchen and get a cup.

Mark had almost reached the door to his office when movement at the opposite end of the hall stopped him in midstride. The door to Steve Buchanan's office was opening, then Buchanan himself appeared. His eyes widened at the sight of his partner.

"Mark, I didn't expect you in today."

"I didn't expect to see you here, either," Mark said in surprise.

Steve smiled uncomfortably. "I suppose not. I just... well..." His voice trailed off, but a few seconds later, he went on, "My memory of the last week isn't as clear as I wish, but I think—no, I know—that I owe you a big thank you."

It was Mark's turn to feel uncomfortable. His partner's marital problems had dominated the first part of the week, but the events of the last few days had all but obliterated them.

Before his near-fatal accident, Mark wouldn't have allowed Buchanan's situation to interfere with his own life. Now his emotions were raw and unsettled. He hadn't helped the man because he needed help; he had helped him in order to avoid a bigger problem to the firm. There had been nothing in Mark's motives that deserved appreciation. In fact, once Buchanan was out of his hair, Mark hadn't thought of him. Not even if he should visit him in the hospital or see how he was doing afterward. Realizing how he had let down his long-time partner and friend sent a stab of guilt through him. Steve's gratitude only added to his discomfort.

"You don't owe me anything," he said uneasily.

Steve smiled. "I know it's Sunday, but could I bother you for a few minutes of your time?"

This was not why Mark had come to his office, and a refusal trembled on his lips. The expectant look in his partner's eyes and his own recognition of how he had failed the man kept him from giving voice to it. Instead, he went into the office and allowed the door to close behind him.

Buchanan gestured toward one of the chairs. "Have a seat."

Mark reluctantly obeyed.

Steve took the opposite chair. "I know I've only been out of the office a few days, but it seems more like years."

There was a feeling Mark could understand, but he didn't say so. The floor-to-ceiling drapes that normally covered the wall of windows had been opened wide, and the afternoon light flooded the office. For the first time, he got a good look at Buchanan. The man was looking a lot better than the last time he had seen him. He was casually dressed in khakis and a pullover sweater. Maybe it was the darkness of the sweater that made him seem pale, but Mark doubted it. Too, Buchanan's features looked more gaunt than he remembered. Could he have lost enough weight in less than a week to make such a difference?

Abruptly, he recognized the silence that had fallen between them and spoke quickly. "How are you?"

Steve opened his mouth, closed it, then smiled ruefully. "I was about to give you my usual spiel, but I'm trying to get away from that kind of thing. To be honest, I'm not great, but I'm better than I was."

Mark nodded, unsure how to respond.

Steve's smile widened. "I don't think I've ever seen you look so uncertain."

At first startled, Mark's sense of humor kicked in. He chuckled, and so did Buchanan. "I'm glad you're doing better," he said.

Steve nodded, and his amusement faded. "I guess I lost it there for a while. I'm not even sure how I ended up in the hospital, and I pretty much slept the entire time I was there, which I really needed, as it turned out. I'm still staying at the hotel, but I'm going to be moving into a condo and…" He shifted in his seat, and his gaze fell away.

Mark resisted the impulse to do a little shifting of his own. He didn't want his partner baring his soul to him. He wasn't used to it, and it made him uncomfortable. Nor did he have a nice, neat solution for the man's problems, and that fact made him even more uncomfortable.

Buchanan abruptly raised his eyes to meet Mark's. "There are a lot of things I need to straighten out in my life," he said, "and I've been forced to the realization that I can't do that on my own. So…I've started seeing a counselor."

Mark hoped his wince wasn't noticeable.

"And I've talked to Deborah Cowell. She's agreed to represent me in the divorce. I'm looking forward to being able to see my children next weekend."

Mark was impressed. Cowell's reputation as a tough, experienced attorney who worked hard for her clients was well known. Steve had chosen well, at least in hiring her.

Buchanan looked slowly around his office before returning to his partner. "I'm going to need to make some changes in my life. I haven't figured out a lot of them yet, but one I have. I need to cut down on the amount of time I spend here. I need to…" He stopped and chewed his lower lip for a minute. Then he sighed. "You know what this whole mess has made me realize? For the past, I don't know how many years, this firm has been pretty much my entire life. Worst of all, I've chosen this firm over time with my wife and my kids. It's too late for me and Melanie, but I intend to fight with everything I've got to make a new life that includes my kids." He paused again and offered a self-conscious smile.

"Listen to me, will you? On second thought, my pontificating is probably boring you." He sighed again. "The main reason I wanted to talk to you was to say that I'm coming back to the firm, but it's going to be different. I can't fall back into the same old habits."

For the first time, Mark saw fear in the man's eyes, a fear that pierced his own heart. Where were his partner's words coming from? They stung him with painful force, and he wasn't sure how much of them were Steve's thoughts and how much of them were thoughts that Mark himself had been resisting for days.

He cleared his throat and spoke calmly, hoping none of his own upset was visible. "You do what you need to do, Steve. The firm will work with you."

The fear left Steve's expression and was replaced with gratitude. "Thank you for understanding."

No, he didn't understand. He didn't want to understand. But something stronger than denial was pressing in on him, and Mark was suddenly terrified that it would overwhelm him in Buchanan's presence. He stood and moved toward the door. "I need to get some things done. I'll see you later."

In the safety of his office, Mark did something he rarely did. He locked the door, then double checked that the lock was engaged. When he was certain no one could invade his privacy, he went automatically to his desk. Just as he was about to sit down, he stopped.

He had come here for a reason, except now he couldn't remember what it was. Fury flared, and he was suddenly furious at Steve Buchanan. How dare he come in today and interfere with Mark's plans? He had come here to... He mentally scrambled to recall his earlier thoughts. He had come to the office in the hope of finding the calm that the events of the last two weeks—not even two weeks, he reminded himself bitterly—had demolished. Instead, he had been sideswiped by Buchanan and his problems.

Mark shook his head hard, but it wasn't enough to dispel his thoughts. Couldn't he catch a simple break? Just for a few minutes? *Coffee.* The memory of that fragrant aroma popped into his mind, and he mentally clutched at it. The distraction of a cup of coffee was just what he needed right now.

When he left the sanctuary of his office, Mark was glad to see Buchanan's office door was still closed. In the kitchen, he found a fresh pot of coffee that was still half-full. After filling a mug, he took a deep swallow. The coffee verged on too hot, but Mark didn't care. He had been right. This was exactly what he needed to clear his head.

"… In less than three weeks…"

What now? Irritation swept through Mark at this new interruption.

"What are you going to do?"

Two voices, young, male. They sounded as if they were just outside in the hall. They were familiar, a couple of the law clerks, although he didn't immediately remember their names.

"I don't know. I guess I need to start packing up the house but"—the naked despair in the young voice was startling—"Cassie is in no shape to go anywhere, and right now I haven't found a place for us to move to."

"I'm sorry, Jay, I wish there was something I could do."

A harsh laugh that almost sounded like a sob cut through the air. "If you happen to come across forty thousand dollars, Russ, I'd love to borrow it."

"I wish I had it, I really do."

Silence fell, and Mark realized he was eavesdropping, even if accidentally. He had the voices pinpointed now. Not in the hall, they were coming from the office next to the kitchen, and with any luck, he would be able to leave without being seen. He was in luck. They were still in the office, and he hurried around the corner of the hall.

The voices faded as he walked away, and the last words he heard were from the first voice, the one called Jay. "I can't believe the insurance ran out. After all the money the hospital's gotten from us, we're going to lose everything because of a lousy forty thousand dollars."

Whatever else was said, Mark could no longer hear them, and he was thankful. His plan to come to the office to relax and gather himself had failed. On top of everything he had already been struggling with, now the problems of Buchanan and a barely known law student added to the dark weight pressing in on him.

Back in his office with the door locked again, Mark no longer felt secure. He tried sitting behind his desk, but that felt uncomfortable. Increasingly disturbed, he moved over to the sofa and set his coffee down on the coffee table. From his position, he could see out the floor-to-ceiling windows to the darkening sky outside. Darkening? He stared at his watch in disbelief. The hours had slipped by without his awareness.

Mark blew out a breath and looked at his desk. He could stay here; he had plenty of work to do. But the thought of work was suddenly unappealing. Until he could get this unrelenting emotional roller-coaster under control, he needed to, wanted to…to what? He closed his eyes and rubbed the bridge of his nose in frustration.

Remember to be good to yourself.

Mark's eyes flew open, and he was across the room before he realized he was standing. He stopped, trembling, for there was no escaping this memory suddenly ripped out of his childhood.

She was lying on the chaise lounge, warmly dressed despite the warmth of the room. Illness made her look older than her years. Yet though her features were gaunt and pale, she was beautiful to him.

He sat on the edge of the lounge, reading the story of a velveteen rabbit to her. Though he felt he was too grown up for the story, she still enjoyed it, so he could enjoy reading it to her. When he finished and closed the book, she reached out with a painfully thin hand to gently caress the curve of his cheek.

"That was wonderful, sweetheart."

He smiled in delight. "I read it good?"

Her own smile faded, and she ran her fingers tenderly through his hair. "You put your heart into it, and that's always good enough."

His smile widened, though he still felt a touch of uncertainty. That wasn't the kind of thing he was used to hearing.

Almost as if she knew what he was thinking, she leaned down to press a kiss in his hair. "No matter what happens in your life, remember to be good to yourself. Promise me, sweetheart."

"I promise," he said solemnly, though he had no idea what she was talking about.

Mark gasped for breath as the intensity of the memory faded as swiftly as it had appeared.

"What is happening?" he demanded aloud, fighting rising panic. His mother had died when he was eight years old. He hadn't thought of her in *years*.

He tried to swallow but his throat was too dry. He remembered—oh, he remembered. He also remembered, though no one knew it at the time, his mother had had less than three months to live the day she made her request of him. *Remember to be good to yourself.*

A shudder ran through him, and Mark turned blindly, staring at nothing in particular, not knowing what he was looking for. He had promised his mother he would remember, but he hadn't. Worse, he had forgotten her. He had allowed his father's critical, dominating presence to wipe away his memories of her. He had buried his childhood in the deepest recesses of his mind. Why were they boiling up now? First his father, now his mother. It made no sense. Mark wanted no part of those memories. He had to—needed to—get a grip.

"Calm down," he exclaimed, gasping for breath, feeling himself verging on hyperventilation. For a few minutes, he teetered on the brink of losing control, but gradually his breathing eased and his pounding heart calmed.

Mark never remembered driving home. Only when he stood shivering in front of the unlit fireplace in his bedroom did he realize where he was. Instinctively, he wrapped his arms around himself. He was so cold. Why was he cold? And he couldn't stop shaking. Why not?

"I'm all right," he said out loud, his teeth chattering slightly. "It's just…just stress and…because I haven't been sleeping well." They were good, solid, ordinary reasons for his distress. Except he had been stressed and tired before and never ended up in this state.

Mark shook his head angrily, as if it would dispel his thoughts. He looked around, trying to take comfort in his familiar surroundings. The large room was well furnished according to his tastes. The sitting area in front of the fireplace was normally his favorite spot, though he also spent a considerable amount of time working at the antique desk on the far wall. The only other large piece of furniture was the bed itself in the center of the room. This had been Mark's sanctuary for years, whether he wanted to work, relax, or sleep. Its familiar comfort was always sufficient to calm him down and ground him. At least it always had. Looking around now, he didn't feel any diminution of the turmoil roiling through his heart and mind.

He took a deep, shaky breath. The room was dark, he realized. Maybe it would help to turn on the lights so he could see more clearly. He took a few steps toward the nearest lamp, only to stop in his tracks when he saw the faint glow; the light was already on.

Mark looked around in bewilderment. No, he wasn't imagining things. All the lights were on; the room should be well lit. Except it wasn't. Why was it so dark?

He gasped at the sudden sensation of weight pressing down on him. He couldn't breathe. He spun around, looking for *something* that would make sense. What was happening?

The dimness increased. Light faded altogether and was replaced by darkness.

This wasn't real. It wasn't really happening. He was—he must be—hallucinating.

Hardly able to move for the trembling that gripped his limbs, Mark raised a shaking hand to his face. He could feel the tips of his fingers brushing his cheek. So he must be awake.

"What's happening to me?" he choked.

As if the words had breached a dam, the emotions that had been swirling through him for days suddenly pored over him, sweeping away everything that was familiar and safe.

"No," he gasped, but the word was swallowed by overwhelming fear.

The pressure, both inwardly and outwardly, was unrelenting. It pressed in on him with ever increasing power until the edges of his vision darkened. Even as he recognized the phenomenon, the darkness suddenly became absolute, driving him into oblivion.

Mark tried to choke back his terror, his head turning frantically. Toward…away from…he didn't know how to get away, how to escape from the darkness that was suddenly all he knew, pressing down on him with actual, terrifying force.

From somewhere deep within him, his brother-in-law's words echoed. *The darkness can be overwhelming…especially if someone is battling it on his own. It might very well have destroyed me if not for God. It took his stubborn love and his perfect light to help me break through…*

As his self-awareness began to crumble under the devastating sensations, a stray thought pushed itself into his awareness. *I wonder, if I believed in God, would I feel this way?* Before the thought was complete, the crushing weight of darkness was gone.

Mark staggered, caught himself, and stood perfectly still, shivering violently. When he dared to look around, he was stunned to see that everything was back to normal. The lights burned warmly in the room and, more importantly, he felt perfectly normal, except he was drenched in perspiration. Still breathless, he collapsed into a chair by the fireplace.

He never knew how much time passed before he became aware of his surroundings again. He was home, in his bedroom. He was safe.

Mark looked around the room again, bewildered. What had just happened… "No," he said sharply. A lifetime of rigid self-control rose up in warning. *Don't try to understand what had happened.* In that direction lay danger—danger to everything Mark had come to believe over the years, to the life he had forged.

It had taken a lifetime of hard, focused work to reach this pinnacle. He had not only survived but overcome his father's harsh criticism and unending denigration throughout his childhood. Today, if William Newman had still lived, he would have to acknowledge that he had been wrong and that his son had proven to be a great success.

Mark winced away from the thought. He didn't want or need the memory of his father insinuating itself in his life. The man had been dead for almost twenty years, and his influence over his son had died with him.

Had it really? What about your thought that you had become him?

He swore as once again that still small voice against which he seemingly had no defense pierced him with an uncomfortable question.

"No," he snarled into the quiet of the room. William Newman was long dead. Mark hadn't thought about him in years. As soon as he got some decent sleep under his belt, the old man would disappear back into forgotten memories where he belonged.

His cell phone buzzed, startling him. He pulled it out, glancing automatically at the clock. Who would be calling him at nine o'clock on a Sunday night? "Newman," he said, privately glad for the crisp normalcy of his tone.

"Hello, Mark. I'm sorry to call you so late, but I finally got hold of the arresting officer, and he told something I thought you should know immediately."

Mark swallowed his protest. He was tired of this; he wanted his life back, not more confusion. *Stop it, Newman. This is no time to turn into a coward.* "What is it?"

"The boy who Brian said was driving gave his statement, and he claims Brian was actually the driver of the car."

"What?" Mark's throat dried. Brian had lied? "How is the other boy, the one who was injured?"

Ramsey's silence made him stiffen even before the man spoke. "He's still unconscious."

Mark gripped the receiver tightly. This couldn't be happening.

"Are you still there, Mark?"

"Yes." He struggled for calm. "It's that boy's word against Brian's now."

"That's right. I promised the officer that Brian would give a statement tomorrow morning at 10:00 a.m. I'll be with him, of course. I, um—"

"Spit it out," Mark said, suddenly angry, though he wasn't sure why.

"I assume you'll want to be there also. I recommend that you not be in the room when Brian gives his statement."

How dare the man! No matter if he was representing Brian, Mark had hired him—and Brian was *his* son!

"We can talk more about this tomorrow," Ramsey added. "If that's okay with you."

Mark took some deep breaths and felt his self-control returning. Suddenly he wanted this conversation over. "Fine," he said curtly.

After he hung up, he went down into the living room. He didn't bother turning on the lights; deep down, he was afraid it might trigger a reoccurrence of whatever had happened in his bedroom. Besides, he didn't need a lamp. The drapes hadn't been drawn, and moonlight spilled through the windows, giving enough light to make it easy to move around.

He desperately needed a drink.

When he reached the bar, Mark automatically pulled out his keys. It took a few seconds of fumbling to find the right one and the lock clicked open. As he opened the cabinet doors, he froze in midmotion then looked once more at the key.

Brian admitted he had been stealing liquor for years, yet Mark always kept the bar locked unless they were having a party. How had his son managed to unlock the doors without a key? He looked more closely at the lock, but there wasn't enough light for him to see any details. He ran a finger gently over the lock and the wood surrounding it. He couldn't feel any scratches or other indentations that would indicate the lock had been picked.

Nausea filled his throat. If Brian had used a key, it must have been this one from his father's key ring. Mark kept his keys in only a few places. Usually they were in his pocket unless he was at work, where he kept them in the center drawer of his desk, or at home, where he left them on the desk in his bedroom. Brian had never been to the office, so he must have snuck into Mark's bedroom at some point. No, that made no sense. There was no way the boy could repeatedly slip into his father's bedroom to borrow his keys without someone noticing.

The headache that had been lurking all day suddenly bloomed full strength.

Mark picked up a bottle of bourbon and put it on the countertop then started to close the doors, only to stop again. On impulse, he pulled out the scotch and vodka and also placed them on the countertop before taking a shot glass from the upper cabinet. He poured a small amount of bourbon in the glass, sniffed it, then tasted it. It was fine; it hadn't been watered down.

After rinsing out the glass, he tried the same experiment with the scotch. That too tasted normal. Hope rose in his heart. Maybe Brian hadn't been telling the truth. Maybe he had just been trying to hurt his father.

He poured out the vodka and sipped carefully, then his heart fell. The flavor of the liquor was definitely less intense than it should be. It had been mixed with water so it looked like the bottle was still full. The lack of flavor wouldn't be noticeable when combined with orange juice or another mixer, but he knew he wasn't imagining it.

Brian had been telling the truth.

Sick at heart, Mark's knees gave way, and he sat down abruptly on the floor behind the bar. He closed his eyes, but it didn't dispel the sudden flood of images that swept through his mind.

Seven-month-old Brian crawling rapidly across the carpeted floor, only to wail in frustration when he ended up behind the sofa and couldn't get out. "He's still trying to figure out how to back up," the voice of a laughing young Geneva explained.

Ten-month-old Brian taking his tentative first steps, only to land in a heap on the floor where he looked up to give his parents an indignant glare, as if it was their fault.

Five-year-old Brian standing proudly in his new khaki pants and plaid shirt, Scooby-Doo lunchbox in hand, ready for his first day of kindergarten.

Mark buried his face in his hands. The memories were fraudulent because he hadn't been there for any of them. He had only seen them later in pictures that his wife had to insist he look at.

He had never been there for his son. He had been too busy proving that he was a better man than the father who had never been there for him. He had been so sure he had proved himself to be the better man.

Now as Mark knelt in the darkness, hot tears burning his eyes, he realized the truth—he had become his father, and his son had suffered because of it. Just as Mark had suffered because of his father.

Mark cringed away from the bitter truth, but there was no escape. He scrubbed at the tears streaking his face and heard an all-too-familiar voice echoing in his mind, *There's no way to go back…no way to make things the way they used to be. But that's not necessarily a bad thing.*

"Go away, Joe," he whispered.

He didn't want to hear it, couldn't bear to hear it. Not when the truth was shouting at him so loudly that a lifetime of denial could no longer withstand it. Until this minute, he had never realized that all of his years of hard work to achieve, to be a success, had somehow turned him into the man he hated more than anyone else in the world.

How was he supposed to live with that truth? How was he supposed to live with himself?

16

"Mark? Where are you? Mark?"

The constant repetition of his name finally dragged Mark out of an exhausted sleep. When he opened his eyes, he was bewildered to see wooden cabinet doors directly in front of him. He shifted his weight and caught his breath as the movement suddenly awoke all the aches created by his awkward position. He was sitting on the floor in front of the bar, his back against the wall, and his body wasn't at all happy with him.

Mark swallowed a groan and began to slowly climb to his feet. He couldn't believe he had fallen asleep like this. What on earth…

Memory slammed into him, knocking the breath from his lungs. Still on his knees, he froze as the memories of the previous night crashed over him. It hadn't all been a bad dream. It had really happened.

"Mark?"

He forced himself upright, clutching at the bar for support. Standing in the entrance to the room, Geneva stared at him in disbelief.

"Mark?" she said again, as if she couldn't believe her eyes.

He stretched and winced as his muscles protested more loudly. How was he supposed to explain this? "Uh, yes." *Good, Newman. That will explain everything.*

Geneva continued to gaze at him as if she had never seen him before. Self-conscious before her wide-eyed stare, Mark tried to smooth the wrinkles out his shirt and winced again as he discovered more muscles that were unhappy at how he had spent the night. He ran a hand through his hair and felt it sticking up in every direction. No wonder his wife couldn't believe her eyes.

"What are you…you didn't sleep here, did you?"

Mark cleared his throat. "Not exactly." He glanced at his watch and stared in shock. Eight thirty in the morning? That couldn't be right.

Looking up, he met his wife's eyes and couldn't decide who was more stunned—Geneva or Mark himself. He cleared his throat. "I, um, I need to take a shower."

She nodded slowly, and he was relieved that she was apparently going to pretend she hadn't found her husband waking up on the floor of the living room. "You're going to be late for work," she noted coolly.

The office. Mark was tempted to swear but resisted. "I'm not going in this morning, at least not yet. Brian and his attorney are going to the police department so that he can make a formal statement. I'm going to be there too."

Her eyes widened. "A statement? Can't this…situation be…dismissed or whatever it's called?"

Mark wasn't about to go into all of the problems that their son was currently facing or the legal ramifications. He settled for part of the truth—the truth Brian's mother most needed to know. "No charges have been filed yet. The police are still investigating."

"Does that mean the whole thing can just be dropped?"

"No. The fact is three underage boys were drinking in a car that one of them was driving. When the police tried to pull them over, they ran away and ended up in an accident." He hesitated, but there was no avoiding the most serious aspect of the matter. "The third boy is still in the hospital—unconscious."

Geneva flinched, and Mark wanted to put his arms around her. He knew she wouldn't accept any comfort from him, and the knowledge filled him with fresh guilt. It might take two people to make a marriage, but he was well aware that it was largely his fault that they had drifted apart over the years.

"Brian isn't responsible," she said hesitantly.

Although Mark was tempted to omit the latest disturbing information that Ramsey had provided last night, Geneva needed to know what their son could be facing.

"We're not certain of that."

"Brian said—"

"I know what he said," Mark cut in. He regretted interrupting as soon as he spoke, but it was too late. He saw Geneva's eyes darken with familiar annoyance and decided to ignore it. "Apparently the other boy who was in the car is claiming that Brian was the actual driver," he explained.

"That's impossible! Brian would never..." Geneva stumbled.

"We never thought he would be drinking in the first place," Mark said, hating the pain he knew his words would cause her. But she needed to understand. "Brian might have lied to try to protect himself."

"I don't believe that."

"Or the other boy might be lying for the same reason— to protect himself." He looked away from her stricken expression. "Speaking of Brian, where is he? And Daniel?" Mark realized belatedly he didn't want to be discussing their oldest son where their younger son could overhear.

Geneva hesitated, as if she wanted to argue his words, then her expression changed to weariness. "Daniel left for school an hour ago. Brian is in his room. He told me he had to miss his morning classes because he had an appointment."

Watching her, Mark thought her lips trembled briefly, but there was no indication of stress in her cool voice when she continued.

"He also said you knew about it. I suppose he was talking about...about making a statement?"

He nodded. For a split-second, her expression changed, another emotion flickered across her lovely features and vanished before he could identify it.

"I'll let you take your shower," she said as she turned away.

"Wait a minute." Mark took a few steps forward.

"Yes?"

He sensed that Geneva had retreated behind her usual mask of cool courtesy, but this was the first time since Joe's revelation about his sister that Mark had had a chance to talk to her. How to ask what was on his mind? He decided to just say it.

"What were you doing at the hospital a few days ago?" He almost winced at his unintended curtness, unsurprised to see her eyes narrow.

"How do you know I was there?"

Bring in Joe or leave him out? "A friend saw you." He hesitated before forcing out the words that had been on his mind since Joe's news. "Are you all right?"

At first, he didn't think she was going to answer. Geneva looked over her shoulder as if she intended to walk away and finally back at him. "A friend of mine is there receiving treatment."

"A friend? Do I know her?"

"She's on the board of directors of the museum with me. You don't know her."

Mark was relieved. Geneva seemed to be telling the truth. Still, that raised another question. "You mentioned, ah, treatment?"

Her lips tightened. "She has stage 4 cancer."

He had no idea what that meant, but his wife's tense posture and clipped tone was enough to tell him that her friend's situation was serious. Once more, he felt the urge to put his arms around her and once more he resisted the desire.

"I'm sorry," he said. He debated leaving it there, but other words forced themselves out. "Is there anything I can do to help?"

Geneva's eyes widened, only to narrow again. "Since when are you offering to help me with anything?"

Mark couldn't hold back his wince this time. "Since now."

"There's nothing anyone can do that isn't already being done." She turned on her heel and walked away.

He looked after her, sick at heart, before slowly heading upstairs.

A long hot shower woke him up, but it did not help him to forget what had happened last night. The memory of the strange darkness that had filled his bedroom— and him—did not disturb Mark; it terrified him. It went against everything he believed about the power of logic and rational thought. He couldn't control his shivering as he toweled off and dressed. Despite the fact the room was nicely warm, the chill lingered. All he could do was try to ignore it by focusing on more important issues.

Three hours later, Mark found himself standing beside a hard wooden bench in the hall of a police station. It had been a long, strained morning. Brian had stayed in his room until his father called him downstairs. The boy hadn't said a word then or during the drive to Ramsey's office. Mark had to cool his heels in the outer office while Stretch met with Brian for nearly an hour. Only when the pair had finished was he brought in so that the other attorney could explain to Brian what to expect during questioning by the investigating officers.

Afterward, they followed Ramsey to the police station. When he was asked if he wanted to be there while his son gave his statement, Mark desperately wanted to say yes. He had failed all of Brian's young life to be there for his son; he wanted to be there for him now. Instead, he caught Ramsey's warning expression that made him hesitate. When Mark glanced at his son, Brian glared back, rejection clear in his eyes. Which was why he had spent the last—he checked his watch for what felt like the twentieth time— forty-five minutes alternately sitting on and standing by this blasted bench.

How in the world had he come to be in this place? A police station was absolutely the last place Mark would ever have expected to find himself. He felt uncomfortable and as if everyone was staring at him, pointing a finger at the man whose son had gotten in trouble with the law. So much for being a highly successful pillar of the community.

All around him, Mark was acutely aware of uniformed and plain clothes officers coming and going, as well as more than a few handcuffed individuals he tried very hard not to see. Snippets of conversations swirled around him, but he didn't pay them any attention. His main focus was the closed door twenty feet away at the end of the hall. Behind that door, his son's life might be in the process of being irrevocably changed, and Mark was out here, useless.

He tried to relax, but he kept seeing in his mind's eye Brian's silent, angry rebuff. For the first time in his son's life, Mark wanted to be at his side to help in any way he could. Whether Brian understood, it was obvious he hadn't wanted his father's presence. The pain of that truth stabbed him in the heart, and Mark closed his eyes. How could he have gone along all these years thinking his life was so wonderful while simultaneously allowing his marriage to wither from neglect and his sons grow up thinking of him as a stranger?

Mark couldn't stand his thoughts, so he tried again for a distraction. He pulled his cell phone out of his jacket and checked for messages. The first was from his partner, Marty Welch. He sounded irritated. "Mark, what in blazes is going on? I just talked to Carolyn, and she says you won't be in this morning. We're supposed to go over the Briscoe merger, remember? I have a meeting with Clancy this afternoon, or did you forget that, too? Call me back—ASAP."

Oh for—Mark rubbed his forehead in frustration. He had forgotten, he who prided himself on his memory. Worse, he hadn't checked his calendar this morning, something he always did religiously. He thought of Welch's question, *What in blazes is going on?* He would give a great deal to be able to answer that question, but he didn't know what the answer was.

About to call his partner back, Mark decided to check his other messages first and was glad he did when he heard the second one, from his assistant.

"Good morning, again, Mr. Newman, it's Carolyn. Mr. Welch was just here. He said you and he were supposed to meet this morning on the Briscoe merger. I'm having Susan go through the files now since I recall seeing your notes from the meeting three weeks ago. I believe those should give Mr. Welch what he needs. Otherwise, nothing new has come up since we spoke earlier."

Mark sighed in relief, thanking the fates yet again for his extremely competent assistant. He listened to the other messages with only half an ear. There was another brief one from Welch that said he had what he needed and not to bother calling back. The others weren't important, until he heard the last one.

"Hi, Mark, it's Joe. I think I've found the right guy for what we were talking about. Give me a call."

The right guy. A shiver ran through Mark. The right guy had to refer to the therapist Joe was recommending for Brian.

Movement on the edge of his vision made him look up, and he saw the door opening and Ramsey and Brian walking out. The attorney's hand was on his son's shoulder, and Mark felt a pang. He knew Brian would not accept such a gesture from him. *Whose fault is that, Newman?*

Mark bristled. He hadn't been bothered by that quiet little voice for hours, and he hated that it had returned. Shoving it aside, he saw that Brian had his head down, so it was impossible to get a sense of what had happened from him. As for Ramsey, he was wearing the noncommittal mask that would-be attorneys learned while still in law school.

"Well?" Mark demanded.

Brian didn't react.

Stretch met his eyes and said quietly, "Let's talk outside."

Of course, Mark chastised himself. This was hardly the place for a private conversation. He and Ramsey had parked next to each other in the lot when they arrived, and by silent consent, that was the direction they walked.

When they reached their cars, Mark glanced around, but there was no one around who might overhear. "Well?" he repeated.

Ramsey looked at Brian, who was still staring at the ground before meeting Mark's gaze. "Brian gave his statement. The officer had some questions that he answered. That was it."

"Have charges been filed?"

Brian flinched, but he didn't raise his head.

Ramsey acted as if he hadn't noticed. "No, they're hoping the boy in the hospital will regain consciousness soon and give his side of the story."

"Will," Brian said.

The men looked at the teenager, and Mark said, "Will?"

Brian raised his head. He was pale, and his eyes were red-rimmed. Mark suddenly understood why the boy had been keeping his head down. "Will is still in the hospital," he said softly. "Terry's the one who was driving."

Mark looked at Ramsey, who said, "Terry Drummond claims that Brian was driving."

"He's lying," Brian put in, a little more strongly than before.

The attorney nodded. "Right now it's Brian's word against Terry's."

Mark nodded too. "So Will's statement will be the deciding factor."

"Not necessarily," Ramsey cautioned. "However, it will certainly be taken into consideration."

"There's another reason for Will to wake up." Brian was suddenly glaring at his father, who was surprised by the hostility.

"What?"

"It'll mean he's getting better."

Mark bit back a sarcastic comment. He was tired and upset, so was Brian. He needed to be careful. "Yes, it will. I didn't mean to imply anything otherwise in what I said earlier."

Brian ran his hands through his hair. "Don't you ever quit?"

"What are you talking about?"

"You! Every time you open your mouth, you sound like a lawyer. I wish just once—" He stopped abruptly, and the jagged end of his sentence was left hanging in the air.

Mark struggled with his slipping temper. He didn't want to have an argument with his son in the middle of a parking lot. For that matter, he didn't want to have an argument with his son, period.

"This has been very stressful for everyone," Ramsey said. "If I can offer my two cents, I think something to eat and then some rest would help us all."

Mark swallowed his anger and held out his hand. "Thanks for everything, Stretch."

"You're welcome." Ramsey shook his hand and smiled. "By the way, good luck with the game tomorrow."

"Game?" Mark stared blankly at the other man and was surprised by a loud snort from his son.

"He doesn't know anything about it," Brian said to Ramsey, who looked at Mark with raised eyebrows.

"The Little League game tomorrow. Your son's team is playing against my son's team."

Brian took a quick step forward that put him squarely between the men, his angry eyes meeting his father's bewildered gaze. "Danny was MVP the last two years. Mr. Ramsey knows all about it because his son plays Little League too, and he's interested in what his son does."

"Brian," Stretch interrupted, "I don't think—"

The teenager swept on, his voice growing progressively louder. "News flash, Dad. Danny's been playing Little League since he was a little kid. You've never been to one of his games, have you? I'll bet you never noticed the trophies in his room. You never noticed—"

"Brian." Ramsey put a heavy hand on the boy's shoulder. "This isn't the place or time."

Brian met the stern gaze and then his father's shocked expression. Abruptly, he pulled out of the attorney's grasp and climbed into the car. Mark stared at him until he felt a hand on his arm.

Ramsey was gazing at him with a mix of compassion and irritation. "I'll let you know when I hear anything. As for the rest, it sounds like you have some very serious thinking to do to get your house in order. If you won't do it for yourself, do it for your sons." With that, he was gone.

Mark stood still, Brian's words repeating themselves in his mind as if on an unending loop, confirmation of his earlier thoughts. Daniel, his youngest, was living a life he knew nothing about.

Is that really such a surprise? Shut up, he thought, but the anger he wanted to feel toward that annoying small voice was crushed by a sudden awareness of the truth. He had never seen, never recognized, the struggles of his oldest son. And what about Geneva? A friend she cared about was in the hospital suffering from a life-threatening illness. He hadn't known. For all these years, he hadn't cared enough about the members of his family to have the slightest idea of what was going on in their lives. How could he have been so blind? How could he have missed *everything*?

Feeling dazed, Mark got into the car, drove out of the parking lot, and headed home. Throughout the drive, he was very aware of the simmering but silent figure sitting next to him, and he couldn't dredge up even a shred of self-justification.

It wasn't until he pulled into the driveway and stopped to wait for the garage door to open that he realized he had been driving on autopilot. He heard Brian open the door and said automatically, "Wait until I've parked."

Without closing the door, Brian turned in his seat to give him a furious glare. "Why? What difference does it make?"

Two weeks ago, even ten days ago, Mark would have responded with cold authority. Today, he couldn't. "You know why. It's for your own safety."

"Oh, please! When did you ever care about my safety? When did you care about anything I cared about? Or Danny? Or Mom?"

Mark was shocked out of his distraction. "Brian, I—" he stumbled.

"Forget it!" Brian flung the door open and lunged out of the car. Mark reached after him, but the boy was already storming up the walk to the side door, and an instant later, he was in the house, slamming the door behind him.

Numbly, Mark leaned over to pull the passenger-side door closed before driving into the garage and parking. He sat still for a long time, distantly aware of the slight *thud* of the automatically closing garage door, then faint pinging and settling as the car's engine slowly cooled.

All his defenses lay in ashes at his feet. All his self-justifications, rationalizations, everything that had enabled him to live his life had disappeared, leaving him feeling bereft. Empty.

His eyes drifted across the view beyond the front window. There in the corner of the garage, still coiled in an untidy heap, was the rope, the same rope that a stranger had used to save his life only days ago.

Mark climbed slowly out of the car, aching in every muscle. He slammed the door shut and stood still, uncertain as he had never been before. Without thinking, he walked over to look down at the rope. He could still smell the dampness of the river water that permeated its fibers. The accident had only happened nine days ago. Who could have imagined that out of it would come such chaos that he no longer recognized his own life?

Mark found himself on his knees, reaching out to touch the rope. It was damply cold and slick to the touch. Why hadn't he thrown it away? He didn't know. At this moment, he realized he was tired, tired to his very bones. He took a deep breath and slowly exhaled. What he really needed was sleep. He still had a few of the pills the doctor in the hospital had given him after the accident. One of those should do the job, give him several hours of solid, uninterrupted sleep.

As he prepared to rise, he realized how dark the garage was with the door closed. Odd, he had never noticed before. *As dark as…* Exhausted and confused as he was, Mark was unable to stop the unwelcome thought before it bloomed fully formed in his mind. The garage was as dark as his bedroom had been last night, that unnatural darkness that no light was able to pierce. With that recognition came another that shocked him with its intensity.

The outer darkness wasn't nearly so dark as the darkness within him.

Mark froze, still on his knees, aware as never before of the all-encompassing darkness that filled him. More than darkness, there was an inescapable chill that drove every sense of warmth out of him. He couldn't move, he couldn't think, he couldn't see. There was nothing but darkness, a darkness that possessed every fiber of his being. He would never be able to find his way out of such darkness, and with that knowledge came utter despair.

A tiny pinprick of light pierced Mark's awareness. There, in the center of his mind. Something deep within him struggled to grasp it, but the effort was too great. The darkness and hopelessness were too great.

The pinprick of light began to grow. From smaller than a grain of sand, it grew rapidly, expanding through his mind, his head, and moving down through his body, filling him with light and warmth, unfreezing the chill, driving the darkness before it, expanding through his chest, his torso, traveling down his arms, all the way to the tips of his fingers, and then down his legs, down, down, all the way down.

An instant ago, Mark had been lost in darkness and despair. Now he was filled with light and a warmth no cold could touch. And so much more. The warmth continued to grow and strengthen, and suddenly Mark recognized what he was feeling.

Love.

A love beyond the grasp of mortal mind.

A love that now filled him, healing, breathing life back into him. Except this time it was life beyond anything he had ever imagined.

He gasped at the sensation of great arms encircling him, embracing him, holding him as no one had ever held him. Tears streamed down Mark's face as he doubled over, unable to think, able only to feel, to experience, to accept. Time ceased while he was caught up in the presence of One he had never believed in, yet whom he now knew was everything he had ever wanted.

"All right," he finally whispered, slipping unaware to the floor, not feeling the chill of the concrete or the damp coldness of the rope that he still gripped. There was nothing but light and warmth and love.

17

Some unfathomable time passed before Mark realized he was facedown on the cold concrete floor of the garage. Yet he wasn't cold. He was warm, with a soul-deep warmth.

He sat up slowly, still overwhelmed by what had happened. More time passed unnoticed before Mark decided he needed to move. He needed to... Something. What? The answer drifted gently to him. He needed to talk to someone.

Joe.

Mark laughed, albeit shakily. Of course. Who better to talk to about what had just happened to him than a minister?

For the first time, doubt arose. Would Joe believe him? He knew Mark's less admirable characteristics, those that Mark had carefully hidden from the world yet never been able to fully hide from his brother-in-law.

Talk to Joe.

The thought came more strongly. Before he could second-guess himself, Mark got up off the floor, then paused to stare at the rope he still gripped. He crouched to lay it down. When he started to rise, something made him pause to give the pile of rope a little pat, then he chuckled at himself.

At some point during his drive to the Ridgeway's, Mark noticed that night had fallen. How long had his experience lasted? How long had he laid on the garage floor unaware of time passing, unaware of anything except what was happening to him? He didn't know, and he didn't care. He laughed again, softly, marveling at the sensation of incredible lightness within him, a lightness that had burned away all the darkness and weight that had been pressing down on him for so long. It was gone. He was free.

Gratitude swelled, and he blinked back fresh tears. "Thank you," he whispered. The words felt so inadequate, but he meant them with all his heart. Surely God recognized that, didn't he? Of course, he did. He was God. What a wonderfully reassuring thought.

When he pulled in front of the Ridgeway's house, he saw the lights were on. For the first time, he thought to glance at his watch. Dinner time. He hesitated, suddenly feeling doubtful. "Maybe this isn't a good time," he thought aloud.

Talk to Joe.

Mark blinked. Had that come from his own desire or from… He shook his head. Stop second-guessing yourself, he thought again. Suddenly determined, he left his car and marched up the path. When he reached the front door, he raised his hand to knock, remembering his last visit here. Little more than a week ago, yet it seemed like a lifetime. How much had changed in so short a time. If it hadn't happened to him, he wouldn't have believed it.

There was a *thump* on the other side of the door, and in the porch light, he could see the door knob turn slightly. He thought he heard faint sounds of high-pitched youthful arguing and laughing overlaid by an adult's cautioning voice.

Abruptly, the door opened, and Beth Ridgeway appeared, looking over her shoulder. "...By the time I get to ten," she warned.

A burst of giggles behind her made Mark smile.

Beth turned back to him, her eyes bright with amusement. "Sorry about that," she said. "I don't know what I was thinking all those years ago when I decided I wanted to be a mom." She took a step back and opened the door wider. "Come in."

"Thank you." Mark entered in time to see three diminutive figures scurrying through the kitchen to the room beyond.

Beth followed his gaze and sighed. "Hopefully they'll stay in the playroom until dinner's done. Would you like to eat with us? It's nothing fancy, just a stew made up of all kinds of leftovers, but we like it."

For a second Mark couldn't speak. He suddenly glimpsed the character of Beth Ridgeway as he never had before; now he understood how she had helped to heal Joe's wounded heart after the loss of his first wife. "I appreciate the offer," he said, hoping she could hear his sincerity. "It smells wonderful but I can't stay."

"Next time," she said.

"Next time," he agreed, smiling.

Throughout their conversation, he was very aware of her hazel eyes studying him, and he couldn't blame her. He was definitely presenting a different picture than the man who had practically pushed his way into her home just days ago.

"I'd like to talk to Joe if he's available. I promise I won't keep him long."

Beth waved a dismissive hand. "Don't worry about that. One of the advantages of stew is that it'll keep indefinitely. Joe's never on time for meals, but maybe you can pull him out of his sermon preparation long enough for him to eat with us."

Sermon preparation? The phrase hinted at a world Mark knew nothing about, and he felt vaguely disconcerted. He mentally shook his head at himself. This was no time for distractions and, it seemed, no time for him.

Trying to hide his disappointment, he edged back to the door. "If he's busy I don't want to—"

"Don't worry about it. Ordinarily, he doesn't even begin thinking about his next sermon until the middle of the week. It just so happens that he and the kids were playing earlier and he got an idea and…" She rolled her eyes.

Mark nodded uncertainly, and Beth patted his arm. "Go on," she urged. "You don't even need to knock. I left the door open last time I tried to get him to come out, for all the good it did. See if you can drag him out of his lair."

Smiling again, he went down the hall and stopped in front of the open doorway. Inside everything looked the same, except this time Joe was standing by his desk, a sheaf of papers in hand, staring vaguely at the bookcase and muttering to himself.

Mark hesitated. Maybe it would be better if he withdrew. Then he began to hear what Joe was saying, and the words stopped him in his tracks.

"The truth is that God has called us out of darkness. God did it so we don't have to, which is a good thing because we never could. We don't have to worry about struggling and striving to climb out on our own. The gospel isn't about us saving ourselves. God has called us out of darkness. Do you notice the tense? It's already happened. And he didn't just call us out of the darkness, did he? He called us out so that we could enter into his marvelous light. Marvelous! Such a wonderful word that the apostle Peter chose to describe the light of God, to describe being in his presence."

Mark almost staggered back in shock. Was this part of Joe's sermon? How could it apply so perfectly to Mark's own situation? How could Joe, all unaware, be speaking to exactly what had happened to him less than an hour ago?

Joe paused to scribble something on the page he was holding. Mark was sure he hadn't made a sound, but Joe's head rose suddenly. "Mark! This is a surprise. Come in." He moved forward, dropping the pages on the corner of his desk.

"I'm sorry, I didn't call…" Mark swallowed. "If this is a bad time…"

Joe's smile faded as he came closer. "Are you all right?"

Mark was startled to feel his eyes fill with tears and Joe caught his arm. "Come and sit down."

He allowed his brother-in-law to guide him to the loveseat and watched as he returned to the door, closing it before coming back and sitting down across from him.

"What's wrong?" Joe said gently.

The worry in his expression made Mark blink back his tears and smile. "Nothing's wrong. Nothing that you don't know about, I mean. I guess"—he paused to take a slightly shaky breath—"I guess you would say something's right. More right than it's ever been."

Joe stared. Slowly he began to smile until it filled his face. "Praise God," he whispered. He dropped to his knees in front of him. Before Mark realized what was happening, Joe threw his arms around him and hugged him fiercely.

Mark had never been hugged by a man before, but what he would have resisted just hours ago now felt like he was coming home. He hugged back, at first tentatively and then, when Joe didn't let go, with more assurance.

When Joe finally drew back, he sat down beside him, keeping one hand on his arm. Seeing the joy in the other man's eyes stirred something deep inside Mark. After circumstances had forced him to realize how his neglect had caused his marriage to wither and Geneva's feelings for him to fade, he couldn't image anyone caring about what happened to him. Certainly not Joe. But despite how he had treated Joe in the past, it was obvious that his brother-in-law actually did care, and he was humbled by the realization.

"Talk to me," Joe urged, still smiling widely. "What happened? I want to hear everything."

"It's kind of complicated," Mark admitted. "It's been a long day…" Just thinking about it made him a little dizzy. "It's been a real roller-coaster."

Joe's eyes softened. "I'm familiar with roller-coaster days."

Mark took another deep breath and felt better. Thinking back over the day, he realized he needed to go further back, at least to last night. Joe listened intently but stayed quiet, to Mark's relief. It was hard enough remembering; he didn't think he could have endured any interruptions or comments about his stupidity or willful blindness. He knew his guilty feelings must be obvious when he described the state of his marriage, Brian's problems, and Daniel's isolation from his father, yet Joe remained silent.

Last night's experience in his bedroom and then again in the garage just a short while ago were hardest to put into words. Mark's vaunted silver tongue that was so helpful in a courtroom or at the negotiating table had disappeared.

Finally, he came to a stuttering halt with a shame-faced look at his brother-in-law. "I don't know how much sense any of this makes."

Joe smiled, happiness radiating from his expression. "It makes all the sense in the world. You're here because God wouldn't let you go."

Despite what had happened to him, Mark still felt uncomfortable at the man's openness. "That's hard to... believe."

"Not at all." Joe patted his arm. "Look where you are, and I'm not talking about being in this room. There have been a lot of prayers ascending for you and your family for a lot of years. I'm more thrilled than I can say to see some of them come to fruition."

"Prayers?" Mark repeated in disbelief.

"Many, many prayers. And let me tell you, you didn't make it easy to pray for you sometimes."

Mark was surprised by his own laughter and a fresh upwelling of the joy that had swept through him in the garage. "I expect I didn't make it easy most times."

Joe laughed too, and in the sound, Mark heard echoes of his own emotion. It was deep and healing, and he felt a surge of thankfulness.

"To be honest," Mark admitted, "I think I'm still in shock."

"That's perfectly understandable." Joe's smile gentled. "You've exchanged the darkness of this world for God's light and presence. It's a huge change, and it will take time to adjust to."

Mark stared at his brother-in-law. "That's what happened. I mean, there was so much darkness I felt as if I was drowning in it. And then suddenly it was all gone, and there was only…" His voice broke.

"Say it," Joe demanded, his eyes glistening.

"There was only light." Mark choked. Only when the pressure in his throat eased could he continue. "It was brilliant yet so warm and so healing…" He stopped again and gave his brother-in-law a helpless look. "It was so…so much. I don't have the words to describe it."

"Praise the Lord." Joe's smile was luminescent. "He's called you out of the darkness into his glorious light."

"Oh!" Mark suddenly remembered. "That's what you were talking about earlier."

"I was." Joe laughed again, a rich, joyous sound that Mark couldn't help but join. After a minute, he continued. "Earlier today when I was playing with the kids, Jonny mentioned that he was glad for the night light in their bedroom because it kept the darkness away." Joe shook his head. "They're currently going through a phase where they think monsters are hiding in their closet, under their bed, wherever, so in addition to praying each night that God will protect them from the monsters, I put in a night light. Between the prayers and the light, the boys are able to sleep without nightmares." He smiled. "At any rate, when Jonny said that, I suddenly remembered the passage in First Peter and knew that's what I wanted to use for my next sermon. That's what you heard me going on about when you arrived."

"That's quite a coincidence," Mark said, feeling more than a little awe.

Joe chuckled. "I doubt coincidence had anything to do with it. As you continue on this new walk God has set before you, you're going to be continually amazed at how he works things out in our lives."

"New walk." The words were daunting.

"You're beginning a journey like nothing you can imagine, Mark. The most wonderful part of it is that you're not going on that journey by yourself. God will be with you every step of the way, leading and teaching you—and using you too—to be his hands and feet to others, provided you allow him to."

"That sounds…" Mark wasn't sure what it sounded like.

"Different than what you're used to?"

"Yes."

"It is," Joe agreed. "But remember, no matter what, you won't be alone. Someone will be with you, someone who knows you better than you know yourself. Through his Holy Spirit, he walks with each one of us every day of our lives."

"I…it all feels…overwhelming," Mark said uncertainly.

Joe suddenly looked contrite. "I'm sure. How can I help?"

Mark considered his brother-in-law's words before falling back on his earlier thought. "It's just so much to take in. I don't know what to do next."

Joe sat quietly for a minute, lips pursed in thought. Then he rose. "Just a second."

Mark watched him go over to the bookcase and stop in front of it, his hand running lightly across the spines of several books before pulling one out and returning to his chair.

"I can't think of a better way to begin than with this," Joe said, offering the book.

Mark took it hesitantly, his heart skipping a beat when he saw what it was. "It's a Bible."

"The NIV Study Bible." Joe smiled. "It's an excellent modern translation, and because it's a study Bible, it includes a lot of notes and maps that can be helpful, and there's also a concordance at the end."

"What's a concordance?"

"Sorry. A concordance identifies a word in a particular verse and lists other verses in the Bible that contain the same word. It can be very useful in your study. The one in this Bible isn't complete, but it does note important words and show you where else and in what context you can find them." His brother-in-law's blank expression made Joe chuckle. "Feel free to ignore it, likewise the other notes and references. You can learn everything God wants you to learn simply by opening the Bible and asking God to help you understand as you read."

Mark nodded in relief and realized he was still running a hand over the cover. "I don't think I've ever held a Bible before."

"Lots of people haven't," Joe said.

Mark looked up at the note of sadness he heard in the other man's voice.

"But it's God's gift to us and the best way I know to get to know him," Joe continued.

"Thank you."

"You're welcome."

Mark looked at the book in his hands. "So what do I do with it? Just open it up to the first page and start reading?"

"That's one way to do it. However, if you want my two cents—"

"I do."

"For a new Christian, I recommend you start with one of the Gospels. Let me show you." He took the Bible back and began flipping pages. When he got a little more than halfway through, he stopped and handed it back. "This is where the New Testament begins. The first four books of the New Testament are called the Gospels and are named after the individuals who tradition says wrote them— Matthew, Mark, Luke, John. There are a lot of similarities between them and also some significant differences."

"So I begin with the first one?" Mark felt a little lost.

"You can," Joe said. "However, I'd suggest that you start with the Gospel of Mark." His smile flashed again. "It should be easy to remember, considering you share the same name. It's believed by scholars to be the first written of the Gospels. I love it for several reasons, one of them being that it gives the reader more of a visual look into Christ's life and ministry than you'll find in the others."

"What do you mean?"

"Don't worry about it. I suggest that when you sit down to read, you begin by asking God to reveal to you what he wants you to learn and then start reading."

Mark gave the Bible a doubtful look. "It's really that simple?"

"God wants us to know him. That's why he gave us this." Joe tapped the Bible. "And he also gave us the Holy Spirit to help us to understand it."

"I feel as if I've landed on a new world. I don't understand anything."

"I'll be more than happy to help in any way I can. Let me know any questions your reading brings up. But most importantly, remember that God wants you to understand. You can trust him to help you with that. Just don't expect it all to happen overnight." Joe leaned forward slightly. "Mark, you're beginning a journey that will last the rest of your life and beyond. Don't fear it. Everyone who accepts Jesus Christ as his or her Lord and Savior is on the same journey. Just remember that through his Spirit, God will be walking with you every step of the way."

Mark was listening intently. He still felt overwhelmed, but he was beginning to realize it was all right to feel that way. There was so much to learn, but according to his brother-in-law, he didn't need to worry about learning it quickly. That was a huge relief considering how drastically his life had just changed.

"I can't believe how much has happened in less than two weeks."

Joe's eyes brightened. "Do you know what started all this?"

"I think so." Mark smiled. "And I bet you do, too."

"I may suspect, but I don't know for sure. Why don't you tell me."

"The accident." Even now the memory chilled him. "I almost died that night. I would have died if not for a passing stranger who risked his life to save mine." He turned regretful eyes on Joe. "I tried to find him, to thank him. I even hired a private investigator."

"And?"

"Nothing. No one else saw him, not at the accident or at the hospital. Why did he disappear so quickly? Why wouldn't he let me thank him?"

"I don't know. Do you have any ideas?"

"No." He met his brother-in-law's inquiring gaze. "Joe, I've worked hard and been very successful. I could have given him a reward. I wanted to. But he just disappeared."

"He obviously didn't want a reward."

"No," Mark said slowly. "Although he did say something…just before he disappeared."

"What? Oh, wait," Joe interrupted himself. "You told me that he said something about how you could thank him by helping someone else who needed a hand. Is that it?"

Mark almost laughed. "Yes. Do you know have any idea what he meant?"

"I think so, and so do you."

For the first time, Mark felt a touch of irritation. "I know you understand a lot more about this Christian business than I do, but that doesn't mean you understand more about life."

Joe chuckled. "I'm not trying to make you think that I know more. I'm just wondering if my suspicions of what your rescuer meant are accurate."

Mark frowned. "Do you think he was a Christian?"

"I have no idea. He could be. Or he could be a card-carrying atheist or something in between. For that matter, he could have been an angel."

"A what?"

Joe's smile softened. "The Bible takes angels very seriously, which tells me I need to take them seriously. Regardless of who your rescuer might have been, I believe the way you respond to the charge he gave you is how you can best thank him."

"Meaning?"

"That's between you and God."

Mark gestured impatiently. "I don't understand."

"I don't mean to be cryptic. It's just that I believe you and God are going to have to figure out how you need to respond to those words."

Suppressing a sigh of frustration, Mark rubbed his forehead. "I guess I've got a lot to learn."

"Don't forget, the Holy Spirit will help you in ways you can't imagine right now. And I'm always available." Joe put a hand on his arm. "It's also important for you to realize that however much your life has changed spiritually, in many ways, it's still the same. Whatever you were struggling with before is still there to be dealt with."

The words cut through Mark. "The boys. Geneva. The firm too."

"Yes."

Without warning, Mark felt his exhilaration collapse. "Nothing's changed."

"Wrong. You've changed. You've accepted Jesus Christ's invitation. That changes everything."

Mark closed his eyes against returning anguish. "So? Brian's still in trouble, he hates me and I don't blame him, my marriage is still in ruins, and I'm a stranger to my youngest son. What difference does it make that I accepted anyone's invitation?"

Joe gripped his shoulder. "It makes all the difference in the world. You no longer have to try to deal with your problems by yourself. That reminds me." He stood up and went to his desk, picked up a piece of paper and returned. "This is the name and phone number of the therapist I suggest Brian contacts."

"Seth Hancock," Mark read aloud.

"Yes. He's an excellent marriage and family therapist, and he specializes in working with youth and teens." Joe's smile came and went. "He's something else I wouldn't have mentioned to you before today. Seth is a long-time deeply committed Christian who lives his faith better than almost anyone I know."

Mark glared. "So you're expecting him to turn Brian into a Christian?"

"No, you misunderstand. I'm recommending Seth because he's an excellent therapist who has a lot of experience working with teenagers. But speaking as Brian's uncle, I'm also glad to know that Seth has a Christian worldview to guide him in his work."

Mark wasn't sure how he felt. All he was certain of was that his son needed help. Did he trust Joe to find the right help for Brian? Meeting that steady gaze gave him his answer. Yes, he did. "All right, thank you." He folded the paper and slipped it into his pocket. "I know Beth was expecting you for dinner. I should be going."

"You don't have to. You're welcome to stay as long as you'd like."

"Thanks but…" His smile faded. "I need to go home. I have a lot to think about."

"Go slow," Joe said, "and keep in touch with God."

Mark suddenly felt uncomfortable. "I'm supposed to do that by praying, right? How exactly does that work?"

Joe sat back in his chair and rubbed his chin. "That Bible is for you to keep, but I'd like to loan you a couple other books." He returned to the bookshelves and, after a minute of rummaging, returned with two slim volumes.

"What are those?"

"I think you'll find them helpful." He gave Mark a long, probing look. "I've known you for a lot of years, and I know you're a highly intelligent, highly educated man with a strong skeptical streak. These books aren't what I would call traditional devotional literature, but I think they may be just what you need. They're two of my favorites." He held them up so that Mark could read the titles. "They're both written by a man named Frederick Buechner. This one, *Peculiar Treasures*, offers thumbnail sketches of various people in the Bible." Joe's smile widened.

"Each one gives what I think of as a humanizing view of everyone from Abraham to Jesus Christ. That view has helped me over the years to know those long-ago people in the Bible much better than I would otherwise. And *Wishful Thinking*"—he held up the other book—"highlights a lot of words from scripture that Christians believe are especially important, words like *faith* and *grace* and *sin* and a lot of others. That's why it's subtitled *A Theological ABC*. Again, Buechner doesn't take the traditional route in his understanding of these words, and again, that's a large reason why I enjoy it so much."

He held them out, and Mark reluctantly took them. His mind felt as if it was whirling. How was he supposed to make sense of everything? By praying to God? The very idea made him uncomfortable.

"Mark." Joe put a hand on his arm again, forcing him to meet his gaze. "The main reason I'm suggesting these books in addition to the Bible is that I don't want you to feel confined or bogged down by old stereotypes. Take prayer for example."

Mark looked at him, startled. Was the man a mind-reader?

Apparently unaware that he had surprised him, Joe continued. "When most people think of prayer, they imagine someone kneeling on the ground, hands clasped, head bowed, murmuring memorized phrases. That's fine for some people. But others would be paralyzed if they tried that route. I can't do that. For me, prayer is focused conversation with my Lord. Sometimes it's silent, sometimes I speak out loud. Sometimes I kneel, sometimes I'm walking or driving my car while I pray. Sometimes when I'm doing the grocery shopping." He chuckled at Mark's wide-eyed look. "Don't call it prayer if that word makes you uncomfortable. Think of it as conversation, a dialogue, if you will. The important thing to remember is that God wants to stay in touch with you. He wants to hear what's on your heart, what you're thinking and worrying about. And he also wants you to hear him."

"Are you saying God wants to talk to me?"

Joe's eyebrows rose. "Isn't that what he's been doing recently?"

Mark felt his face warm. "Last night? And, um…"

"And today in the garage." Joe nodded. "And probably several other times that you haven't mentioned. And he can also talk to you through that," he added with a nod at the Bible.

You're an idiot, Newman, he decided. Maybe something of what he was feeling showed because Joe smiled sympathetically.

"I know you were feeling overwhelmed when you got here, and I probably just added to that. I'm sorry. Don't forget, you don't have to figure this out overnight, so don't try."

Mark sighed. "So now I read this"—he held up the Bible—"and…"

"Take it a day at a time. Ask God to help you understand what he wants you to understand. When you have a question, any question, ask him about it and also ask him to help you to understand any answer he may give you. Offer up your relationships with Brian and Geneva and Danny, and ask for guidance, and for healing. Usually, change takes place gradually, so don't expect an overnight miracle."

"Isn't that what happened to me?" Mark smiled.

Joe laughed. "It feels like it, doesn't it? But I'm here to tell you that I've been praying for you since you and Geneva first began dating. Over twenty years, it's been. Hardly overnight."

Mark swallowed, stunned all over again. "It's hard to believe you've been praying for me all these years. And for Geneva?"

Sorrow darkened Joe's eyes. "I accepted Jesus Christ when I was fourteen years old," he said quietly. "I've been praying for her every day since."

"I don't understand." Mark frowned in thought. "You've been praying for her longer than for me, yet...what happened to me today...I mean, I accepted..." He stumbled. It was hard to go against a lifetime of conditioning. "I, uh, accepted him too today." Suddenly he was terrified he was wrong. "That's what happened, isn't it?"

"Yes," Joe said. "You belong to Jesus Christ now."

It was the first time anyone had said the words out loud, the first time Mark had actually thought it through. It sounded so odd, like something an old-style religious revivalist might proclaim. It was going to take some time before he would be able to wrap his mind around all that had happened.

Setting that aside, he returned to his question. "Why has this happened to me when it hasn't happened to Geneva? You've been praying…" It was definitely going to take him time to be able to say that word without mentally stuttering over it. "You've been praying for her a lot longer than for me."

"It's not about time," Joe said with unusual heaviness. "God meets each of us wherever and whenever he finds us. For you, it was today. For Geneva…only God knows. Like all of us, she has free will. One thing I am certain of"—the pain in his eyes softened—"as much as I love my sister, God loves her more, and he will leave no stone unturned in trying to win her to him."

Mark felt a pang when he thought of his wife. Even though his first excitement was easing and the memories of all he was still struggling to deal with were returning, he was aware of a sense of peace deep inside that he had never known before. He had no idea what the future held, but he suddenly wished with all his heart that Geneva might know this same peace.

"Maybe if I told her what happened to me," he said slowly, "how everything's changed for me, she might—"

"Go slow," Joe interrupted. "On the one hand, I'd love for her to hear your story. On the other hand, if her heart isn't ready to hear, it could drive her even further away. Talk to God about it first. Ask him to show you the right way to go with Geneva."

Mark sighed. "It's all so complicated."

"It seems that way sometimes, but it's really not as complicated as you think. Keep talking to God, keep listening, and let him lead. You can forget everything else we've talked about so long as you remember that."

"I'm not going to forget any of it," Mark said as he stood up, "though it'll take time to understand. Thank you for these." He held up the books.

"You're very welcome." Unexpectedly, he gave Mark another hug. "Welcome home, Brother."

Mark flushed, warmed by both the words and the gesture.

When they broke apart, Joe said, "Before you leave, would you mind if I pray?"

There it was again, the stab of discomfort Mark felt every time he heard the word. Nonetheless, he couldn't resist the request.

"Please."

Placing one hand on his brother-in-law's shoulder, Joe bowed his head and said, "Our Lord and our God, we come to you with full hearts, offering our thankfulness and joy that you have brought one more of your children home to you. I pray you will bless my brother, Mark, and help him to know you and your will for him. In Jesus's name, we thank you for hearing us. Amen."

"Amen," Mark echoed. To his surprise, his discomfort had faded and been replaced with a sense of rightness. "My first prayer," he said, smiling slightly.

"Your first recognized prayer," Joe corrected, also smiling. "I have a feeling you've been talking to God for quite a while. You just didn't realize it."

Was that possible? Obviously, it must be. Ministers knew about those kinds of things, didn't they?

"Thank you," Mark said again.

Joe's hand still rested on his shoulder, and he gave it a squeeze. "It was my pleasure and my joy. You know my phone number. Keep in touch."

That was an easy promise. "I will."

18

Driving home, Mark struggled with the fading remnants of his earlier exhilaration and a growing awareness that despite what had happened in the garage a few hours ago, nothing had changed in his life.

Wrong. You've changed. You've accepted Jesus Christ's invitation. That changes everything.

Joe's words still echoed in his thoughts when Mark pulled into his garage. He parked and turned off the ignition; the car went quiet, and the headlights disappeared.

As he sat in the dark, reviewing what had happened, how his life had been turned upside down in such a short time, he gradually became aware once more of the pile of rope in the corner of the garage.

More than anything else, it was that blasted rope that convinced him of the truth of what had happened to him today. And not only today. Ever since the night of the accident, despite all that had gone wrong, he felt as if he had been moving in this direction the entire time, as if all the disparate events had led him, inexorably, to his new relationship with God. Maybe Joe was right in that he had actually been headed toward this day for a long time, but Mark was certain his journey of the past several days had played a crucial role.

He sighed and rubbed his forehead, realizing all over again how tired he was. Pulling himself wearily out of the car, Mark walked into the house, glancing at his watch when he entered. It was almost seven thirty; he wasn't surprised to find the kitchen empty, although, he sniffed, he could tell the boys had eaten. It smelled like beef stroganoff, and his stomach growled hungrily. *Later*, he told it, and he continued through the house.

There were no lights on in the dining or living rooms, and Mark moved through the shadows, feeling the knot in his stomach growing. He needed to talk to Brian, to Daniel. And he needed to talk to Geneva.

As much as Mark wanted to share what had happened to him with his family, he didn't need Joe's warning to make him hesitate. If he were to tell Brian or Geneva what had happened to him today—he winced away from the thought of their likely reactions. What was that old saying? Talk was cheap. He could talk until he was blue in the face, but it meant nothing compared to the life he had lived and his abysmal relationships with his wife and sons. It was those relationships they would believe because they had experienced them, experienced him. It was going to take time and a lot of evidence of his changed priorities before any of his family would be ready to believe, much less accept, what had happened to him.

When he reached his bedroom, Mark automatically removed his jacket and tie and hung them neatly in the closet. "Now what?" he said aloud. Everything had changed, but he had no idea what he should do next. His wandering eye found the books that Joe had given him, still lying on the bed where he had dropped them.

Was he supposed to pray now? It was an intimidating thought. Despite Joe's reassuring words, Mark feared he wouldn't be able to pray correctly or properly—or at all. It was such an archaic concept. How was he, living in the early twenty-first century, supposed to add that concept to his life in a way that would be—he sighed again—meaningful?

"What do I do?" he said out loud, feeling a little foolish. "I don't know what to do, where to begin."

A thought came to him, and he picked up the books. *Wishful Thinking*, that was the one he wanted. Tentatively, Mark paged through the book, and sure enough, he found an entry entitled "Prayer."

"'Everybody prays,'" he read aloud, "'whether he thinks of it as praying or not. The odd silence you fall into when something very beautiful is happening or something very good or very bad. The ah-h-h-h! that sometimes floats up out of you as out of a Fourth of July crowd when the sky-rocket bursts over the water. The stammer of pain at somebody else's pain. Whatever words or sounds you use for sighing with over your own life. These are all prayers in their way. These are all spoken not just to yourself but to something even more familiar than yourself and even more strange than the world…According to Jesus, by far the most important thing about praying is to keep at it.'" Rising emotion stopped Mark. This was like nothing he had ever heard before. Granted he knew almost nothing about praying, or about religion in general, yet what he was reading now spoke deeply to him, almost like that silent communication he had experienced in the garage a couple of hours ago.

Although Mark hadn't thought about it for many years, memories of the births of his sons came flooding back to him now, along with his long-ago feelings—the utter awe and all-encompassing joy that filled him when he first held Brian and again when he held Daniel. According to this book, those moments *had* been prayerful moments.

An even older memory nudged his thoughts, the day he had married Geneva. He had been scared to death yet so excited he could hardly think. And that night too. Geneva had wanted their honeymoon to be special, and because he loved her, Mark honored her request, so that night was the first time they came together. Thinking back, he realized that time had also been, in a very real sense, a joyously prayerful time.

With growing relief, he returned to reading. He was intrigued by the examples the author used from the Bible. Luke was one of the Gospels, he remembered Joe saying. Another example came from Matthew. That too was a Gospel. It was the passage from the Gospel of Mark that resonated most powerfully. A desperate father, a seriously ill son. The father's dialogue with Jesus struck Mark hard.

"Jesus said, 'All things are possible to him who believes.' And the father spoke for all of us when he answered, 'Lord, I believe; help my unbelief!'" Pain squeezed Mark's heart. That was him, Mark Newman. When the pain eased, he read more.

"What about when the boy is not healed? When, listened to or not listened to, the prayer goes unanswered? Who knows? Just keep praying, Jesus says."

Unanswered prayer? Mark was confused. Didn't that contradict the idea that God was always listening? He kept reading, and as he did, a new kind of pain edged with an emotion he couldn't name began to press in.

"Even if the boy dies, keep on beating the path to God's door, because the one thing you can be sure of is that down the path you beat with even your most half-cocked and halting prayer the God you call upon will finally come, and even if he does not bring you the answer you want, he will bring you himself. And maybe at the secret heart of all our prayers that is what we are really praying for."

Mark sat still, aware of but ignoring the tears sliding down his face. "I don't understand," he whispered, "but I know what happened last night and in the garage today, and I choose you, whatever that means. Thank you for…for not giving up on me. I know I gave you plenty of reasons to do that, but you didn't. I don't understand." His breath caught on a half-laugh, half-sob. "I guess you're going to be hearing that a lot from me. I don't understand what's going on. But I thank you with all I am that I'm here now, and I know you are too." He swept a hand across his face.

"I've screwed up so badly I don't know where to start. I guess you already know all about it. The worst part of it is that I've hurt the people I'm supposed to be closest to— Geneva, Brian, Daniel. How can I…" He closed his eyes, but it didn't stop the fresh tears. "I don't know what to do to help them, to heal the hurt I've caused them, to fix all the wrong that I've done to them." He laid the book aside and bent over, wrapping his arms around himself as if that could hold back the pain. "I'm sorry," Mark choked. "I'm so sorry."

There was nothing but pain and guilt and regret. He deserved it; he deserved it all. How could God not despise him as he despised himself?

The pressure eased; his breath came easier. Something brushed his consciousness, feather light, and he felt as if someone had stroked his cheek. The pain began to subside, taking with it the guilt and regret that had paralyzed him.

Wonderingly, Mark straightened up and touched his face. "Was that you?" He didn't know why he was whispering. "I don't know why you want anything to do with me, but Joe says you do. He knows a lot about you. I guess it's because he's spent most of his life getting to know you."

That triggered another memory. "I guess it hasn't always been smooth sailing between you and Joe. But you hung in there with him even when he didn't want you to. That's what he told me." The more Mark thought about that, the more wondrous it seemed. "I remember hearing—I don't know where or when—that you're both the Creator of the universe as well as its Redeemer." Hearing the words as he said them aloud made him smile through his tears.

"I'm sorry, I'm laughing at me, but I guess you already know that. A week ago, even a couple of days ago, I would have laughed at the idea. Me, Mark Newman, believing in that kind of…nonsense." He absently wiped the tears from his face. "But it's not nonsense, is it? And here I am." His brief levity faded. "So now what do I do? How do I undo the damage I've caused to the people I love most?" The last words caught in his throat, but he pushed on. "Help me, please," he whispered.

The next morning Mark had an early morning meeting with clients. It was midmorning by the time he finished, and he walked back to his office. Halfway down the hall, a figure suddenly burst out of the library and almost ran into him.

"Oh sorry, Mr. Newman!"

The young man took a quick step back, juggling the files and books in his arms. In that instant, Mark recognized him. It was the law student Jay Russell. He flashed back to what he had unintentionally overhead about the young man's family situation. Though Mark hadn't meant to eavesdrop, he still felt a little guilty.

"That's all right," Mark said, stepping aside.

In the privacy of his office, Mark sat down and dropped the messages on his desk. It seemed wherever he went, he ran into people who were struggling with their own pain.

If you really want to thank me, the next time you run across someone who needs a hand, give him yours.

His breath caught in his throat. What a time to remember the words of his rescuer. What exactly did that mean? As a new Christian, how was he supposed to react to that challenge? There was so much about this new life Mark didn't understand, but one thing he knew. No matter how true his commitment to Jesus Christ, he simply couldn't help all the people in the world. And those he was in a position to help, such as Geneva and Brian, didn't want his help. They didn't want anything to do with him.

He rubbed his head, which was aching again. So much for the distraction of coming to the office. All it had done was remind him of all that was wrong in the lives of people surrounding him.

In his mind's eye, he suddenly saw Jay Russell again, and was startled by a new thought. He considered it for a while before coming to a decision. It didn't take long, and when he was finished, he found himself facing the same thought that he had awakened with this morning. Surely this wasn't an answer to the prayer he had prayed last night before falling asleep?

"No," he muttered aloud. "This can't be from you, Lord, can it?"

The thought refused to leave him alone, and by midafternoon, Mark surrendered. After checking in with Carolyn and being assured that everything was under control, he ran out of excuses. Reluctantly, he left the office.

The next half-hour of driving went by much too quickly, and Mark found himself pulling into a parking lot he had never visited before.

"This is a bad idea," he muttered for what was probably the tenth time. He parked his car near the chain-link fence and noted only a few other cars in the vicinity. Even after he turned off the engine, he continued to sit in the car. "I shouldn't have come," he grumbled. He looked down at the key still in the ignition. All he had to do was turn it again, and he could leave.

He started and looked around in bewilderment. What was that? The car wasn't moving. There were no other cars nearby and no people, although he could hear laughter and voices in the distance. Nonetheless, he had the distinct impression that someone or something had bumped into the car.

Whether it was his imagination or something else, Mark decided to get out. Once outside, he took a deep breath before trudging slowly toward the sound of the commotion. A twenty-foot wall blocked his view, but he could hear the noise getting louder as he approached.

The gate was open, and he walked through. Several more paces brought him out from behind the building, and Mark stopped at the sight of the baseball field spread out before him. A group of young boys in uniforms were scattered across the diamond, throwing the ball back and forth and shouting encouragement and instructions to one another. He turned to survey the bleachers. Down among the first rows were several women and a surprising number of men, several chatting with each other, occasionally laughing. Between them and the kids out on the field, it was a happy-sounding noisy scene.

Mark suddenly felt self-conscious in his suit and tie. For some reason, he hadn't expected to encounter any adults. Most of the watchers were casually dressed. Even the two men in suits had removed their jackets and ties.

A shout across the field made him look in that direction in time to see the teams running off the field.

"The game's about to start," one woman said happily to her companion.

No one seemed to have noticed him, and Mark slipped quietly into a seat in the bleachers as far as he could get from the others. Once he was sitting, he felt less conspicuous, but his discomfort did not lessen.

What was he doing here? Well, he knew what he was doing here. Why had he come? That was the real question.

He had no idea how to make things better with the members of his family. Telling God about all that was on his heart had kept Mark up most of the night. At some point, he remembered Joe's suggestion about asking God to lead, so he had done that. He had also asked God to show him what he could do to begin to undo the damage he had done to his relationships with his wife and sons. Sometime after that, he had fallen asleep.

When Mark was awakened by the alarm this morning, the idea was already firmly planted in his mind. He had done his best to ignore it, following his usual routine that led him to the office and a morning filled with meetings. But the idea refused to leave him alone; instead, it seemed to grow stronger, more intrusive, as the day wore on. And here he was.

He cast a resentful look skyward and was immediately ashamed. Although he was uncomfortable being here, although he would have preferred not to come in the first place, he couldn't escape the thought that he was here as a result of God answering his prayer. How that actually worked he had no idea. He hoped that time and God would clarify that.

"Mark?"

He froze then forced himself to look up to meet astonished eyes. "Hello, Stretch."

"I thought...when I was walking over here, I thought I recognized you. But I..." Ramsey stopped, fumbling.

Mark felt a smile tug at his lips. "Surprised to see me?"

"Well, yes I am," Stretch said frankly.

"I'm surprised too," he admitted.

Ramsey's eyebrows rose, and he smiled. "You mind if I sit here?"

"No." Mark was surprised to realize he was speaking the truth. With the other man's arrival, his own feeling of discomfort began to fade.

Ramsey settled down beside him. He peered out at the field and gave a satisfied grunt. "Good, the game hasn't started yet."

Mark glanced at his watch. "Isn't it time?"

"Yes, but when I was walking by the field, I overheard one of the coaches saying that the umpire was stuck in traffic and would be ten minutes late."

Mark chuckled. "I wonder if that excuse would work in the Major Leagues."

"I seriously doubt it." Stretch laughed. He gave him a quick look before returning his gaze to the field. "It should be a good game. The last time these two teams met, it went right down to the wire. Bottom of the last inning, two out, two strikes against him, and the boy hit a home run that won the game. By one run." He shook his head admiringly. "It was a heck of a game."

Mark wanted to ask how Daniel had done in the game but swallowed the words. He was a stranger in his youngest son's life, and he had a long way to go before he would deserve the title of Dad. But something in the other man's statement caught his attention. Hadn't the other attorney mentioned that in a previous game his son had been on the opposing team?

"Is your son on Daniel's team?"

Ramsey grinned. "No, the other team. Everyone's been looking forward to this rematch between Danny's team and Sean's team, especially the boys. Sean had trouble getting to sleep last night, he was so charged about the game."

"Sean's your son."

"Uh-huh, one of three. We've also got a fourteen-year-old and an eight-year-old. I'm constantly amazed our house doesn't collapse under all the chaos of three boys. I told Lauren once she was lucky to have blond hair because it wouldn't show the gray that the kids caused her." He chuckled. "Talk about putting my foot in my mouth. I meant it as a joke, but she didn't take it that way."

Mark smiled, feeling increasingly relaxed. He was grateful for Ramsey's casual words with no questions or accusations.

"Here they come!"

Ramsey's voice broke into Mark's thoughts, and he focused on the field. What looked like a small army of boys in uniforms were spreading across the field. There were two different kinds of uniforms—one was predominantly blue, and the other was white with green trim.

"There's my boy!" Ramsey beamed and waved and shouted encouragement.

"Where?"

"He's walking past home plate. There, see? Our team will be batting first, so you're going to see Danny pitch right away. There he is."

Mark spotted the small figure in blue trotting out to the pitcher's mound, and his throat tightened. That was his son. "No. 7," he murmured.

"That's Danny." Stretch smiled even as he shook his head. "He's got a great arm and even greater control. Amazingly so for a twelve-year-old. Unfortunately, that spells bad news to the other teams."

If Daniel was such a good athlete, did that mean he might want to pursue a professional sports career one day? Shame filled Mark; he had no idea. He had been too busy making a success of his life to bother with being a father. *A success.* The word suddenly tasted bitter.

There was no way he could fix this.

No sooner had the thought crossed his mind when he remembered—he couldn't fix this, but God could, provided Mark allowed him to help. Sitting in the bleachers with a Little League game about to begin, Mark closed his eyes and whispered under his breath, "Please, Lord, help me to do what needs to be done so that I can one day be a true father to my sons."

Father. Wasn't that one of the names of God in the Bible?

Mark swallowed to try to dispel the pressure in his throat. He suddenly decided he was going to look up every reference to *father* he could find in the Bible. Maybe that would help him begin to get an idea of what he needed to do in order to become who he needed to become for his sons.

19

"Ow!"

He started and opened his eyes to see Ramsey groaning beside him.

Ramsey gave Mark a pained look. "For being such a nice kid, Danny shows no mercy when he pitches. First up, first out, how are we supposed to win against that?"

Mark had missed it. Chagrined, he turned his attention back to the field. Although he had never had time for sports, he had picked up enough miscellaneous information over the years to be able to follow the game. When he finally decided to come this afternoon, he hadn't been sure what to expect other than a bunch of kids playing baseball, which made the teams' performances all the more impressive.

Watching, Mark realized he didn't have the expertise to note all the fine details of play. When an outfielder on Daniel's team wasn't able to get under the ball to catch it and a runner scored, the groans that reverberated across the field surprised him until Ramsey enlightened him.

"Didn't keep his eye on the ball." Ramsey shook his head. "A common error, the coach is probably tearing his hair out."

"But it's just a game," Mark protested. Why did people get so worked up by children playing sports? He was surprised by Stretch's look of exasperation.

"It's not just a game. Play-offs are starting in a couple of weeks, and both of these teams are contenders." He studied his companion. "Stick around for a few more games, and then we'll see if you still feel the same."

Mark had no problem picking up the subtext. Ramsey thought that if he was exposed to Little League games on a regular basis, he might become as enthusiastic as the other adults here seemed to be. Maybe so. If it would help him take a few shaky steps toward building a relationship with his son, he was willing.

It was a beautiful day to be outside, sunny and not too warm. After a couple of innings, he found himself thoroughly involved, though most of his attention remained on his son. He was surprised and impressed by Daniel's abilities. He walked only one runner, gave up just one hit, and struck out or made the other runners pop up the ball for easy catches.

Mark didn't expect much when it came Daniel's turn to bat. Ramsey had explained earlier that while an excellent pitcher, the boy was only an average hitter. Nonetheless, Mark was gripped by an intensity that surprised him, an intensity that broke through his normal reserve and took him to his feet cheering on his son.

The first time he did it, he saw Daniel's head swing in his direction. Unsure if the boy could see him, Mark waved while calling encouragement. "You can do it, Dan!" he yelled enthusiastically and yelled even louder when Daniel's swing caught enough of the ball to send it bouncing past the pitcher's outstretched mitt. Daniel raced down the line and slid into first, barely avoiding the baseman's attempt to tag him out.

"Yes!" Mark exclaimed. "Did you see that? An average hitter, huh?"

"I saw," Ramsey chuckled. "That was pretty good. I'm betting seeing you here gave him extra incentive."

"You don't really think…" Mark felt oddly shaken by the words.

All amusement faded from the other man's face. "Yes, I do."

Mark looked away. After years of ignoring his sons, he didn't deserve to have his presence matter to Daniel.

He watched the rest of the game, trying to take it all in even while knowing it was impossible. On one level, the sight of little boys playing baseball was strangely warming. On another, watching his son participating in a game at which he excelled was humbling. Despite his father's neglect, Daniel had managed not only to survive but to create a life filled with friends and activities. Daniel had done this despite his tender years, despite his father.

Mark swallowed. He deserved to feel guilty for what he had done, but he couldn't escape the thought that God didn't want him to continue to wallow in it. It seemed too easy—to ask for forgiveness for his failings and then it was all behind him. He did his best to ignore the troubling thought and focus on the field and began to realize how important this game was to the kids. They were cheering each other on, running and throwing as if their lives depended on it. At the center of it all, for Mark, was his twelve-year-old son. He was amazed at the boy's coolness despite the pressure of a close game. Daniel only got on base one more time when he was walked, but another teammate hit a triple that enabled him to score.

Mark watched and marveled, regretting that it had taken twelve years of his son's life to have his father finally see him doing something he loved. If he occasionally had to blink back unwanted moisture in his eyes, Stretch Ramsey didn't appear to notice.

By the end of the fifth inning he was exhausted. "I don't know how much longer I can keep this up," he admitted.

Ramsey chuckled. "I know what you mean, but there's just one inning left."

"One?" That didn't sound right.

"Usually, there are just six innings in a Little League game."

"Six? I thought…" Mark stopped, embarrassed. He had assumed the game would have nine innings, like a Major League game, because that was all he knew.

"Here we go." Ramsey's grin was wide with anticipation. "Two to two, one inning to go. It should be a whale of an ending!"

On the heels of his words, Mark saw his son trotting out onto the field again, and his throat tightened. The boy's uniform showed the effects of the game, streaked with dirt and grass stains from running (and sliding) the bases as well as his occasional dives trying to catch balls that were batted back at him. A streak of dirt also ran down the side of Daniel's face that Mark didn't know how he had gotten.

He had to chuckle at the sight of the disheveled but determined little figure, a chuckle composed of equal parts of amusement and pride. And love. How could Mark have had this little boy in his life for twelve years and not realized how much he loved him? How could he have allowed anything to come between him and his son?

I'm so sorry, Danny, Mark thought in the privacy of his heart. *I have so much to make up for, but I promise that with God's help, I'll learn to be the kind of father you deserve.*

The crowd yelled, and Ramsey groaned.

Mark looked out into the field. "What?" he demanded, angry with himself for missing what had happened.

"Two pitches and Danny gets him to pop up," Stretch moaned, shaking his head. "One out and the inning's just started."

"Yes!" Mark yelled belatedly. "You go, Dan!"

This time there was no doubting it. For a second, Daniel turned his head, and his eyes met his father's.

Mark felt tears welling up at the shock in the boy's expression. Forcing them back, he grinned broadly. "You can do it, son!"

For another beat, Daniel continued to stare at him before turning back to the next batter.

Nerves fluttered in Mark's stomach. "I didn't mean to distract him. I shouldn't have said anything."

Ramsey smacked him on the arm. "Don't be thick," he said. "You're here. That means more than you can know to Danny."

It was still hard for Mark to believe that his presence could mean so much to Daniel. But this wasn't about Mark; it was about his son. He needed to remember that.

The second out was harder to get. The young batter ended up with a full count, three balls and two strikes, then fouled the next several pitches. The two young athletes battled, while Mark felt his heart rising in his throat with each pitch.

"Come on, Sean!" Ramsey urged.

Mark was startled. He had gotten so wrapped up in his son's performance he had forgotten that Stretch's son was playing for the other team. "That's your son trying to get a hit off my son?" he demanded.

"Yep," Ramsey said without taking his eyes off the scene.

"He helped score a run in the third inning," Mark remembered.

"Yep. And it looks like Danny's getting tired."

"He is?" Mark stared harder.

"It's not surprising. He's pitched a heck of a game. But you can tell"—his words were cut off by an exclamation, and he jumped to his feet—"run, Sean!"

Sean had finally got a solid hit and the ball soared high in the air.

"Go, go, go!" Ramsey was yelling.

"Get that ball!" Mark heard himself shout.

The center outfielder was backing up, backing, backing, one hand raised to shield his eyes from the sun while the other hand waited, mitt ready.

Ramsey groaned. "So close!"

"Yes!" Mark yelled happily as the equally happy outfielder turned in a circle, mitt still raised to show the ball nestled firmly within.

The third out came unexpectedly fast, when the next batter hit a pitch straight back at Daniel. Mark's heart leaped in his throat, then his legs felt suddenly shaky when his son caught the ball.

"Way to go, kiddo!" he yelled jubilantly. He fell back down to his seat, suddenly limp. Something of his feelings must have showed because Ramsey chuckled.

"It takes a lot of energy watching the kids play, especially when our kids are involved." Ramsey said.

Mark nodded. He was tired, yes, but he also felt good in a way he couldn't identify. "I'd say I was sorry that Daniel's team won, but that would be a lie."

"I wouldn't believe you, anyway." Ramsey stretched and yawned. "It looks like these two teams are going to be playing again during the play-offs."

"Really?"

"There's only one other team with a better record than ours. They've got two of the best hitters in Little League and one of the best pitchers. However," he added with a grin at Mark, "Danny's a better pitcher, and Sean's team has a great infield. The play-offs should be a lot of fun."

"I'm looking forward to them," Mark said, recognizing the truth in the words after he spoke them. As fun as it had been watching the boys playing this afternoon, it had been more than fun that kept him focused on his son. Seeing the players walking off the field, he had a thought. "Where are they going?"

"Back to the buses. Except for the kids whose parents are here and will be driving them home."

Eagerness warred with uncertainty in Mark. He wanted to take Daniel home, but would his son want to come with him?

"I need to pick up Sean." Ramsey was standing now. "You coming?"

Mark followed him off the bleachers, but instead of heading toward the parking lot, Stretch went in the opposite direction, walking around the perimeter of the field until they came to an exit that led to a smaller parking lot. Two buses were parked, and the players were milling around them, talking and laughing and occasionally high-fiving each other.

"Now where's that kid of mine?" Ramsey muttered.

Mark wondered about his own son. Thanks to the crowd of boys, he didn't immediately see Daniel.

"Sean," Stretch called, and one of the green-and-white uniformed boys turned and waved. He had been talking to another boy, this one in the other team's uniform, who also looked around. Mark's breath caught when he recognized his son. Daniel stared at him, not moving for a minute, then he trailed after his friend.

Despite a hard-fought six inning game, Sean Ramsey was still bouncing when he reached his father. "Hey, Dad, what'd you think?"

"Great game," Ramsey said heartily, tousling his son's already mussed red hair. "Right down to the wire."

"Yeah, too bad we didn't win, but we'll get 'em next time!" The last was said over Sean's shoulder, obviously directed at Daniel, who grinned smugly.

"In your dreams," Daniel jeered.

Mark was watching, totally absorbed at this side of the son he had always considered shy and withdrawn. He had never imagined that Daniel had a secret life—no, not secret. If Mark had paid any attention to his son, he would have known. It wasn't the first time this afternoon the thought had crossed his mind, but it still tasted bitter.

"I've got to admit, Danny," Ramsey said, "that was a heck of a performance."

"Thanks, Mr. Ramsey."

The boy's voice softened and held a new note of hesitancy. Mark didn't understand it until Daniel looked at him. In those expressive blue eyes he saw a world of emotion—surprise, confusion, nervousness, and hope.

It was the last two emotions that broke Mark's heart. He spoke without thinking. "He's right. You pitched a great game."

Daniel's eyes shone so brightly Mark felt blinded. His son glanced at his friend, then at his friend's father.

Ramsey cleared his throat. "We'd better head for home. Mark, I'll be talking to you. And Danny"—he pointed his finger at the child and waggled his eyebrows—"you keep pitching like that, and no one's going to have a chance against you."

"Hey!" Sean protested. "I almost got a hit off him today."

Ramsey put an arm around his son's shoulders and pulled him against him. "Foul balls do not make a hit, buddy."

The boy huffed indignantly and squirmed away from his father. "Dad, we're in public!"

Daniel snickered. "So much for your reputation."

Sean glared at him. "Not one word, Newman."

"Come on, we've got to go." Stretch swatted his son on the back.

"I'm going, but I gotta ask you something, Dad."

"Mark, later," Ramsey said as he started walking away. He turned to his son. "What do you want to ask?"

"When are you going to get glasses?"

"Hey!"

The pair headed off, laughter trailing behind them.

Mark watched them go before turning back to his son. Daniel was still watching him. The emotions Mark had seen earlier were no longer visible, except for uncertainty. Guilt rose, dampening his pleasure. He had only himself to blame for his son's insecurity. For a minute, he felt paralyzed, unsure what to say or do. A man's voice called out, and Mark looked over automatically. It was one of the coaches, standing by the bus and waving the boys over.

Daniel looked too, then at his father. He took a step away, hesitated, then another step. "I guess, um, that I should—"

"Would you like a ride home?" Mark interrupted. He couldn't bear the look in his son's eyes. Worse than uncertainty, the expectation of disappointment broke his heart all over again.

Daniel stopped. "With you?" he said doubtfully.

Mark smiled, hoping the tears in his throat could not be heard when he spoke. "Of course, with me."

Daniel looked at his teammates filing into the bus, and Mark realized he couldn't breathe when the boy started walking after them. Suddenly he was running, and all Mark could do was watch his son racing away from him. The tears pressed harder against his eyelids, and he lowered his head so no one could see while he fought for control.

This was his fault, no one else's.

He breathed shallowly, afraid the pain would overwhelm him if he tried to draw in deeper breaths. In a minute, in a few minutes, when he had his emotions under control, he would go back to his car, and he didn't know what he would do.

"Okay, I'm ready!"

Mark jerked his head up to see Daniel standing in front of him again, bright with anticipation. Confused, he looked toward the bus and saw the coach still standing there, ushering the last of the boys inside.

"I...I thought," he stammered, "you were going with them."

Daniel looked at the bus. "I had to tell the coach I was going home with my dad."

The simple words almost undid Mark. He nodded, swallowed, then smiled. "Let's go."

He was very aware of the small figure—the small, silent figure—beside him while they walked to the car. Remembering Sean Ramsey chattering with his father, Mark suddenly couldn't stand the silence. "Tell me about the game," he said, barely hiding his desperation.

Daniel looked up at him, brows drawn together. "But you saw it." Confusion gave way to trepidation. "Didn't you? I thought I saw you before."

"Yes, I saw," Mark said quickly. "But I don't know what it was like from your perspective."

"My perspective?" Daniel wrinkled his nose.

Mark smiled at the expression. "What it was like for you."

Daniel nodded slowly. "Okay."

Mark didn't realize it until later, but he had hit on the perfect subject to keep his son talking. Throughout the drive home, Daniel gave him an inning-by-inning summary of the highs and lows of the game. The names of the players meant nothing to Mark, so he occasionally had trouble following what the boy was saying. It didn't matter. It was enough to listen to his son's voice and try to ignore his lingering sense of guilt. He didn't want anything to get in the way of his enjoyment of this rare time with his son.

They were only a few blocks from home when Daniel finally began to run down. "I didn't think we were going to be able to pull it out at the end," he said. "Those other guys are really tough. They beat us last time."

"I know," Mark said. "But even though they were tough, your team was tougher today."

"Uh-huh," Daniel agreed, sounding preoccupied.

Mark wasn't sure what had triggered it, and he debated how to respond. Before he decided, Daniel said, "You knew they beat us last time?"

"That's right."

"So…you've been following my team?"

The uncertainty in the young voice hit him in the stomach like a fist, and seconds passed before he could breathe again. For a minute, he contemplated an extravagant lie but immediately gave up the idea. If he was going to have any chance of rebuilding a relationship with his youngest son, it couldn't be by lying. Only the truth would work, though Mark flinched from it.

"Stretch—Mr. Ramsey told me at the game today." He glanced sideways and saw the small shoulders slump and barely heard the soft "Oh." Mark hurried on, not giving himself time to chicken out. "I'm ashamed to admit it, but today is the first time I saw one of your games, Danny."

"Ashamed?" Daniel repeated, and Mark heard bewilderment in his son's voice.

"Yes. You see, I owe you a big apology." It was strange; the words hadn't been as hard to say as he had expected.

"You do?"

"Yes, I do." Mark hesitated. How did he explain what he was just beginning to understand about himself? *Keep it simple*, he decided.

When they turned onto their street, he reached up to the visor and pressed the automatic garage-door opener. By the time he pulled into the driveway, the door was fully up, and he coasted into the garage and parked. The rope still lay piled in the corner, and when Mark saw it, he felt his resolve stiffening. After turning off the engine, he unfastened his seat belt and turned to face his son who was watching him.

The sight of that young face twisted Mark's heart. Daniel deserved so much more than he had received from his father. It was impossible to go back, but things could begin to change today, this moment.

"I haven't been a very good father," Mark confessed, trying to keep his voice steady. He saw Daniel's eyes widen and forced himself to continue. "I got so busy with work I forget to spend time with you and your brother." *And Geneva*, he thought but kept it to himself. This wasn't about Mark's marital issues. "I know you must have felt…ignored sometimes and…" His voice cracked, and he took some deep breaths before going on. "I'm very sorry, son. You're a great kid, and you deserve better. You always have. I can't change the mistakes I made in the past, but I would like to try to be your dad." His throat closed up, and he waited for several beats until the pressure eased. "Would that be okay with you?"

It was the sixty-four-thousand-dollar question, and he had no idea how his son would answer it. Daniel was still staring at him as if he had never seen him before. The thought only added to the pain in Mark's heart, though he did his best not to show it.

"What does that mean?" the boy finally asked cautiously.

It meant more than Mark could say, more than he thought he understood at this point. At least he had some ideas that he hoped were good ones. "I'd like to watch more of your games, spend more time with you, doing things that you like to do." He tried to smile. "I'm afraid that other than baseball, I don't know what any of those things are."

Daniel looked away, as if thinking. After a minute, he said quietly, "I, um, I like camping."

Mark blinked back tears at his son's willingness to expose himself. "You do?"

"Uh-huh. I went camping last summer with Eric Machado and his family." Hesitancy was replaced by growing confidence as Daniel warmed to his explanation. "It was really fun, even though his sister was a pain." He wrinkled his nose at the memory. "She's seven and wanted to do everything we did, but she's too little."

"What kinds of things did you and Eric do?"

Daniel smiled and the lightening of his expression warmed Mark. "We went swimming in the lake a lot, and we explored too, and we made boats out of twigs and leaves. They floated really good. And I helped Eric find some rocks for his collection. He has lots of rocks. And we hiked a lot, and Mr. Machado taught us the names of the trees and how to recognize different kinds of plants. Did you know that Indians used to make all kinds of remedies from plants?"

Mark smiled too. This chattering little boy was someone he didn't recognize but wanted desperately to know better. "I think I remember hearing about that when I was in school. It sounds like you had a lot of fun."

"I did." Daniel looked up at him, suddenly serious. "Do you like camping?"

"To be honest, I've never been camping. But I'd like to," Mark added hastily at his son's look of disappointment. "You could show me all the things you learned."

"I could do that," Daniel agreed, his smile restored. His stomach chose that moment to growl loudly, and Mark chuckled at his son's surprise as Daniel stared down at his midsection.

"It sounds like someone is hungry," he teased.

"I'm starving!" Daniel exclaimed as if he had never eaten before.

"Well, let's go do something about that."

Before he opened the car door, Mark reached out to give his son's shoulder a gentle squeeze and was rewarded with a brilliant smile. Though he wouldn't have thought it was possible, his heart swelled with even more love, this time edged with gratitude. It was nothing less than a miracle that his youngest child, the child he had so shamefully ignored, was willing to give Mark a second chance at being a father. Such acceptance, such forgiveness, how would he ever be able to thank Daniel for that?

By being the kind of father Daniel needs.

The words came from deep within, and Mark blinked back fresh tears. There was only one Person who could have effected such a miracle.

Thank you, Lord, he whispered from the depths of his heart.

20

Daniel pushed the door open and hurried inside. Following, Mark was startled to hear the boy yelp in delight, "Chicken and dumplings, my favorite!"

Chicken and dumplings were a favorite meal of his son? Mark had just learned something else about Daniel.

"Don't you even think about sitting down until you've washed your hands," a vaguely familiar voice said with a laugh.

Mark reached the kitchen and saw Amy Kittredge, the housekeeper. Her eyes widened in surprise at the sight of him, and he smiled as he closed the door behind him. "Good evening."

"Good evening, Mr. Newman." She turned her attention to Daniel. "Well? I don't see you washing your hands yet. Have you changed your mind about eating?"

"Nope!" Daniel hurried to the sink.

Mark watched him, delighted to see his son relaxed and happy. Obviously, the boy had a good relationship with the housekeeper, and he was glad to know that. He looked back at her and met her intent gaze. Recognizing both confusion and apprehension in her eyes, he tried to set her at ease.

"Is everything all right? I didn't think you stayed this late."

"Everything's fine as far as I know. Mrs. Newman called a couple hours ago to ask if I would spend the night."

Mark's eyebrows rose involuntarily. "Spend the night?"

"I washed my hands," Daniel said, suddenly appearing. His expectant smile dimmed when he looked from one adult to the other.

Amy Kittredge patted his shoulder. "Then sit down. I've been keeping the food warm in the oven. Let me set it out, and you can dig in."

"Great." Daniel eyed his father uncertainly. "Are you, um—"

"I'm going to eat with you," Mark said quickly, hoping he was reading his son's expression correctly. "If that's all right."

"Sure." The shadows left Daniel's eyes, and he was beaming again. He went directly to the breakfast nook and sat down.

Amy laughed, gave Mark another uncertain look, then went to the stove.

"Dad? Are you going to sit down?" Daniel asked.

"Yes, I am," Mark assured the eager boy. "Let me just run upstairs and drop these." He gestured at his suit jacket and tie that he had slung over his shoulder.

"Okay, but you better hurry. I don't know how much I'm going to leave for you."

Mark stared at his son but realized he wasn't imagining things. The glint of mischief in Daniel's eyes was genuine, and he was overwhelmed by this grace. Unable to speak, he smiled again before leaving. In his bedroom, he started to hang up his jacket and tie then changed his mind. After today, his suit would need to go to the dry cleaners.

Mark laughed softly at himself, awed by the new emotions that had somehow been released within him. "I don't think I'll ever understand all that your grace involves," he whispered, "but thank you for helping me to recognize it the other day in the garage and with Daniel today."

He went to his desk, took the Bible Joe had given him and set it gently on the bed. *Tonight*, he promised. Tonight he would sit down and open this book and begin to know the One who had reached down from heaven and lifted him out of the darkness that had become his life.

Mark ran a gentle hand over the Bible, marveling at how the Creator and Redeemer of the universe had gone to such effort to reach his fallen children. For the first time, he realized it would take more than a lifetime to understand. What a journey that would be.

Right now, he needed to get back downstairs. Daniel was waiting for him. The joy of that simple fact almost brought him to tears again.

Where was Brian? The new thought broke into his happiness. Suddenly fearful, he couldn't wait to get back to the kitchen. He wouldn't be able to relax until he knew his older son was all right.

He walked out of his bedroom and hesitated. Maybe Brian was already in his room. He hadn't seen the teenager since Brian stormed out of the garage—had it actually just been yesterday? Mark had been left sitting in his car, drowning in despair. Then when hopelessness seemed to be all he would ever know, God swept into his heart, driving out all the chill and darkness and filling him with warmth and life and a joy that passed understanding.

Mark had never believed that the term "broken heart" was anything other than a colorful colloquialism. Now he knew better. The thought of his oldest son, still torn by anger and fear and worst, by despair, hurt him as he had never known he could hurt. Last night he hadn't dared approach Brian, and this morning when he woke, the boy had already left for school. As glad as Mark was for being able to spend part of the day beginning to connect with his youngest son, he also desperately wanted to begin to rebuild his relationship with his older son.

Patience. It wouldn't, couldn't, happen overnight.

Mark sighed again at the unwelcome thought but couldn't deny its truth. First things first, he needed to go downstairs and join his son for dinner. He hoped he would get a chance to talk to Amy Kittredge about Brian, but he'd play that by ear.

After a quick glimpse in Brian's room—which was empty—he went downstairs. When he walked into the kitchen, he found Daniel eating and the housekeeper sitting opposite him, drinking a cup of coffee and listening while the boy replayed the game for her.

Mark couldn't help smiling as he approached. "You missed an exciting game," he said.

Amy Kittredge smiled in return. "So I hear."

"Dad." Daniel stopped to swallow his mouthful. "Come on, while it's still hot."

There was an edge of uncertainty in both his expression and his voice, as if he expected his father to turn into the reserved, neglectful man he had known all his life.

Mark swallowed a pang of regret. "It smells delicious."

"It is," his son garbled around another large bite.

Amy Kittredge rose. "Would you like something to drink?"

Mark was struck by a sense of déjà vu. It took a few seconds before he remembered she had asked him the same question that first day they met, less than two weeks ago. It felt more like a lifetime.

"Coffee would be great, thank you," he said as he sat down across from his son. Fragrant aromas came from the covered bowl in the center of the table, and Mark realized he was hungry. A memory of the beef stew he had recently eaten in this kitchen flashed through his mind, and his stomach rumbled.

Daniel laughed and quickly covered his mouth. After swallowing, he lowered his hand and said, "I think you need to eat right away."

Amy laid a plate and silverware in front of Mark. "Dig in."

He picked up the serving spoon and served himself a large helping of the chicken, then the dumplings from the other bowl.

Daniel swallowed another mouthful and gestured with his fork at an aluminum-foil-covered platter. "Biscuits," he identified. "Amy makes the best biscuits."

"Thank you, kind sir," she said, smiling as she moved back to the stove.

Daniel was right. The biscuits were delicious, particularly with the chicken and dumplings. The vegetables included in the meal were tender but not overcooked, and Mark had to force himself to eat slowly, savoring the different flavors that made up a wonderful whole.

"Do I taste onions?" Mark asked.

"Pearl onions," Amy acknowledged, "and carrots and peas." She gave him an amused look. "Do you want me to list all of the ingredients?"

"No, thank you, I'll just enjoy them as I eat."

Ten days ago, Mark couldn't have imagined sitting in the breakfast nook eating with his youngest son while the housekeeper stood by, kibitzing. Once again, he was reminded of how much had changed in his life during a startling short period of time.

"I take it that Brian already ate?" he asked.

Amy's smile faded, only to return when Daniel looked up from his meal. "Yes," she said matter-of-factly.

Mark heard the lie she tried to hide. He was careful not to react; he didn't want Daniel to pick up his concern. As soon as the boy was out of earshot, Mark would ask the housekeeper about Geneva's and Brian's whereabouts.

It took longer than he expected. Daniel seemed to be enjoying this time with his newly approachable father and was in no hurry to bring it to an end. Not until Mark asked if his son had any homework did the boy reluctantly get to his feet.

"I'll see you later, I guess," Daniel said.

Mark's throat tightened at the return of the boy's uncertainty. "Count on it," he said firmly and was rewarded by a smile. Daniel probably feared his father would return to his old habits. Only time would be able to convince the twelve-year-old that he had changed. Or so Mark prayed.

He waited until the boy was gone before turning to Amy Kittredge. "Where is Brian?"

She looked away briefly before meeting his gaze. "I don't know. He came home after school but left again about a half-hour later. I haven't seen or heard from him since."

Mark took several deep breaths. He was not going to lose control. "Is this typical?"

"It's…it's not unusual," the housekeeper admitted.

The old habits he had just been thinking were gone abruptly roared back to life. "Why didn't you—" He stopped, biting back angry words. Amy Kittredge was a housekeeper, not a parent. It wasn't her duty to keep track of the boys. *Lord, help me. Please.* Seeing annoyance flare in her eyes, he raised an apologetic hand. "I'm sorry. I know it's not your responsibility. Did he say anything about where he might be going?"

"No. Maybe you could try his cell phone. I don't have that number."

But she expected he would. A fresh wave of guilt swept through him. He had no idea what that number might be. "I'll try that," he agreed, hoping he looked more confident than he felt. "Can you tell me what my wife said when she asked you to spend the night?"

Amy cradled her coffee cup in both hands. "She said she didn't think she'd be home so could I stay the night. Luckily, I was free, so I said yes."

Geneva wasn't coming home tonight. She had planned not to come home tonight. At least that ruled out any kind of accident. So what was she doing? Several possible scenarios ran swiftly through his mind, each one worse than the last.

"Mr. Newman?"

"Yes?" he said distractedly.

"Your wife didn't sound…that is…" The woman looked a little lost. "I couldn't help thinking when I heard her that she was, well, sad." Amy Kittredge looked uncomfortable.

Sad? He thought back to that brief, difficult conversation with his wife about her friend who was ill. Was that it? Is that where she was? Although he rarely used it, Mark did have her cell phone number programmed in his own cell phone. As soon as he was alone, he would try calling her. He only hoped she answered. For now, a change of subject seemed to be in order.

"You say you've stayed overnight before?" he asked. They had two guest rooms on the second floor, but he had never seen the housekeeper wandering around up there.

"Yes." Amy pointed at the window that overlooked the backyard. "In the guest cottage."

Mark nodded, hoping his surprise was not noticeable. He had forgotten about the little one-room cottage at the rear of the property. "Of course," he said, suddenly unable to sit still another minute. He rose. "Thank you for the delicious meal."

"I'm glad you enjoyed it."

Back in his bedroom, Mark first called his wife's cell phone. He left a message when the voice mail came on, then turned to the file cabinet. Sure enough, he found a paid bill with a number on it he didn't recognize. When he tried it, he heard his oldest son's voice. "Hey, you know who you called. Leave your number, and I'll call you back. Maybe."

He sighed, but when the voice mail clicked on, he said matter-of-factly, "Brian, please call me. I'm at home so you can use that number or else my cell phone." He left the number and hung up, fighting back rising frustration.

Standing in the middle of his bedroom, Mark felt a little lost. He needed to talk to Geneva; he needed to talk to Brian. But he wasn't certain what to say to either his wife or son. Neither of them would be impressed by an apology or a promise to do better. Only his actions could show them that he was sincere and that wasn't going to happen overnight.

He paced around the room, feeling as if he needed to be doing something but unsure what that was. Then he remembered; he'd promised God to spend time with the Bible. That led to another thought. Just a few hours earlier, he wanted to look up the term *father* in the Bible. This was the perfect opportunity.

Picking up the Bible, Mark went to his desk and sat down. He pulled out a legal pad from a desk drawer and opened the Bible. It fell open halfway through, and he began to flip the pages. Suddenly he stopped. A verse leaped out of the surrounding text as if it had been highlighted. "Be careful, or your hearts will be weighed down with dissipation, drunkenness and the anxieties of life, and that day will close on you unexpectedly like a trap" (Luke 21:34). Brian's face appeared before him, and Mark closed his eyes in pain. Joe had warned him against wallowing in guilt, but it was hard not to. Suddenly angry with himself, he jerked to his feet. He had something to do before he did anything else.

He took bottle after bottle out of the liquor cabinet. One by one, he poured the alcohol in the sink until they were all empty. Then he took the bottles out to the garage and put them in the recycle bin.

His actions didn't ease his pain, yet he felt as if he had passed a test. Perhaps for the first time in his life, at least for the first time in more years than he could remember, he had done something for someone else that could not benefit him.

What about going to Daniel's Little League game earlier today? asked that now-familiar small voice. *Didn't that count?*

No, Mark knew better. He had gone to the game in the hope of beginning to undo years of neglecting his son, as well as—he hoped—beginning to heal the breach in his relationship with Daniel. Was this action any different? Mark had emptied out the liquor cabinet as one small step to aid his older son in the boy's battle with alcohol. It was just one aspect of a healing process that was going to take a long time. Standing there, he prayed that the end of that process would result not only in physical healing for Brian but also the healing of their relationship.

He rubbed his forehead, trying to massage away the beginnings of a headache. "Isn't anything simple, Lord?"

The air in the garage was chilly, but Mark didn't want to leave. He had turned on only one of the overhead lights when he first entered, but it was bright enough to see clearly. Inexorably, his gaze turned to the coil of rope. He reached down to touch it; the hemp was still damp, and the faint musty smell he had noticed earlier was stronger.

Why did he still cling to the rope? It had saved his life ten days ago, granted. And maybe, it had served as some kind of conduit, triggering his awareness of the overwhelming presence of God.

Tears pressed against Mark's eyelids. Regardless of any other reason, the rope was a reminder of his near-death and rebirth both physically and spiritually. On impulse, he gathered the rope up in his arms and carried it out of the garage to the backyard patio. There, he began to lay the rope out in a long line, edging the patio and running up and down the walkways. When Mark finished, he stood back to survey his work. This time of night, the rope was little more than a narrow shadow on the ground. He was glad he hadn't laid it out on the large lawn. The automatic sprinklers that kept it green and lush would ensure the rope never dried.

Now the rope could dry properly. Once that happened, Mark was going to coil it up and find a permanent place for it in the garage. Maybe he had become sentimental in his old age; he didn't care. He wanted to remember all that had happened in the past weeks. Every time he looked at the rope, he would remember.

He paused on the patio and looked up. There were no clouds tonight and the stars glittered brilliantly in the night sky, like countless diamonds thrown across black velvet.

"Thank you," he said softly. "I know it's not going to be easy but"—he swallowed—"thank you for giving me the opportunity to try...and for the certainty that you'll be part of it."

21

Mark went back inside, and when he reached his bedroom again, the first thing he did was to check his cell phone. Neither Geneva nor Brian had returned his calls. He took a deep breath; a look at his watch reminded him that it was only a little after nine p.m. There was no reason to think the worst.

The sight of the Bible on his desk beside a legal pad reminded Mark of his earlier plan. When he sat down, he deliberately didn't look at the verse that had struck him so hard less than an hour ago but turned directly to the end of the Bible. Then he had to skip backward, past several maps that he decided he would look at later, and finally stopped when he reached the concordance.

Mark's eyebrows arched in surprise at what he found. Joe had said this was only an abbreviated concordance yet there was over a column of verses listed under *father*. It seemed logical to begin with the first reference.

"Honor your father...

"Anyone who curses his father...must be put to death."

His heart sank as he read through several verses. How could you honor someone you despised?

He hadn't thought about his father for years, and he hadn't even realized it until recently. The returning memories weren't slipping smoothly into his consciousness but dropping into place as jarring thuds, shaking him to his core.

When Mark was growing up, his father, William Newman, had been a highly successful businessman and president of the largest bank in the city. He ran the institution with an iron fist that was usually hidden by a smooth exterior. Unfortunately, he ran his family the same way.

Sitting at his desk now, the Bible open before him, Mark cringed. Instead of dealing with those memories, he had buried them. Now almost twenty years after his father's death, the memories were returning, as sharp and painful as ever.

"I tried," he whispered, "For years, I tried so hard to please him, but I couldn't." He scrubbed roughly at stinging eyes. "Nothing I did pleased him. All he ever did was criticize and condemn. I was an embarrassment. He was ashamed I was his son..." His voice cracked, and minutes passed before he could speak again.

"I was afraid of him. And I...I hated him." He took several breaths until the pressure in his throat eased. "I still hate him," he confessed in a whisper. "I swore I would be a better man. More successful, a better husband, a better father. So how…how did I turn into him?"

The pain was crushing.

Some interminable time later, he realized the pain receded, not a lot but enough to enable Mark to refocus. He looked down at the text again and sighed.

"I have so much to learn about you, Lord, and about what you want for me, but I believe you don't want me hating my father. Except…I don't know how not to hate him. I don't know how to forgive him." He squeezed his eyes shut. "I don't want to forgive him," he admitted. "He doesn't deserve it, not the way he treated me and…" He swallowed, but it didn't ease the pressure in his throat. "And my mother. Lord, I can't believe I haven't thought of her all these years. She died when I was…" Regret filled him. "I was seven? Eight? I don't remember." The shame bit deeply. "I suppose I was trying so hard not to think about him I forgot about a lot of other things too."

It was no excuse. Now that he had allowed himself to remember, Mark clearly recalled how much she had loved him, and his feelings of regret and shame deepened. So did his confusion. Where did he go with all of this? Would confessing his countless shortcomings to God change everything? Would it relieve his guilt, change his feelings about his father? It sounded much too simple and also impossible.

"I don't know what I should do about...about all this. Please help me to figure out what to do."

Mark waited while the minutes ticked by, but no inspiration struck. Maybe this was another one of those situations that fell into Joe's it-would-take-time for change to happen. Finally, he rubbed his eyes and looked again at the Bible under his hand. He was reluctant to read anymore, considering the admonitions he had already encountered. Still, he couldn't shake the feeling that he needed to continue.

As he expected, he found additional verses containing the same kind of language, but he noticed a new trend. Now the Bible was identifying God as a father, and Mark wasn't sure what to make of it. His concept of father was negative in the extreme, and although he didn't believe that God intended fathers to be like William Newman, Mark was increasingly convinced that he wouldn't be able to change his own attitude about the concept of fatherhood. He could only hope that Joe knew what he was talking about. He sighed again. Here was another issue he needed to raise with the only expert on Christianity whom he knew—his brother-in-law.

Wait, here was something. "As a father has compassion on his children, so the Lord has compassion on those who fear him" (Ps. 103:13).

Mark sat back with a frown. Fear? God wanted people to fear him? That didn't fit with his slight knowledge of God, and it certainly didn't fit into what had happened to him in the garage—was it just yesterday? It was hard to believe. It seemed the more verses he read the more questions he had. His eyes turned to the beginning of the psalm.

> Praise the Lord, O my soul;
> all my inmost being, praise his holy name.
> Praise the Lord, O my soul,
> and forget not all his benefits—
> who forgives all your sins
> and heals all your diseases,
> who redeems your life from the pit
> and crowns you with love and compassion,
> who satisfies your desires with good things
> so that your youth is renewed like the eagle's.

The words began to blur, and he stopped reading to wipe his eyes. This was the God he had encountered in the garage; this was the God he wanted to know better and to follow, whatever that meant.

When he reached the New Testament passages, Mark found more verses identifying God as a father. He was particularly intrigued with the verses in the Gospels in which Jesus identified God as *his* father. The relationship within the Trinity and the Trinity itself totally confused him, but remembering Joe's comments, he was reassured by the thought that he wasn't the only one confused.

"No one has seen the Father except the one who is from God; only he has seen the Father" (Jn. 6:46).

Mark scratched his head. There was more going on here than a simple identification of God as Jesus's father. He needed to start making a list of the questions he wanted to ask Joe.

By the time he finished reading the *father* references listed in the concordance, Mark was glad this was an "abbreviated" concordance. He felt as if his head was about to explode with all his questions.

He carefully closed the Bible and looked at it for a long minute. How relevant to today were the contents of a book that was written how long ago? Hundreds of years? Thousands?

"I don't know what to think," he said softly. "I can't find a simple description of what a father is supposed to be. I guess the verses identifying you as a father are the closest but…" Mark shook his head in frustration. "You're God. How am I supposed to be like you?"

He glanced absently at his watch and straightened so fast he almost slid off of his chair. It was almost midnight. A quick look at his cell phone confirmed he had no messages waiting. Where were Geneva and Brian?

Mark was on his feet before he realized it and went swiftly down the hall. Stopping in front of his eldest son's room, he cautiously opened the door. The hall light brightened the room enough so that he had no problem seeing the figure in bed. His back was to the door so Mark couldn't be sure, but Brian appeared to be deeply asleep.

He closed the door as gently as he had opened it. Irritation was swallowed up by relief, and he leaned shakily against the door. Brian hadn't returned his call, but at least he was home, safe. Tomorrow they would talk.

Turning in the opposite direction, Mark went down the hall to Geneva's room. This time, the hall light wasn't sufficient. He cautiously pushed the door wider until he could see the bed, but it was too dark to tell immediately if it was occupied. After several seconds passed, his eyes began to adjust, and he saw that the bed was perfectly made and perfectly empty.

Despite there being no need to remain quiet, Mark left as quietly as he had arrived. For a minute, he was sorry he had emptied all the bottles of alcohol, then regretted the thought. He didn't need a shot of Dutch courage. There was something else, or more accurately, someone else, to hang on to. It was still a new thought, and Mark silently apologized for his delay in remembering.

He returned to his bedroom and sat down in front of the fireplace. Just because Geneva hadn't returned was no reason to think something had happened. He thought back to Amy Kittredge's words, "She said she didn't think she'd be home so could I stay the night. As it happened, I was free so I said yes." Amy had said something else too, and Mark was dismayed that he'd forgotten it. Geneva sounded sad on the telephone.

His wife had sounded sad, and he hadn't known anything about it. A curse almost escaped his lips before he caught it. Was Geneva at the hospital with her sick friend? He didn't know who the friend was, how sick she was, or even what hospital the woman was in.

Mark sighed. Was there any way he had not messed up as a husband and a father?

Don't linger on what can't be changed, but focus on what can be.

"Lord, I don't know what to do," he whispered.

When he thought of his wife, he felt a deep-down pang of regret and sorrow. The feelings were not only because of his own failure as a husband but also because Geneva did not know what he had discovered in the garage. Even though the intensity of that initial exhilaration had eased and the memories of all he still had to deal with in his life had returned, the weight of those memories was not as heavy as before.

Even more striking, beyond the guilt and regret and confusion and frustration, the new sense of peace deep within him remained. He had no idea what the future held, but he knew now what he had never known before—he didn't face it alone. Someone was with him now, supporting him and helping him in ways he didn't yet understand.

Mark wished with everything in him that Geneva might know the deep-down peace that now resided in his heart.

Where did he begin to undo the damage he had done to his marriage?

Be a friend.

He started at the unexpected thought.

Joe would know what hospital Geneva's friend was in, except it was much too late to call him, especially considering the topic. Though Joe hadn't said anything until recently, Mark was sure he had been aware of his sister's marital problems for a long time. It was only natural that Joe would take his sister's side, even if he hadn't said so explicitly. Calling him after midnight to ask what hospital he had seen Geneva visiting would be the same as admitting Mark had no idea what was happening with his wife.

Mark pressed the heels of his hands against his burning eyes. It was all well and good to decide he needed to be a friend to his wife, but it was much less than what was needed. How in the world could he fix something that had been broken into so many pieces he didn't know where they all were?

You can't.

The thought pierced him so quickly he didn't realize how much it hurt until after the fact. "I can't," he whispered in the darkness. "But you can, Lord, can't you? Will you?"

Even as he asked, he knew the answer. God would help insofar as he was allowed. That was the main issue. Both Geneva and Mark had to want to save their marriage, had to be willing to do the hard work needed to save their marriage. Thanks to the active intervention of God in his life, Mark was ready to do whatever needed to be done. Was Geneva?

The truth cut him to the quick. He didn't believe she was, and he had no one to blame for that but himself. Again he thought of that old saying: "Actions speak louder than words." For some eighteen years, Mark's actions had damaged his relationship with his wife. Geneva would not believe any apologies at this late date. He was going to have to show her by his actions that he was no longer the man she had known all these years. The biggest question, would she give him the time to prove he had changed? Would she be willing to eventually accept him as a friend? He feared the answer.

Mark realized he was pacing and stopped. This wasn't accomplishing anything; he knew it, but he didn't know what he should do. Sleep would be an impossibility.

It's God's gift to us and the best way I know to get to know him. Joe's words echoed in his mind. Mark thought back to their conversation. "God's gift," he recalled. That's what his brother-in-law had called the Bible.

The best way I know to get to know him. Mark had so much to learn about this Person, this One he now called Lord. And he had some undisturbed time on his hands. He turned to look at the Bible where he had left it on his desk. Joe had recommended he start with one of the

Gospels in the New Testament, the same Gospel that bore his own name.

He felt some of the tension knotting his stomach begin to unwind, as if confirming the direction of his thoughts. "All right," he said quietly. "But I don't have a hope of understanding any of this on my own. Joe said you would help me to understand if I asked, so I'm asking. I'm going to need your help."

Again he sat down at his desk, turned over a page of his legal pad, then opened the Bible. After some searching, he found the Gospel of Mark and focused on the first words, "The beginning of the gospel of Jesus Christ, the Son of God."

A shiver ran through Mark, and he didn't know if it was of fear or anticipation. After a moment's thought, he made a note on his legal pad: *The Gospel doesn't waste any time in throwing down its gauntlet. Here at the very beginning it makes its claim clearly. This is about Jesus Christ, the Son of God.*

A sudden fierce joy swept through Mark. He was glad this was all new, that it had not become ordinary or trite through overfamiliarity. The old saying was sadly true—familiarity breeds contempt. This was an extraordinary story before him, and he was deeply grateful that he recognized its extraordinariness. What an amazing, unearthly claim. Not "a" son of God, but "the" Son of God. Mark took a deep breath and was surprised by its shakiness, then set it aside to focus on what he was reading.

He had a vague memory of hearing about John the Baptist at some long ago time. It was a very different sensation finding the man here, speaking out of an ancient volume.

"'After me will come one more powerful than I, the thongs of whose sandals I am not worthy to stoop down and untie. I baptize you with water, but he will baptize you with the Holy Spirit.'"

Another shiver ran through Mark. What an amazing testament. He would never be able to comprehend this with his own finite, human mind. Thank God that he was willing to help Mark to understand.

He continued reading. When Jesus appeared on the scene, Mark felt his excitement rising. Here was the man who was also God according to this book. The same Person Mark had encountered in the garage yesterday, the day before yesterday, now. Just thinking about it took his breath away.

"As Jesus was coming up out of the water, he saw heaven being torn open and the Spirit descending on him like a dove. And a voice came from heaven: 'You are my son, whom I love; with you I am well pleased.'"

Mark sat back, trying to comprehend what he was reading. Jesus was a grown man at this point. John baptized him, and then… Mark shook his head in awe. This seemed to be a concept he had ran across in his distant past and dismissed—the Trinity. Here was Jesus, here was a voice from heaven—God, the Father—and here was the Holy Spirit. They were all involved with Jesus coming to this world, with his ministry in and to this world.

These weren't distant cosmic forces. Jesus was a living, breathing man. God the Father called Jesus "my son, whom I love," and said that he was "well pleased" with him. Even if Mark hadn't already encountered God face-to-face, so to speak, in his garage, these verses would have told him that God was real and personal and cared about him—him, Mark Newman. Unbelievable, but this book said it was true.

He kept reading and kept being surprised—Jesus driving out an evil spirit, Jesus healing a woman and then healing many more. So there was more going on here than Jesus coming to this world to die for humankind. He took the time to show people who God truly was and how they should live. He healed. He loved, even the most unlovable. Such incomprehensible mercy.

There were so many glimpses of Jesus praying, preaching, and healing injured souls. According to this book, Jesus's ministry eventually made him too well known to enter towns openly, so he stayed outside "in lonely places."

Mark had to brush away more tears when he read the last verse in the first chapter: "Yet the people still came to him from everywhere."

He blew out a deep, shuddering breath. If he had lived two thousand years ago, would he have been one of these people? The truth pierced his heart. Mark Newman hadn't come to Jesus; Jesus had come to him—in the garage of all places!—and overwhelmed him with his light and love. If not for the mercy and grace of Jesus Christ, Mark knew he would never have found his way "home," as Joe called it.

His eyes turned to the notes he had scrawled during his reading. What struck him most was a recurring theme— "at once," "immediately," "without delay." The phrases reappeared over and over again in the first chapter. Mark didn't know what the other Gospels had to say about Jesus, but here in this Gospel, he was left with an inescapable conclusion: Jesus had been in a hurry. He had gone from place to place as if he had no time to lose, preaching and teaching and healing. What was one to make of that?

He rubbed his tired eyes. There was so much Jesus had to do, so many people to heal, to teach, to convict of the truth of his words. He had an entire world to save and little time to do it. It was no wonder he had been in a hurry.

The Son of God. The title sent a chill through him, then a flush of warmth. The Son of God, the Second Person of the Trinity, chose to leave heaven to come to this fallen, dark world, bringing the light of heaven with him to offer to his lost children. Mark hadn't lived in a vacuum all his life. Even though he had never opened a Bible before this week, even though he had never gone to church except for the occasional wedding or funeral, he had heard of the Christian teachings behind the holidays of Christmas and

Easter. He knew how the story of Jesus's sojourn on this earth began and ended.

"How am I supposed to grasp all this?" he thought aloud. "Just one chapter of your Gospel has me reeling. How am I supposed to understand, really understand, all this?

His gaze wandered around the room until it stopped on the Buechner books Joe had loaned him. Maybe there was something in those books that would help him to understand. No. Mark looked forward to reading what the books had to offer another time. Here and now, he wanted to understand God's written word, and he sensed no one could help him to understand as well as God's Spirit.

There was so much to comprehend in this first chapter. Mark carefully tore out his pages of notes, set them aside, and settled down to reread the chapter again. Maybe it would take a lifetime to understand all that God had revealed in the Bible. Regardless, he was determined to understand as much as he could.

22

Time disappeared as he read and reread, praying occasionally over this verse or that. Mark was so absorbed in his study that he jumped when the soft strains of a piano concerto began to fill the room. He blinked and shook his head before realizing the alarm had gone off on his clock radio.

Mark looked at his watch. He had been up all night exploring the first chapter of this Gospel. Then he smiled because he couldn't think of a better reason for missing a night's sleep. He yawned and stretched, wincing as stiff muscles protested. It was time to begin getting ready for the day, but now that his thoughts were no longer occupied by his Bible study, worry returned in a rush.

On the heels of that thought, he sat up. Was that a door he had just heard close? He rose and went to his own door and opened it. No one was in sight. Maybe Amy Kittredge was downstairs? He thought it was too early for her to begin work, but since she had spent the night in the cottage, she might be planning to start her day sooner than usual.

Mark listened for another minute, but only silence greeted him. He went to Brian's room and knocked on the door. When there was no response, he opened it. The covers had been thrown back on the bed, but there was no sign of the teenager. Then he heard the faint sound of the shower running behind the closed bathroom door. He exhaled in relief, closed the door, and went to Geneva's room. Again, there was no answer to his knock. When he opened the door a few inches, he saw the bed exactly as he remembered—neatly made with no indication that it had been slept in.

A knot formed in his stomach. Geneva hadn't been home all night. Was she still at the hospital? *Or…* A new thought nudged its way into his consciousness. Had she found someone else to take his place? Someone who treated her as he had not done for years?

Mark closed the door and returned to his own bedroom. As if on autopilot, he took a shower, shaved, and dressed. When he went down to the kitchen, he found it empty. Two bowls and glasses were on the counter beside the sink, and he took that to mean Brian and Daniel had already eaten.

The pantry door opened, and Amy Kittredge appeared. She was balancing several tomatoes in her hands and almost dropped them when she saw him.

"Mr. Newman, I didn't realize you were up."

"I'm sorry if I surprised you."

She smiled and put the tomatoes in the sink. "That's all right. Can I get you something to eat?"

"No, thank you."

He was just walking into the living room when he saw Daniel trotting down the stairs. The boy smiled tentatively at the sight of his father. Mark suppressed a wince at his uncertain expression and spoke heartily, "Good morning."

The boy's smile widened. "Hi, Dad."

"You look ready to go."

Daniel nodded at the same time he reached the floor. "My ride should be here"—he glanced at his watch—"any minute. And Mrs. Randall doesn't like to wait."

"Who's Mrs. Randall?"

"Mike's mom."

It was hard to resist the next question that immediately rose to mind. Mark hesitated because he felt he had already lost points not knowing who Mrs. Randall was. Considering how involved Daniel was in Little League, Mark tried a little logical deduction that he hoped would not make him sound as stupid as he felt. "He's on your team, isn't he?"

Daniel beamed. "You remembered!"

His son's delighted expression made it impossible to lie. "Actually," he admitted, "I guessed."

The truth didn't seem to bother the twelve-year-old. "It was a good guess. You—"

A sudden pounding on the front door made them both start. Daniel immediately hurried over and flung it open.

"So what's the hold-up—"The accusatory words stopped abruptly as the shaggy-haired boy standing on the door step saw Mark.

"Mike, this is my dad," Daniel said, and the innocent pride in his voice made Mark's throat tighten. He didn't deserve it, but not for the world would he say so. It would only confuse and likely hurt his son, and Mark had already done too much of that.

"Uh, hi," Mike Randall said uncertainly, his feet shuffling in an obvious desire to escape.

"Hello." Mark smiled and gave his son's shoulder a pat. "You have a good day."

"Thanks, Dad. You too!"

With that, both boys were gone. Mark watched them hurry down the walk to the cream-colored SUV parked at the curb. Mike dived in first, Daniel on his heels. The faint sound of laughter drifted back to him, and he was pleased to hear it. At least his son was beginning the day in high spirits. He hoped it lasted.

After the SUV drove off, Mark decided to check on his oldest son. He didn't know exactly when Brian needed to be at school, but since Daniel had left, it was a certainty that the teenager needed to be leaving soon. Mark hoped he would have a chance to talk to him first, but if not, he would find out when Brian would be home this afternoon.

There was no response when he knocked on the bedroom door, and he turned the handle. "Brian?"

Silence answered, and Mark pushed the door wider. The bed was still unmade, but this time, the bathroom door was open, and he could see inside. Damp towels lay in a heap on the floor, the only evidence that the bathroom had recently been inhabited.

He walked slowly out of the room, increasingly troubled. When had Brian left? There hadn't been much opportunity for him to leave without being noticed, just the few minutes when Mark was in the kitchen. Had his oldest son deliberately snuck out to avoid a confrontation with his father? He took a deep breath, trying to ignore the ache in his throat, unsure what to do next. Chasing after Brian wasn't an option.

He was tempted to wait around until Geneva appeared, but he had no idea when that might be. A glance at the clock on the wall showed he was going to be late to work even if he left now. Mark sighed again. It seemed as if he would have to put off a talk with his wife too.

After retrieving his briefcase, he went out into the kitchen, intending to leave by the side door. Through the glass panel, he saw Geneva come out of the garage, and he stopped. The door opened, and she took a step inside before she saw him.

For a minute, they simply looked at each other. It was long enough for Mark to see his wife's exhaustion and pallor. The suspicion that had briefly crossed his mind earlier faded away. Wherever Geneva had been, she hadn't been enjoying herself.

"Are you all right?" he asked.

Geneva blinked, then blinked again. Without a word, she started to walk by him, but Mark stepped in her way.

"Geneva? What's wrong?"

"What's wrong," she repeated, as if it was a statement, not a question. "Nothing."

Mark knew he was pushing, but he couldn't let it go. "Something's wrong," he insisted. "Is it your friend? The one in the hospital?"

Geneva squeezed her eyes shut before she surprised him with a glare. "You were never interested in Peg when she was alive. Why care now that she's dead?" Her voice broke on the last word while tears suddenly shimmered in her eyes.

Mark stared at her, shocked. Before he could think of a response, she brushed past him and hurried toward the stairs. He wanted to follow her to help, somehow, but a second thought kept him still. Geneva wouldn't accept any comfort he tried to offer. She wouldn't believe he was serious. Pain and fresh regret filled him, and he took a deep, shuddering breath. While he had been home happily working his way through a chapter in the Bible, Geneva had been spending the night in a hospital with a dying friend. Mark hadn't known. If he had, would he have cared? The bitter truth was that before his encounter with Jesus

Christ in the garage two days ago, he might not have been that concerned.

Thanks to his conversation with Joe, Mark knew God didn't want him wallowing in guilt, but it was hard to avoid. He was unhappily certain of one thing. Staying here would accomplish nothing. Geneva would not accept anything from him, especially not now.

When Mark walked into his office later that morning, the receptionist, Charlotte Ingram smiled at him.

"Good morning, Mr. Newman. Here are your messages."

He took the small pile from her. "Thank you. Is Carolyn in?"

"Yes, sir. She's in the small conference room."

"She's meeting someone?" Mark tried not to sound surprised. He had been so distracted recently he had little idea what was happening at the office.

"With the Raymers," Charlotte confirmed. "An initial conference."

Now he remembered and was ashamed he had forgotten. "Ask her to see me when she's done."

"Yes, sir."

Thinking of the work that waited for him on his desk, Mark decided he needed a cup of coffee first. A few feet from the kitchen, he heard voices and had a sudden sense of déjà vu. Unlike the last time, this time he frankly eavesdropped.

"….Pinch me because I still think I'm dreaming!"

He recognized Jay Russell's voice but unlike before, it now bubbled with excitement.

There was laughter that sounded like it came from two or three people. A female voice said, "And the hospital wouldn't say who paid it?"

"No. I know it wasn't the insurance company, but I don't have any rich relatives, so I don't have a clue!"

There was more laughter and congratulations while Mark listened with relief and pleasure.

"How's Cassie doing?" a different female voice asked.

"A 110 percent better. With all her medical bills paid, the hospital isn't going to bother us anymore. She doesn't have to go anywhere. Neither of us do. We're staying in our home, and no one can kick us out!"

Mark quietly withdrew, smiling inwardly. He would get coffee later. When he reached his office, he made sure the door was firmly shut behind him before he relaxed. "Thank you for the idea," he said into the quiet of the room.

That the idea had been divine intervention, he had no doubt. He recalled his earlier depressing thought from a few days ago—there was no way he could help all the people in the world who needed help. But as God had helped him to understand, he was capable of reaching out to those people in his own circle. Or more accurately, God could use him to reach out to them.

If only he could help the members of his own family. The thought sent a shard of pain through him. That quickly, his good mood disappeared, and he sank into the nearest chair. "I don't know what to do," Mark whispered. He knew he had said these words before, but they were just as true now.

For a few minutes, he sat in silence, trying not to let the ache in his heart overwhelm him. Then he rose abruptly and went to his desk. Pulling his telephone closer, he dialed the number that was now engraved in his mind. The familiar recording clicked on, but this time it was interrupted in the middle by a breathless voice.

"This is Joe Ridgeway."

Breathing a sigh of relief, Mark said, "Hello, Joe, it's Mark."

"Mark! It's good to hear from you. How are you doing?"

Mark couldn't resist a wry laugh. "I think the best word to describe how I'm feeling at the moment is confused."

Joe's answering laugh was sympathetic. "Is there anything I can do to help?"

"Well, to be honest I could use your ear."

"It's yours," Joe said promptly. "I'm tied up this morning, but what about this afternoon?"

"Are you free for lunch? My treat." Considering how much time he had taken from Joe recently, Mark thought it was the least he could do.

"I never turn down a free meal." His brother-in-law chuckled. "But it would have to be a late lunch, after one."

"One thirty? At Remington's?"

"Wow, I don't think I've got anything in my closet that would be appropriate."

"Anything other than shorts or jeans will be fine. Or would you prefer another restaurant?"

"Are you kidding? I'd never be able to afford that place on my own, so since you're paying, I'll see you there at one thirty."

Mark hung up, still smiling. Even though he suspected his brother-in-law would have no magic answers for him, the thought of being able to share his struggle made him feel better.

The intercom buzzed, and he pressed it. "Newman."

"Mr. Newman, it's Carolyn. Charlotte said you wanted to see me. Is this a good time?"

Right, the office. Life went on despite his emotional and spiritual upheaval. Giving himself a mental shake, Mark said, "Yes, it's fine."

While he waited, he looked through the messages and stacked them according to importance, except for two his assistant could handle. A few minutes later, there was a light knock on his door and Carolyn Colby appeared.

"Good morning, sir."

"Good morning, Carolyn. Come in." As she approached the desk, he noticed she was carrying some files. "What have you got there?"

She sat down in one of the chairs in front of the desk and laid down the files, except for the top one that she handed to him. "This contains my notes based on the original intake and my meeting with the Raymers this morning. It looks like it's going to be a real mare's nest," she added. "Some of the family want to sell their controlling interest in the company, but other family members are opposed."

"Which side has the majority?" Mark questioned as he skimmed through her notes.

"Those who want to sell, but just barely."

"With the future of a nation-wide chain of pharmacies at issue," he noted.

Carolyn nodded but remained silent, allowing him to concentrate.

When he finished reading, he looked up. "How adamant are the two groups?"

"Very, at least as of this morning."

Mark considered the information. "All right, let's schedule a meeting for me to meet with them."

"Which side?"

"Both." He smiled at her raised eyebrows. "I expect a lot of arguing at first, but if we're going to find some middle ground, everything will need to be kept above board. No secret meetings, no playing one side against the other."

"Yes, sir."

Mark gave his assistant credit. She showed no surprise at this change of tactics. Throughout his career, Mark had done what he needed to do to win. While he had always avoided outright illegal tactics, he had skated close to the edge more than once. It was the way the world worked, or so he had always thought. As a new Christian, things suddenly seemed a lot less murky, a lot clearer, and he was tempted to cringe under the remorseless light of truth that pierced him.

He reminded himself this wasn't the time for soul-searching. "What else have you got there?" he asked.

They worked their way through the files that needed to be taken care of this morning, and he gave Carolyn the messages he wanted her to deal with. After she left, Mark started returning calls which took him through the rest of the morning. Ordinarily, he became so immersed with his work he lost all track of time, but today he remained aware of the hours passing and wound up his last telephone call twenty minutes before his scheduled lunch with his brother-in-law.

The Remington was on a side street in the heart of Old Town Pasadena, and Mark enjoyed the brisk ten-minute walk from his office to the restaurant. Just as he reached the front door, he heard a familiar voice behind him.

"Mark!"

He turned. "Hi, Joe. That's what I call timing."

"On both our parts, I'd say," Joe returned with a grin.

The restaurant was designed to look like an upscale nineteenth-century English-style pub with lots of dark, shiny wood, old fashioned-looking fixtures and chandeliers, but with modern lighting. Mark had eaten here many times in the past, and the hostess who approached them gave him a warm smile.

"It's good to see you again, Mr. Newman. Lunch for two?" she asked.

"Yes. We'd like the alcove booth, please." The alcove booth was Mark's favorite, for it offered both room to stretch out as well as privacy.

"Of course." She snatched up two menus. "Please follow me."

After they were settled and received their menus, Joe looked across the table with raised eyebrows. "What would you have done if this booth wasn't available?"

Mark paused in his review of the menu to consider the question. "You know, it's always available when I come here." He shrugged. "I guess I would have had to sit somewhere else."

"So no big fuss?"

"Ah." Now he understood what the other man was getting at. "To be honest, in the old days, I would have kicked up a fuss."

"The old days? Such as three days ago?"

The gentle humor in Joe's voice didn't sting, but it reminded Mark of something he had been thinking a lot about.

"It's amazing how much has changed in my life in just a few days."

"I don't think it's about how much has changed in your life but rather how your life has changed."

Mark tried to smile, but it wasn't a good effort. "And yet some things haven't changed at all."

"I thought we agreed that you're going to take it one step at a time."

A waitress dressed in an outfit that went along with the nineteenth-century high-class pub interior appeared at the table. "Good afternoon, gentlemen," she said brightly. "Can I get you something to drink?" She smiled between them.

"I'll have a glass of iced tea," Joe said.

The words of his usual drink order came automatically to Mark's lips, but he caught them before they could escape. The effort sent him into a spam of coughing that, when it finally ended, left him wheezing and teary-eyed. Joe slapped him on the back several times, and only when Mark was finally able to catch his breath did he settle back in his seat.

"Better?"

Mark nodded, coughed again and looked up at the anxious waitress. "Uh, make that two."

"Yes, sir." She made a note on her pad. "Are you ready to order, or would you like a little more time?"

They ordered, and after she was gone, Mark finally met Joe's concerned gaze. "The food is very good here. You'll enjoy that steak sandwich."

"I don't doubt it. Are you sure you're all right?"

Mark picked up his spoon and studied it carefully while he tried to come up with the right words. "Have you ever heard that saying, 'Old habits die hard'?"

Joe nodded. "Yes."

"And?"

"And what?"

Mark sighed in frustration before finally giving up on the silverware and sitting back to meet his brother-in-law's calm gaze. "Do you think it's true?"

To his surprise, Joe chuckled. "Anyone who has ever made a New Year's resolution knows it's a true saying. Change is always difficult. That's just a fact of life."

Mark decided there was nothing to do but throw himself in the deep end. "Last night I emptied all of my bottles of liquor down the sink."

Joe's eyebrows rose, but he only nodded.

Mark glared. "You don't make it easy, do you?"

That got him a slight smile, but when Joe spoke he said, "Why don't you tell me what's on your mind."

"I just almost ordered my usual drink." Mark rubbed his face in frustration. "I got rid of all of the alcohol in the house last night, and now I almost ordered—" He stopped abruptly.

"Take it easy," Joe said calmly. "Let's not try to combine apples and oranges here."

"What do you mean?"

"Why did you get rid of all of the liquor in your house?"

Why? Just thinking of why sent a surge of pain through Mark.

"Because of Brian." He looked beseechingly across the table.

Joe met his eyes, and Mark recognized the expectation. He blew out a breath and forced himself to go on. "I know it's not going make a big difference, but I thought…actually I wasn't thinking," he admitted. "It was a knee-jerk response to a verse I ran across in the Bible." He closed his eyes in an effort to recall it. "I don't remember the exact words, but it was something along the lines of 'Be careful or else your hearts will be weighed down with drunkenness that will turn into a trap.'" Mark opened his eyes and sighed. "That's a bad paraphrase, but it just hit me right between the eyes, and I suddenly realized there was something I could do for Brian. Get rid of all his easy access to the alcohol in our house."

"And?"

"And?" Mark repeated in confusion. "I'm not sure what you're getting at. I know it's not going to be that easy. Even if Brian is willing to accept help, it's going to take a lot of time and work for him to be able to…" He stopped, suddenly overwhelmed with the hard road in front of his son, especially knowing he was at least in part responsible.

"Stop it."

Joe's voice was low, but it cracked like a whip and startled Mark out of his preoccupation. He looked across the table again and was pierced by the other man's gaze.

"You're right that Brian has a long road in front of him," Joe went on, "but there are a lot of people who want to help him. He won't be going it alone. For that matter, you didn't put him on that road originally."

"I—"

"I'm not done. Accepting responsibility for one's mistakes is part of being a responsible adult. I'm glad you're willing to do that, but it's not all on your shoulders. Regardless of why Brian originally began drinking, the fact is he's not a little boy any longer. There's no way to go back, no way to change or to regain what was missed the first time around. Some people never accept that, and they end up missing out on all that life still has available to them."

The words felt like a blow, and Mark wanted to look away, but he couldn't.

"This is where you need to begin," Joe said, his eyes almost burning in intensity. "Certainly you want to ask God to help you recognize your mistakes. If there are apologies to be made, ask God to help you apologize appropriately. Then you need to ask Him to help you to let go of those mistakes because he's forgiven them. Now they're only a useless weight on your back that you don't need and God doesn't want you carrying. Remember, the more you cling to them, the more they'll interfere with God's plans for you."

Mark rubbed his face, suddenly feeling very tired. "Didn't you already say this or at least some of this?"

Joe's smile was warm. "I've known you for almost twenty years. I figure you need to hear it more than once."

"I'm trying."

"I know."

Mark shifted uncomfortably. "There's so much to learn."

"I know," Joe repeated. "Just remember, it can't all happen overnight."

"Follow God as he leads. One day at a time," Mark added, unable to refrain from a touch of sarcasm.

Joe's smile widened. "Yes."

"Including when I read the Bible?"

"Especially then."

"More than once when I opened the Bible these past few days," Mark admitted, "I saw a verse that seemed to speak directly to me right there and then."

Joe nodded. "That's God's grace. Just don't expect it to happen every time you pick up the Bible. God wants us to know all of his written word, not treat it like a Christian version of an Ouija board."

Mark laughed at the thought just as the waitress appeared with their orders. After she was gone, he picked up his fork.

"Would you mind if I say the blessing?" asked Joe.

Feeling his face warm, Mark laid the fork back down. "Sorry."

Joe shook his head. "Nothing to be sorry about. I keep telling you—"

"It's going to take time."

"Exactly."

When Joe bowed his head, Mark did the same. He was acutely aware they were in a public place and was grateful for the privacy of the alcove, which was immediately followed by another surge of guilt. Forcing it away, he listened to Joe.

"Lord, before we eat, we pause to thank you for this good food you have provided. And we thank you for the blessings you pour out on us every day. We ask that you bless this food and our time together. May we be nourished physically and spiritually to better serve you and our brothers and sisters. In your name, we pray all these things and thank you for hearing us. Amen."

"Amen," Mark echoed.

23

There was silence while they ate, and Mark debated what, of all his jumbled thoughts, he wanted, no, needed, to share.

He felt Joe's eyes on him and met his enquiring gaze. "Yes?"

Joe smiled. "Since you asked, I have a question for you."

"Which is?"

"How are you doing?"

That was the fifty-thousand-dollar question and trust his brother-in-law to ask. "I'm not sure I know. Oh, did I tell you about Daniel?"

"No."

Mark recounted his experience of a Little League game and his subsequent talk with his youngest son. Joe listened intently.

"That's wonderful, Mark. A wonderful beginning."

"I just hope I can follow through with him."

"You can if you want to. God wants your family to be healed and whole. He will help you. You have to remember to ask."

Mark nodded. "After ignoring Daniel most of his life, I can't believe how..." He hesitated.

"How forgiving he is?"

"Yes."

"Children are remarkably forgiving of those they love. Adults would do well to emulate them."

"I wish..." Mark swallowed. "I don't know if Brian will ever forgive me. I don't know if I'll ever be able to forgive myself for failing him and Daniel so badly."

Joe took a bite of his sandwich and chewed, then munched down a few of his ranch fries. After washing it all down with a swallow of iced tea, he sat back in his seat. "And?"

Again with the "and." Slightly annoyed, Mark used his earlier response. "And what?"

"I've been a minister for over twenty years. I've learned a lot about people during that time. It's obvious you have more on your mind."

"I don't know where to begin," Mark admitted.

"What about just saying the first thing that comes to mind?"

The first thing... "I've let down all of the people closest to me, especially Geneva."

It was hard to admit to Geneva's brother. Mark wasn't sure what to expect, but when he finally forced himself to look up, there was no shock or anger on Joe's face.

"Keep going," Joe said quietly.

Mark swallowed again, but it didn't ease the pressure in his throat. "I recently learned that a friend of Geneva's was hospitalized, but I didn't say or do anything about it. Last night, she didn't come home, not until this morning." Emotion stopped his voice, and he took a few deep breaths before he could continue. "Sometime during the night her friend died."

"I know."

Surprise yanked Mark out of his regret. "You know? How?"

"I spent the morning with Geneva. She told me…a lot of things."

Mark opened his mouth to ask for more information but stopped himself. He eyed Joe uncertainly, and once again the older man seemed to read his mind.

"What people tell me is confidential. There may come a time when Geneva decides to share with you what she told me, but that's up to her."

Mark felt a combination of regret and relief. It was good to know that nothing he told his brother-in-law would ever be shared with anyone else, but he wished he knew what Geneva said.

"I don't think she'll ever tell me."

"Don't be so sure." Joe was smiling again. "Among my favorite verses is one that says, 'All things are possible with God.' Jesus Christ himself spoke those words."

"I wish I could believe that."

"Believe it. I've seen it happen more than once in my own life, as well as in the lives of many other people."

Mark licked his lips. Maybe one day he would believe Joe's favorite verse, but he didn't think it would happen today.

Joe set his plate aside and leaned forward. "There is something very important you need to keep in mind. The Bible doesn't promise that bad things won't happen to Christians. What it does promise is that God will be in the midst of those bad things with us, carrying us through them."

The intensity in Joe's voice was reflected in his eyes. Mark couldn't have looked away if he wanted to.

"We're never alone, Mark," Joe went on. "Through his Spirit, God is with us every step we take, every day of our lives. Do you understand?"

"I'm trying to," he said honestly.

"Fair enough. Here's something else for you to think about. God isn't up there." He pointed toward the ceiling. "One of the promises God gave in the Bible is that through his Spirit he is right here with us. He's down here in the trenches with us, in the blood and the muck, in the pain and the joy of our lives. He's beside every single one of us, every moment of every day, whether we accept Him or not."

Mark knew his brother-in-law wasn't a mind reader, but the way the man kept unwittingly speaking to his concerns was startling. Joe's words touched something deep inside, warming and reassuring, reminding him that he wasn't taking this new walk as a Christian by himself. God was walking beside him, walking with him. His heart ached with sudden longing.

"I wish I knew how that translated to being to be a better husband and father."

"You love them."

It was a statement not a question, but Mark answered it anyway. "Yes. I didn't realize how much until God blew his way into my life and made me see everything differently. But"—he groped for the right words—"as much as I love them, it doesn't take away the…the damage I've done or change how they see me or their feelings for me."

"God's love has changed you," Joe said matter-of-factly. "He loves you, and he loves Geneva and Brian and Danny. Don't try to diminish something so important."

Mark glared. "I know love is important. Even before I became a Christian I knew that. But as much as I love them, they don't love me. After the way I've ignored them, why should they?"

Joe picked up his fork and stabbed absently at the remains of his sandwich. "When it comes to humans, things are rarely simple. Here's a question for you. What do you think is the opposite of love?"

Mark blinked in surprise at the abrupt change in subject but decided to see where his brother-in-law was going. "Hate, of course."

"Most people think that, but they're wrong."

"What do you mean?"

"Think about it. Both love and hate involve strong emotions directed at the individual who inspires that emotion. Love and hate aren't opposites. On the contrary, they're two sides of the same coin."

Mark thought about it before nodding grudgingly. "All right, I see your point. But…I'm not sure what that means."

"Here's another question for you." Joe leaned forward again. "Since love and hate are two sides of the same coin, what's their opposite? What is the opposite of love? Of hate?"

"You have all the answers, so you tell me."

"All the answers?" Joe chuckled. "I wish. Come on, Mark, think about it."

"I didn't come here for guessing games." The words came out a little more strongly than Mark intended, but his brother-in-law didn't seem bothered.

"All right," Joe said easily. "Whether we're talking about love or hate, the opposite is indifference."

"What?"

"Loving or hating someone involves intense emotions—emotions that show the other person matters to us. Whether positively or negatively, they matter. Indifference, on the other hand, doesn't involve any kind of emotion. If you're indifferent to someone, you don't care what happens to them."

"Once you explain it, it's obvious," Mark said slowly. "But what does all this have to do with my family?"

Joe gave him a reproving look. "Don't play ignorant. I happen to know you're a very intelligent man."

"Thank you, I think."

"Come on, do I have to spell it out?"

Mark suddenly felt very tired. "Joe, in the last two weeks I've been on a roller coaster like nothing I've ever known before, a roller coaster that culminated in God sweeping into my life and turning it upside down. Now I'm just trying to figure out what I'm supposed to do next and I'm da—that is, I don't know."

"I'm sorry." Joe looked contrite. "The point I'm trying to make is if Geneva and/or Brian didn't have strong feelings about you, they wouldn't react so strongly to you."

"Yes, but"—Mark took a deep breath, the better to help him to force out difficult words—"you already pointed out the feelings can come from hate as easily as love. I don't think love is involved in their feelings for me."

"I disagree. Remember what I said a minute ago about how when humans are involved, things are rarely simple?" He waited for Mark's nod before continuing. "As someone who works with people on a daily basis, I've learned a great deal about human relationships. I don't know exactly what

Brian feels about you, but it's more than just one emotion." He reached out to put a hand on Mark's arm. "Some of those emotions may be negative, but I don't believe they all are."

"So what? So long as he doesn't want to talk to me, doesn't want to have anything to do with me, it's irrelevant. As for Geneva—" Mark stopped when his cell phone buzzed in his pocket. He pulled it out and was about to turn it off when the display caught his attention.

For a split second, he was puzzled. The telephone number was only slightly familiar. Suddenly he remembered, and his heart skipped a beat. More bad news?

"Excuse me," he said quickly before answering. "Newman."

"Mark, it's Stretch Ramsey. I just got word that the boy in the hospital, Will Morgan, has regained consciousness. One of the first things he said was that Terry Drummond was driving the car, not Brian."

Mark closed his eyes as relief washed over him. "Thank you, God," he whispered. Brian still had a lot to deal with, but one huge hurdle to his future had just been removed.

"Mark? Are you still there?"

Ramsey's voice brought him back, and he replied, "Yes. Have you told the investigating officer?"

"I didn't have to. The hospital called him first, and he went straight over there. I found out a short time later."

"So what does this mean for Brian?"

"That's still to be determined, but I think it's likely that we'll only be looking at probation and maybe court-mandated counseling."

Mark took a deep, shuddering breath and fought back tears of thankfulness. *Thank you, Lord*, he thought again. *Thank you that the injured boy is going to be all right, thank you that he was able to clear Brian, and thank you for this new chance for Brian.*

"Thank you, Stretch," he said after he regained control. "For everything."

"It's not over yet, but I'm very encouraged. I'll talk to you again when I know more."

"Thank you," Mark repeated before disconnecting.

Joe was looking intently at him. Still smiling in relief, Mark gave him a summary of the conversation. When he finished, Joe smiled too.

"Thank you, Lord," Joe murmured.

"That's what I was just thinking."

"Is he going to tell Brian, or will he leave that to you?"

"He didn't say." As he spoke, Mark realized the truth. "Which means he expects me to tell Brian." His heart sank. "I don't think my son is going to accept anything I say."

Joe put his hand on Mark's arm again and gave it a little shake. "I know looking at the big picture can be overwhelming, so don't look at it. What you need to remember is that you can't change things overnight but you can change them over time."

"How?" The question was wrung out of Mark's heart.

"God will help, but you can't sit back and expect him to do it all. It's going to take an outsider's viewpoint to help you and Brian work through what needs to be worked through—as well as to help you and Geneva do the same."

"You're talking about a professional counselor."

"Yes, I am. There's no shame in recognizing that you can't do this alone. On the contrary, it takes a great deal of strength to be able to take that step."

Mark didn't want to do it. Consulting with a counselor seemed like admitting he was a failure. But Joe was arguing otherwise. Maybe, just maybe, his brother-in-law was right. He knew Brian needed counseling. But getting the teenager to that point was another matter.

"I don't think Brian will agree to see a therapist."

"You want him to, and Geneva wants him to. You can present it to him as a way to ensure the court will be lenient with him."

"Wait. Geneva wants him to?"

"Yes, she said so this morning." Joe smiled again. "That was one thing she said I could pass along to you. What about you? Are you willing to be an example for your son?"

Mark winced. "You don't pull any punches, do you?"

"Never have," Joe returned, his smile widening. "The question on the table is, do you have the guts to act on what you know is the right thing to do?"

Mark sat back in his seat and contemplated his empty glass. As if sensing he needed a break, Joe concentrated on finishing the coleslaw that had come with his meal. The silence that fell between them was surprisingly comfortable. Mark waited until the older man had finished before speaking.

"I know you can't say anything about what you and Geneva talked about but based on that conversation, do you think I have a chance of saving my marriage?"

"It takes two people to make a marriage," Joe returned quietly. "You and Geneva need to talk. Equally important, you need to listen to each other. I don't believe either of you really wants to end your marriage. But repairing it is going to take a lot of work, and you're going to need help."

"God?"

"His involvement goes without saying," Joe said in a "duh" tone of voice that made Mark grin. "The two of you are also going to need an objective third party."

Mark's brief amusement faded. His brother-in-law was not going to let the idea drop. "Marriage counseling," he said with another sigh. "I don't know if Geneva would agree to that."

"Would you?"

The direct question caught him off guard. When he thought about it, he knew the answer, as distasteful as it felt. "If that's what it takes, yes. But Geneva..."

"That's why the two of you need to start by talking."

"You don't believe in taking the easy road on anything, do you?"

That won him a laugh. "Unfortunately, it's been my experience that the easy road doesn't get you anyplace that's really worth going to."

"Great."

"So what do you plan to do next?"

Mark laid down the spoon he had been turning idly between his fingers. "Go back to the office and get some work done. Tonight, I want to spend some time with Daniel, and then I need to talk to both Brian and Geneva." The thought made his stomach roil uncomfortably, and he hoped he didn't give any sign of his apprehension.

"I think that's a good plan," Joe said. "I have an appointment, so I'm going to have to leave, but thank you for lunch. You're right—it was delicious."

"I'm glad you enjoyed it."

The afternoon raced by, in part, Mark thought, because he was uneasy about the evening. Spending time with his youngest son would probably be the high point and he was looking forward to it. Every time he thought of Daniel's open-hearted acceptance of the father who had always been so distant and unavailable, tears came to his eyes. Such easy forgiveness, such whole-hearted love, was beyond understanding. He felt both humbled and exalted. His old plans for his children had vanished. Now he wanted nothing more than to become a true father, to be part of

Daniel's life and help him to grow up to become the man God wanted him to be.

Mark left the office earlier than usual because he wanted to be able to eat dinner with his family. The thought excited him almost as much as it frightened him. He couldn't remember the last time they had eaten together as a family, and he felt fresh shame at the thought. When he reached the house, he was pleased to see that Geneva's car was in the garage. One step in the right direction. He started up the walk to the side door, but a sudden impulse turned him toward the gate to the backyard.

When he reached the patio, he saw the rope that he had laid out along the perimeter. He knelt down and laid a hand on the coarse fibers, pleased to discover that it was finally drying now that it was out in the sunlight. As he knelt there, he thought over the days since the accident. That he had come to this point still staggered him. A pang of gratitude mingled with pain filled him. *Grace*. It was all about the unbelievable grace of God. Something he knew he would spend the rest of his life trying to understand and thanking God for.

A few minutes later, he went through the french doors and then through the house to the kitchen. Hearing voices as he approached, he wasn't surprised to find both Daniel and Brian sitting in the nook eating something that made his stomach growl hungrily.

"Something smells good," he said.

To his chagrin, both boys jumped at the sound of his voice. He hadn't meant to surprise them and was both pleased and saddened by the faces that turned toward him—Daniel's was smiling and welcoming, while Brian's face was a blank mask.

"Hi, Dad," his youngest greeted him. "You're home early." Hope brightened his eyes. "Can you, uh, I mean..."

"I came home early so I could have dinner with you," Mark said and hoped his smile wasn't as tentative as he felt.

"Cool!" Daniel said happily. "Brian, isn't that great?"

Brian mumbled something and dropped his eyes to his plate. Daniel looked at him, and his smile faltered.

Pretending he didn't notice anything, Mark went to the cabinet and took out a plate. "Is there enough for me?"

"Sure," Daniel said. He looked anxiously at his brother, but Brian kept his head down so he turned back to his father. "Amy just left, but she always makes lots. We can't ever finish it all."

"Lucky me," Mark said with a chuckle.

Daniel's smile returned, and he scooted over when his father approached.

Recognizing the silent request, Mark sat down beside to his youngest son. "So what do we have here?" he said as the reached for the nearest bowl.

"That's garlic mashed potatoes," Daniel explained. "They're yumlicious!"

"Yumlicious, is it?" Mark grinned. "Anything else here, yumlicious?"

"Everything." Daniel pointed at the oblong pan covered by aluminum foil. "That's chicken cach…cash…" He huffed in frustration. "Brian, how do you say it?"

"Cacciatore," Brian answered, though he didn't look up.

"That's it! And that"—he pointed at the covered bowl in front of him—"is carrots. Baby carrots with…" He hesitated, brows scrunched in thought, then he smiled triumphantly. "Melted brown sugar. My favorite. Amy's a great cook."

Mark's smile widened at his son's blissful expression. "In that case, pass it over here."

Daniel did the passing; Brian never looked up. As Mark filled his plate, he said, "So how did your day go?"

Daniel straightened, beaming. "I got an A- on my history report."

"Excellent! What was it about?" It felt oddly as if Mark was entering unchartered territory, but he tried to set aside his discomfort and speak naturally.

"We're studying the Revolutionary War," the boy explained between bites of food, "and I had to write a report on how George Washington became the commander of the Continental Army."

He spoke with great animation, and Mark listened to the details of the A- report that segued into the boy's day. The silent, brooding presence across the table was distracting, but he did his best to ignore it. This wasn't the time or place to talk to Brian. For now, he focused on his youngest son, enjoying this first glimpse into Daniel's daily life that heretofore he had ignored. Once again, he marveled at the child's generous, open-handed offering of affection. Mark made a silent promise to both his son and God that he would not betray that affection again.

"And at practice this afternoon," Daniel rambled on, obviously happy with his father's attention, "the coach said he was really proud of us. Not just for winning but because we worked hard all season. And now we're in the play-offs!" Some of his animation faded. "And the first team we're probably going to face is the Cougars."

That was the same team Stretch Ramsey's son was on. Mark smiled at the memory of sharing a bench with Ramsey and at how he had gotten sucked into the game by the other man's enthusiasm. "You beat the Cougars yesterday," he reminded.

"I know, but the time before that, they beat us." Daniel sighed mightily. "They're really good."

"So is your team," Mark said firmly. "I saw you play yesterday, remember? You all did a great job."

Daniel beamed. Across the table, Brian raised his head. "You saw Danny's game?"

Mark almost winced under the disbelieving look, a look he knew he deserved. "Yes, thanks to you."

"Me?"

"If you hadn't told me about the game, I would have missed it. And," he added to his youngest son, "I've missed way too many of your games. I don't want to miss anymore."

"Really?" Daniel's eyes glowed. "That's great."

He didn't deserve this, Mark thought again. Then again, he didn't deserve God's forgiveness either, yet he knew he had it. *Forgiveness.* True forgiveness must be part of God's grace, and the knowledge left him abjectly grateful.

Brian looked from his brother to his father, and Mark saw a shadow of emotion cross his face. Suddenly the teenager was on his feet. Without a word, he carried his plate that still held half of his meal over to the sink and then walked out of the kitchen.

Mark sat still. He knew that giving into the all-too familiar feeling of guilt wouldn't accomplish anything except to delay him in doing what God wanted him to do. He knew it, but it was hard not to fall back into that trap.

He realized Daniel was gazing unhappily at him. Mark managed to smile and gave the small shoulder a squeeze. "You finish eating. I'll talk to Brian."

"Is he mad because you came to my game?"

"No. He's not mad at you, Danny. Don't worry about that."

"Okay." The boy still looked uncertain but also oddly pleased, and Mark realized it was because he had used his son's nickname. He rose, picking up his empty plate with one hand while he tousled the boy's hair with the other.

Daniel's smile widened, and he tried to duck away. "Dad!"

A thrill of pleasure swept through Mark at the sound of the happy laughter. He still had a long way to go, but this felt like a good beginning.

24

A few minutes later when he climbed the stairs, he wished he could be as hopeful about his older son. *One step at a time*, he reminded himself.

When he reached his son's bedroom, he knocked on the door. "Brian? May I come in?"

There was no answer.

Mark was saddened but not surprised. He knocked again. "Brian?"

After waiting through another minute of silence, he took a deep breath and opened the door to see Brian at his desk by the window. He didn't look around when his father entered.

The sight of the slumped, defeated young figure sent a stab of pain through Mark. He got right to the point. "Your friend, Will Morgan, has regained consciousness."

Brian's head shot up. "Is he going to be okay?"

"I believe so." He gave his son his most reassuring smile. "Will said that the other boy, Terry, was the one who was driving."

"That's what I told the police," Brian said, and Mark heard anger in his voice. "They didn't believe me, but they believed Will?"

Mark sat down on the edge of the bed so that he was at his son's level. "It wasn't that they didn't believe you, but it was your word against Terry's. The police didn't know who to believe. Will's statement backs up yours."

Several emotions crossed Brian's young features, so quickly Mark had trouble identifying them. For a split second, he saw relief before it gave way to the familiar emotionless mask. For the first time, Mark recognized the expression as a mask, and he swallowed hard. He debated whether to bring up Stretch's expectation about sentencing and decided to hold off. Ramsey was hopeful, but he couldn't guarantee anything.

When he discarded that topic, Mark was left with just one other. For a moment, he wavered, tempted to flee. He opened his mouth only to close it again because a sudden lump in his throat made talking impossible.

After clearing his throat he tried again. "I owe you a huge apology, Brian."

The teenager stared at him with wide eyes. "What?"

It was hard to say the words, to admit the truth, but Brian deserved nothing less. "For years, I've been obsessed with being a success in my profession, so obsessed that I neglected my family." Meeting his son's gaze took everything he had. "I neglected being a father to you."

Brian blinked, his lips twisting, and Mark knew he had shocked the teen. He wasn't surprised when the shock was immediately followed by anger.

"Why tell me something I've always known?"

Mark tried not to flinch at this direct hit. "I'd give a great deal to be able to change the past, but I can't. I am..." The words caught in his throat and he coughed to clear it. "I am more sorry than I can say for not being there for you when you were growing up."

Brian stood up so fast he knocked his chair over. Ignoring it, he turned his burning gaze on his father. "So you've apologized, big deal. Like that changes anything. Am I supposed to say all is forgiven and fall into your arms now?"

The raw anger in his son's voice cut through Mark like a knife. It was nothing more than he deserved. Yet for Brian's sake, he had to keep trying to break through the walls his neglect had helped create.

"No," he said quietly. "I don't expect that. What I hope is that you'll give me the opportunity to show you by my actions that I want to change things between us. You have no reason to believe me now, but perhaps, in time, you will see that I mean what I say."

In a way, the suspicion that darkened Brian's eyes was worse than anger. "What's in it for you? Is making up to me supposed to keep Mom from divorcing you?"

Shock pierced Mark, and he fumbled for a response. "What is between your mother and me is something she and I need to deal with. Why I'm here now has nothing to do with her. I don't have a hidden agenda, Brian. The only thing I care about is learning to be a real father to you and Daniel."

"Talk is cheap."

"As I said, I don't expect you to believe me at this moment. What I'm asking for is the opportunity to prove to you I mean what I'm saying." As he repeated his earlier assurances, Mark wondered how many times he would have to say them. It was impossible to tell what the teenager was thinking. All he could do was wait and pray.

"Why now?" Brian demanded. "Why wait sixteen years to decide you want to be my dad?"

Mark had heard the term *heartbroken*, but only now did he understand what it actually meant. He waited until he could speak without breaking down to answer. "I loved being a father when you were born. It wasn't until sometime later that I…" He stopped, trying to find the right words.

"Got tired of it?" Brian challenged.

"No!" With a heavy sigh, Mark admitted, "I allowed myself to get distracted. I didn't realize how badly for a very long time."

"So what?" All of a sudden you had a dream or something that made you realize you screwed up?"

Mark tried to smile. "You're not so far off. My accident was a big wake-up call." He suppressed a shudder at the memory. "I suppose almost dying can do that to a person. It wasn't until—Brian!" He was startled to see all the color drain from his son's features, leaving him paper-white. Mark jumped forward, catching the boy's arm as he swayed and lowering him back to the chair. "Take it easy," he instructed, fighting back his own panic. "Breathe deeply, slow and steady."

Brian obeyed, and gradually some color returned to his face, and he pulled his arm out of his father's grasp. "What are you talking about? Almost dying? I thought you just drove your car off the road."

Mark stared at his son before rubbing his face. "I'm sorry. I…guess I have some explaining to do."

Quietly, without excitement or drama, he related the story of his accident and a stranger's rescue. He was relieved to see Brian's shock fade, but his interest didn't. He listened silently until his father was finished.

"How come you didn't tell me all this before?"

"To be honest, so much has happened so quickly in the last two weeks." Mark stopped and shook his head. "It's been hard to keep track of everything."

"Almost dying doesn't seem like something you'd forget."

For now, Brian's curiosity outweighed his anger with his father. Mark supposed it was something to be expected of a sixteen-year-old. "I haven't forgotten," he said quietly.

"I guess not." Brian looked slightly abashed. "Who was the guy who rescued you?"

Mark thought back to Joe's litany of possibilities and smiled. "He didn't stick around long enough to introduce himself."

"He just left?"

"Yes."

"He risked his life to save you and then just walked away?"

Mark didn't blame Brian for being so incredulous. He felt the same. "That's right."

"That's just...unreal."

Mark nodded, realizing belatedly that the news of his near-death had broken through the armor of Brian's anger. He doubted he would get a better opportunity to say what was on his heart. "It is," he agreed. "But in a way, I'm very grateful it happened."

"Grateful you almost died?"

Mark almost smiled. "It forced me to begin to reevaluate my life."

"I guess," Brian said, his anger apparently still on hold. "Like the part about not being a dad?"

It was hard not to wince at the uncompromising judgment. "Yes," he said simply. "And I'm learning that part of being a father includes having to make difficult decisions."

The wary look was back in his son's eyes. "Like?"

"You need help in dealing with what's been happening in your life," Mark said, all the while praying for the right words.

Brian bristled. "I'm fine."

"I wish that was true." Mark swallowed again to try to ease his throat's tightness. Earlier, he had thought about bringing up his son's problem with alcohol. Now he realized it wasn't the time. "I know you're a very bright young man, so I also know that deep down, you know you aren't fine." "You're a fine one to talk! You think you're Mr. Perfect or something?"

"No," Mark said softly. "Just the opposite. It's hard to admit, but I need help too."

It was a painful admission but worth it when he saw the teen's anger diluted by fresh surprise. It enabled Mark to push on with what he needed to say.

"I'm not sure how that's going to work, but both your mother and I want you to talk to someone. Not one of us," he added hastily, seeing refusal form on the boy's lips, "a counselor."

"I don't want to."

Mark smiled ruefully. "I know. I don't want to, either. But sometimes life is too difficult to deal with on our own. During those times, it can be helpful to have an objective outsider to help us gain perspective." He wished he sounded smoother, more confident. At least Brian wasn't looking as angry as he had earlier.

"You're really going to talk to someone?"

Mark hadn't expected that question but, after a moment's thought, realized its inevitability. He didn't want to see a therapist; he didn't want to allow his most painful, most deeply buried secrets to see the light of day. But if his agreement would sway Brian…

"I will if you will," he promised.

Brian looked away for a minute, and Mark held his breath. When the boy's eyes turned back, he saw reluctant acceptance in their depths and swallowed once more, this time in relief.

"Well… okay," the teen finally said in grudging tones.

"Okay," Mark said quietly.

Brian looked at his desk, and Mark sensed the boy had had enough for now. He stood. "I'll let you get back to what you were doing. Don't stay up too late."

The teen looked unexpectedly amused. "Careful, you're starting to sound like a dad."

Pain mingled with pleasure in Mark, and he hoped he kept them out of his smile. "Get used to it."

He closed the door behind him and leaned against it while taking several deep breaths. Only now did he admit to himself how afraid he had been when he walked into Brian's room. Afraid he would not be able to come up with the right words. Afraid that Brian would refuse to listen. Afraid, most of all, that he had lost his son permanently.

Mark still wasn't sure he had said what needed to be said, but he felt more hopeful now than he had a few minutes ago. "Thank you, Lord," he whispered into the darkness of the unlit hall. He felt limp with sudden exhaustion. The thought of his bed drew him, but there was another conversation he still needed to have. And he was looking forward to that one even less than the one with Brian.

Mark straightened, took a deep breath, and went down the hall to Geneva's room. He knocked on the door and waited. There was no answer, but he knew she was in there; light edged the bottom of the door.

He knocked again. "Geneva? I'd like to speak with you."

The silence stretched out. The more time that passed, the greater grew his discomfort. If she refused to answer...

The door opened, and Geneva faced him. She was backlit from the light in her bedroom but her features were in shadow. "Yes?"

"Could I come in for a minute?"

For a few seconds, she didn't react, and Mark feared she was going to refuse. Then she stepped back and opened the door wider. Relieved, he walked in and heard the door close behind him. Mentally gathering himself, he turned to face her.

Geneva stood quietly as if unaware of his gaze. She was wearing a silk robe that he recognized; he had bought it for her years ago for her birthday. Or had it been an anniversary gift? He couldn't remember and felt obscurely guilty for the lapse. Despite the soft, flattering lamplight, she looked tired, and he didn't think it was his imagination that her eyes were bloodshot. It wasn't surprising, considering her loss last night.

"I didn't know your friend, Peg," he began, "but I can be sorry for a life cut short too soon, and I am. I'm especially sorry you had to go through it alone."

Her head came up at that. "You think it would have made a difference?"

Mark heard an edge of anger in her voice, but it was an edge softened by something else—grief. Sorrow twisted his heart. "Not in the ultimate outcome," he acknowledged. "But maybe I could have shared the weight you were carrying."

Geneva's eyes narrowed. "Why? Why claim to care now?"

Mark would have liked to tell her the whole truth about how his life had been abruptly transformed by Jesus Christ. But Joe's warning still echoed in his ears, and he knew this wasn't the right time.

"The accident really shook me up," he said. "It forced me to take a long, hard look at my life." He paused, frustrated with himself at how hard it was to force out the words of his confession. "I wasn't happy with what I discovered, especially the way I had been treating you and the boys. I'm so sorry, Geneva."

"Sorry for what?"

The words were soft, but the intensity in her tone could not be missed. He sensed that she wouldn't accept anything less than the truth, so he gave it to her.

"For failing you in so many ways for so many years."

"You should be."

Bitter, painful truth. Of course, she would feel that way. He nodded slowly, praying she wouldn't leave it at that. "Is there any chance for us?" he asked softly. "I'm willing to do whatever you say, if it means that we still have a chance for a life together."

Geneva looked away. He saw her hands turn into fists before she shoved them in the pockets of her robe. After a minute, she looked back, her beautiful features without expression. "You're leaving it in my hands to say yay or nay?"

Mark closed his eyes briefly. *Please, God, help me. Please help her to hear what you want her to hear.* When he opened them again, he spoke without giving himself time to think about what he wanted to say. "I know I have a great deal to make up for. But if you aren't willing to give me a chance, then there's no way this can work. I'm not saying I deserve a chance, just that nothing can work without it."

She looked past him, not meeting his eyes. "If you had asked me yesterday, I would have said no."

"And today?" Mark had to force himself to keep breathing.

"Today..." Geneva repeated so softly he could barely hear her. Her chin quivered, and she rubbed fiercely at her eyes. "Today I'm dealing with something I never expected, losing one of my dearest friends to a vile disease. I spent practically the entire morning with my brother cursing God or fate or whatever was responsible. And then"—she sniffed—"then I cried like I've never cried before."

Mark ached to put his arms around her, but he didn't dare. Perhaps someday, if they were able to heal their relationship, she would accept his comfort. Not today.

One thing was clear. As his life had recently been turned upside-down, so her life had been turned upside-down in the last twenty-four hours, even if in a different way. Geneva was being more open with him than she had in years; it was a bitter irony that her openness was in response to the loss of a close friend.

She turned abruptly away and disappeared in her bathroom. He caught a glimpse of her reflection in the mirror while she grabbed some tissues and wiped her eyes. When she reappeared, she looked calmer. "Why try?" she said bluntly. "Why not give up this marriage as a lost cause?"

Fear held him silent for a beat before he pushed past it. "I remember how we were in the beginning. Do you remember, Geneva? It was wonderful."

She met his gaze squarely, unsoftened. "That was a long time ago."

"I know, but I still remember. Do you?"

"What if I do? What difference does it make today?"

Be honest, he reminded himself. Only honesty had a chance here. "I know we can't go back, but when I remember how it once was, how we once were..." He took a few steps toward her, reaching out a hand. "Geneva, I'm willing to work as hard as I have to, do whatever I need to to have that again. Maybe this isn't the right time to ask but"—he shrugged helplessly—"but here we are. Can you find it in your heart to want it too?"

She looked away again, and he saw her swallow. "You're right, this is a bad time. I'm very tired."

Dear God, now what? For a minute, his thoughts skittered frantically, and it took an almost physical effort to slow them down. In his mind's eye, he imagined himself scooping them up and handing them over to the One he knew was here. *You, Lord*, Mark prayed. *Let it just be you.*

"What about tomorrow? Can we talk then?" he asked. "Please?"

Geneva shook her head slowly as if in negation, and his heart dropped to his feet. Then surprisingly, a slight smile lifted the corners of her lips, and his heart soared again. "You never quit," she said. "Not even in the very beginning. How many times did I say no before I finally agreed to go out with you the first time?"

Mark chuckled, holding tightly to the faint fluttering of hope in his heart. "At least half a dozen." He debated whether to leave it at that but couldn't. "So can we talk tomorrow?"

She sighed. "Do you believe we can work through all the...all that needs to be worked through?"

"Not without help," he said and tried a small smile. "As it happens, I have a brother-in-law who knows several good counselors. I'm sure he could provide us with a referral."

"I'm sure," she agreed dryly. "You'd be willing to do that? To see a counselor?"

A part of him still resisted the idea, but Mark pushed it aside. The stakes were too high to fall back on old insecurities. It was time to move forward, and by God's grace, they would.

"Yes, I would."

Geneva looked surprised by his firm tone. After a minute, she nodded. "All right, we'll talk tomorrow."

Tears of relief and gratitude pressed against his eyelids, and Mark forced them back because he didn't want to scare her off. "Good." He smiled.

She nodded slowly, then stopped, her lips tightening. His heart missed a beat. Was she having second thoughts already?

"What is it?" he inquired.

"Brian." She looked beseechingly at him. "He needs help too. But I don't think—"

"He's agreed to see a counselor too."

Her eyes widened in shock. "He has? When?"

"Just a little while ago. I went to his room to talk with him, and before I left, he agreed."

"He...how?"

Mark's smile felt painful yet oddly liberating. He didn't even try to understand what he was feeling. "I think mainly because I admitted that I had failed miserably as a father and was willing to get professional help."

Geneva's hand went to her throat; she looked shocked beyond the ability to speak, and he grinned in spite of himself. It was enough to bring a faint smile to her face. "So before you came here, you already agreed to see a professional."

"Yes. And now I have even more reason to keep my promise. Both to Brian and to you."

"And Daniel?"

"Of course."

For the first time, she gave him a genuine smile. "All right."

The tiny fluttering of hope grew in his chest. "All right," he said softly. There was much more he would liked to have said, but he sensed it was time to retreat and give her some space. "I'll let you get some sleep. And tomorrow..." He hesitated.

"We'll talk," she said, still smiling. It was a smile that held grief and loss and exhaustion, but he saw something else this time, something that sent him out of her room with a full heart.

25

Two days later, Mark sat in his parked car and wondered yet again what he was doing. When he got up this morning, he hadn't intended to be here. He had spent a good part of the day at the office, forcing himself to do the work before him. Finally, a little over an hour ago, he gave up the struggle against a nagging feeling he couldn't identify and left early. He had known where Brian would be, and almost without steering, the car made a beeline to the same address.

The neighborhood was in one of the older areas of Pasadena, and the houses were almost entirely bungalows from the early twentieth century Arts and Crafts movement. The particular bungalow he was parked just down the street from had been renovated and now housed two separate offices. He ignored one of them, an architectural firm. It was the second office that Mark was interested in.

His eyes kept returning to the front door of the second office. A simple plaque proclaimed that this was the office of Seth Hancock, PhD, marriage and family counselor. Brian had been in there, he check his watch, almost an hour.

He knew he was taking a risk. If his son found him hanging around outside, it could undo any positive gains Mark had made during his discussion with the boy a couple of nights earlier. He wasn't sure what had drawn him here. Maybe that persistent, unnamable feeling? If so, what caused it? Had he been worried that Brian would change his mind and not show up for his first meeting with the therapist? If that was the case, Mark could discard that concern, for the teen's blue Toyota Rav4 was parked on the opposite side of the street.

Knowing Brian had followed through on his promise relieved Mark's mind, but he could not bring himself to leave. For the first time since his near-fatal accident, he thought that the pieces in his life were beginning to fit together again, this time in a totally new pattern. He had begun to restore his damaged relationship with Danny, and Geneva had agreed to see a marriage counselor with him. Although she refused to make any promises, for the first time in a long time, Mark felt hopeful about the future of their marriage.

As for Brian, whether he had truly accepted the fact that he needed professional help, Mark didn't know. At least the boy was here, willing to take the first steps of what would likely be a difficult but, his father hoped, ultimately healing journey. These were all encouraging signs for which he was deeply grateful. They were proof—if he needed more proof—that God was working in the lives of those he loved, even if they didn't yet know it. As much as he wanted to share with his wife and children what God was doing in his own life, he didn't know how or when to speak up. Earlier he had been troubled by this hesitation, but he now recognized that God himself would reveal when the time was right.

And what of his professional practice? Mark had been so focused on his family that he hadn't considered how much God was needed in the law offices of Newman, Buchanan, and Welch. Fortunately, God had been ahead of him there too. He thought back to the law student Jay Russell and his ailing sister and smiled. Before Mark even realized the need, God had inspired him to step in to assist the youngsters. They had no idea of the anonymous donor who had paid the medical bills and forced the insurance company to leave them alone. Mark would never tell anyone, for fear he might be given the credit when all credit belonged to his new Lord.

Even with Steve Buchanan, Mark now understood, as he couldn't have before, why his partner had found himself in an impossible situation. Thankfully, he seemed to be doing better, but the only way the man's life would truly change for the better would be when he came to know Jesus Christ as Lord and Savior. Mark ached to share this marvelous news, but something—Someone—held him back. He needed to wait on God's timing and trust it would happen.

He leaned back in his seat and exhaled. Even though he was new at all this, he understood enough to know that he couldn't rush ahead of God. He had to follow, always being open to his Savior's leading in reaching out to others. The thought exhilarated him and also filled him with uncertainty that he would be able to fulfill God's will in his relationship with others. At least he could begin praying for each man and woman who worked at his firm. Where God would take him, well, Mark had placed himself in God's hands, and he couldn't think of a safer place to be, regardless of what the future might hold.

Thinking over all that had happened since his accident both saddened him and filled him with inexpressible joy. Feeling as if his heart was about to split apart under the weight of all his myriad emotions, Mark had to say something to let them out.

"Thank you, Lord," he murmured in the quiet of his car. "Thank you for bringing to pass that which I never could have. Thank you most of all for not giving up on me." Wait, hadn't he said that before? No matter, it was worth repeating. He smiled to himself. Thanking God was probably going to be part of his daily life for as long as he lived. Fair enough.

He sighed, trying to rub the stiffness out of his neck, then saw the door open. A familiar young figure trotted down the steps and headed straight for his Toyota. Mark sighed again, this time in relief that Brian seemed too preoccupied to notice his surroundings. Although he had parked a block down under the shade of a giant oak, Mark's vehicle was hardly invisible. Fortunately, Brian never looked around, and a minute later, the little SUV drove off.

Mark glanced at his watch and was a little surprised to see it was almost five o'clock. No wonder the traffic was increasing. Rush hour had begun. It was time he too headed home before he got caught up in the inevitable traffic jams. It was a good idea, but he couldn't bring himself to turn the key in the ignition. Nor could he dispel the annoying, nagging feeling that had been troubling him all day. He didn't understand it. Work had gone as well as could be expected, Brian had kept his first appointment. Everything about the day had also gone as well as he could have hoped. So where was the uncomfortable feeling coming from?

Mark's gaze turned back to that solid wooden door. and there it was—the real issue. Brian had taken the first critical step in his recovery, but his father had not. Mark had made a promise to his oldest son that he had yet to keep. He tried to swallow, but his throat was too dry. Brian had had the courage to act on his promise. How could Mark look his son in the eye if he failed to do the same?

Marriage counseling for Geneva and himself, yes, he could do that. But this step right now wasn't about his marriage; it was about Mark himself.

I know I promised, Lord, but I didn't mean so soon!
Did you intend for Brian to delay?

No. He needed to begin as soon as... Mark's thoughts faltered as he heard them. Excuses. He was trying to, what, make a deal with God? To try to evade his promise?

Not daring to give himself time to think about it, Mark quickly exited the car and marched up the sidewalk, turning in when he reached his target. At the front door, he raised a hand to knock and hesitated, then he shook his head at himself. No, no more delays. Ignoring a sudden burst of nerves, he gave a single knock and pushed the door open.

What had obviously once been a living room had been turned into a waiting room. He was relieved to see it was empty. Mark looked slowly around the room. The furniture looked almost as old as the house but was still in good condition. A beam of light from the setting sun reflected through the stained-glass windows on either side of the front door, and he couldn't help smiling at the colorful refractions of light—green and blue and gold—that danced around the room.

The distant sound of a door closing yanked his attention back. A hallway led to the back of the house, and at the opposite end, Mark saw a figure appear.

"Hello," he said hesitantly, quelling the desire to make a hasty retreat. His stomach churned with nervousness, and Mark prayed he wouldn't get sick.

The figure approached and turned into a tall, slender man dressed in khakis and plaid shirt, the sleeves rolled up to his elbows. A riot of dark curls haloed his head. The man looked younger than Mark had expected, then he realized his mistake when the overhead light glinted off the gray sprinkled heavily through the curly hair.

The man stopped a few paces away. "I'm Seth Hancock. I don't believe we've met."

"No." Mark held out his hand. "I'm Mark Newman, Brian's father."

Recognition lit the therapist's eyes, a recognition that was immediately followed by caution. He shook hands, saying, "It's good to meet you, but I wasn't expecting to, at least not today."

"I know, and I'm sorry for barging in on you," Mark said, stumbling a little in his discomfort.

Hancock studied him thoughtfully. "I assume you know I just met with Brian."

"Yes."

"If you expect me to tell you what we talked about—"

"No," Mark interrupted. "That's between you and him. I hope someday my son will be willing to tell me about it, but it will be up to him."

"I'm relieved to hear that. So what can I do for you?"

"I…" Mark hesitated, wanting more than ever to flee. Instead, he tried to clear his throat and said, "If it's not too late in the day, I think I would…I would like to talk."

One dark eyebrow rose, and Hancock nodded. "All right. This way."

The therapist's office had probably once been a bedroom. Now it was filled with an old desk and shelves on every wall. As Mark entered, he glanced at the nearest shelf and smiled involuntarily at the row of Agatha Christie novels. During his teenage years a lifetime ago, he had loved reading her books.

Maybe Hancock had official publications from his field somewhere in the room, but Mark felt oddly reassured by the fact that the first books he noticed had nothing to do with counseling. When he looked at the other man, he was still smiling. "Christie?"

Hancock chuckled. "My second favorite, after Chesterton's Father Brown stories." He gestured at the chair beside his desk. "Why don't you have a seat?"

For no reason he could identify, the brief foray into mystery novels eased some of Mark's nervousness. Or maybe it wasn't the novels so much as the fresh awareness that he wasn't alone. He was here to keep a promise he had made to his son and to God. Although he was just at the very beginning of his Christian walk, Mark was convinced of the most important point—God was with him here and now. *All right, Lord, I'm here*, he thought. *Even though I have no idea what I'm going to say, I'm here.*

Trust me.

The thought came quickly and strongly, almost jolting Mark in his chair, and he found he was able to meet the therapist's gaze without flinching.

"What would you like to talk about?" Hancock asked.

Mark took a deep breath and tried to relax, reminding himself that God was here with him and he could do this, take the steps that needed to be taken to become the man God wanted him to become.

"I'm not sure…where to begin."

The therapist smiled. "How about whatever's on your mind right now?"

Mark settled himself a little more comfortably in his chair. "Right now, what's most on my mind is how badly I've failed my family."

Hancock's eyes were steady, nonjudgmental. "Go on."

Another surge of nerves made him hesitate, then something else pushed him forward. *All right, Lord. Let's get to it.*

As Mark began to talk, the last of his nervousness faded and was replaced by a growing certainty that he was on the right track, headed in the direction God wanted him to go. Together with his Savior.

It was a good feeling.

CPSIA information can be obtained
at www.ICGtesting.com
Printed in the USA
LVOW04s2054120816
500060LV00016B/195/P